One *good* Thing

Other Works

Fiction

Carolina's Legacy Collection:
Any Good Thing: A Novel
This Good Thing: A Novella
Every Good Thing: A Short Story Compilation
One Good Thing: An Epistolary
"Our Good Thing:" A Short Story

The Crux Anthology
"Ealiverel Awakened"
Edited & Compiled by Rachael Ritchey

Nonfiction

Finders Keepers: A Practical Approach to Find and Keep Your Writing Critique Partner
Joy E. Rancatore and Meagan Smith

A Gift for You

One *good* Thing

JOY E. RANCATORE

LOGOS & MYTHOS PRESS
SLIDELL, LA, USA

ONE GOOD THING

Cover Design and Layout by Rachael Ritchey, RR Publishing

www.joyerancatore.com
www.logosandmythospress.com

One Good Thing is a work of fiction. Any resemblance to actual persons, living or dead, or actual events is coincidental. Historical events, places and people have been carefully researched by the author, and any deviations from timeline or actual battles and procedures were chosen for the purposes of the story. Names, characters, businesses, events and incidents are products of the author's imagination, as is the town of Bellum.

Disclaimer: "Neither the United States Marine Corps nor any other component of the Department of Defense has approved, endorsed, or authorized this book."

ISBN 13: 978-1-7331387-9-6 (paperback)
ISBN 13: 978-1-954465-00-8 (e-book)

Library of Congress Control Number:2024901543

Logos & Mythos Press LLC
Slidell, LA, USA

To the characters who
challenged an author's bold declaration of
"I will never write romance!"
and to the readers who fell in love, too.

Every day—no matter how bleak it seems—find One Good Thing for which to be thankful. When we focus on that one good thing—when we choose to find it—our hearts can't help but be uplifted because they're lifting out of ourselves—our selfish, inward-looking selves—up toward the Creator and Sustainer of all, including us.

Sunday, May 26, 2002

I have loved Jack our whole lives, and this journal records our highs and lows. Now it holds today's catastrophic revelation: I kind of hate him.

He told me goodbye in a letter sent through my dad.

Who does that? He wouldn't even deliver it in person.

Jack made a decision that wasn't his alone. He ran away from me, from us, from his mom. He also ran from himself.

I understand why he ran from Bellum, hometown of his past, pain and grief. I saw the looks and heard the whispers I hoped and prayed he wouldn't. At my graduation, I saw how the ache of betrayal in his eyes melted across his drooped shoulders into pseudo-apathy.

Later that night, I journaled about why he left then. Most of my classmates and their parents—and even the teachers—drifted away from us whenever Jack was by me. He left that night for me, so I could celebrate with everyone else. Now, he's left me.

A few more months, and we would have left here together for college. He didn't need to leave this way. He didn't need to leave me behind.

He had the nerve to write that he has to "find another future." Well, he was and is my future, so he better get over himself. He's not as broken as he claims, and shouldn't the people he thinks he keeps hurting decide if we deserve better?

Now, I'm stuck here, trying to figure out what's next. I spent too much of my senior year waiting on Jack. Now, I've got no scholarships for the fall, and because I didn't accept any offers, I don't have a spot at any school. I know it's not a huge deal. In many ways, it's probably better this way. It's just ... it wasn't the plan.

The plan was me and Jack. We were going to Georgia Tech if they accepted his GED. Whatever the future held, it held for us ... together. Wherever that took us wouldn't be Bellum.

A town this size squeezes its inhabitants, more constrictive than cozy. As the preacher's daughter, I should know. I've grown up in a fishbowl as Exhibit A.

> "Can you believe what that preacher's daughter's wearing?"
>
> "That preacher's daughter giggles too much."
>
> "That preacher's daughter frowns when her daddy's preaching. She's gonna be a rebellious one."
>
> "That preacher's daughter's hair's too red. I bet she has a wicked temper."

And then there was the time I was destined to turn up "in the family way" because I hugged Jack at church.

If this town judged me, they condemned Jack without hope of parole. The whole town blamed him for things that weren't his fault.

What happened that gosh-awful day on the Cutter land was an accident—a horrible, terrible accident. I have told Jack that. Daddy's told him that. His mom's told him; so has the sheriff. None of us can make him believe it—probably because everyone else in Bellum screams "murderer" at him.

Daddy's no longer the preacher after this morning. I'm not mad about that. He aimed today's sermon at all the townspeople with their childish hatred. He gave these judgmental people a piece of God's mind, and I've never wanted to shout "Amen!" more.

He'll be fine focusing on the Mission. Mama talked to me about that before she died. She explained how Daddy has a special gift for helping addicts see the truth of the Gospel and picture what life without drugs or alcohol could be. She also told me he would take a while to figure out he should be there instead of behind the pulpit. She never told me why, just that she was used to Daddy taking his sweet time figuring things out.

Maybe Jack needs time, too.

I'm still mad at the whole letter thing, so he's not going to waltz back and have everything hunky-dory.

He needs to hurry up and return, though. I can't imagine my life without him. He was in it the day I was born, and we've done everything together—crawl, walk, learn, live.

Plus, his mama is my second mama. Ms. Becky and I talked today. That's another thing I'm so mad I could spit nails about: he left his mama with a letter, too. I'd like to punch him for her and me.

Between the cracks of Ms. Becky's words, I heard her pain. Jack's leaving is breaking her heart. She's lost so much in her life; Jack should've known better. Ms. Becky misses her son, but I think she knew he was going to do this. She thinks he's like his dad, but he's not. He won't stay gone forever.

Surely, he won't.

Ms. Becky and I talked about the guilt Jack's felt over Abbie Mae's death on the road through the Cutters' land. She told me Jack's nightmares returned after that accident, and he rarely slept through the night. His screams would wake her.

She teared up when she admitted how lost she's felt as a mom since my mom's been gone. They talked through everything that had to do with us kids.

Life isn't the same without Mama—not for me or Daddy or Ms. Becky or Jack. Mama was the captain of our joint family team. Since the cancer ripped her away, we've been leaderless.

I miss her.

What would she say if she were here today? I suppose that's not a fair question. If she'd been here, things wouldn't have gotten so bad in this town. Everything would have been different after the accident. Mama had a way of calming people's anger and soothing their hurt without talking about the actual issue.

As a little girl, I believed my mama was magic. I still do. She had this special way with plants and with people. Both grew straighter and more productive when she had a hand in their growth.

I think she would've been proud that Jack and I were dating. I think, too, that she would have been guiding us and helping us figure out the whole relationship thing and the whole "planning-for-the-future" thing, without sounding like she was counseling us.

How would she handle this mess, though?

I've spent the past ten minutes trying to figure that out. All I came up with is an image of Mama dragging Jack over by his ear to apologize. She never did that, but the visual makes me laugh.

Mama always made me laugh when I needed it most, usually when I didn't want to feel better.

Regardless of what Jack does next, I have big changes coming. Daddy and I agreed we'd like to move. He said wherever we go is up to me. One minute that responsibility feels like an awful burden; the next it feels like a gift. I don't want to go to college too close to here, but I don't want to be far from Daddy either.

Losing one parent made me realize how great they are. Maybe if Mama hadn't died I'd be fine moving across the country by myself and visiting on holidays and breaks because I'd believe they'd always be here. Instead, I want to be able to live at home with Daddy if I want.

Besides, he'll need someone to cook for him from time to time. As smart as he is, that man will never learn to cook anything other than pancakes. He even burns canned soup. I swear, I have no clue how he manages that.

He told me I don't have to make a decision any time soon. Practically, I should decide sooner than later, but I'm relieved to feel no pressure.

As Mama once told me, "Making decisions under pressure is a recipe for future disaster. Remember the time I trusted a pressure cooker for the church potluck?"

I'm going to accept this in-between year before I start college as a good thing and move forward.

Without Jack.

That's the part I cannot stomach right now. I can't picture any part of my life without him at the center, especially this next one. I suppose Jack's not the target of my hate after all. I mostly hate that he left me behind in this town of pointing fingers and wagging tongues.

Why would he run from me?

We were going to get married and have a family. It's what we always knew would happen, even before the first time he kissed me beside Mama's roses when we were ten years old.

He's my only for always. Now my always is dark.

Friday, May 31, 2002

Dear Rachael,

Why am I writing this letter I have no intention of mailing?

Maybe I'm not ready to say goodbye. Maybe I don't have to move on because I never really can—or deserve to. Maybe I've gotten used to this whole letter-writing thing.

One thing I know is my brain's filled with a swirling mess of confusion and rage and ... something. I need to figure out whatever that "something" is and assign some sense of order to it. I want to understand the chaos in my mind.

You always loved journaling. I'm not a "Dear Diary" kind of guy, though. I'd rather pretend to tell my thoughts to you than to lines on a page.

Maybe I just want someone to talk to—someone who knows me better than anyone else; someone who won't put up with my crap; someone who can uncover my heart, my soul, my hidden self ... the good and the mostly ugly. Even if it's make-believe.

Or, maybe I need you so much it terrifies me. I'm a mess, but you always saw something beyond that. Maybe writing with you in mind will help me make sense of the confusion twisting inside me, until one day I see something else there, too.

You likely hate me right now. You should.

Don't take it out on your dad. He couldn't have stopped me from leaving. It was what I needed to do. Now you'll be free to lead the life you were always meant to, without being chained to me.

I regret my decision to leave you behind in that hell of a town with all its blame and reminders of the damage I've caused. But, not a moment goes by that I'm not reminded of the train wreck I am and would be for you.

The biggest benefit for me is I'm not in Bellum anymore. After Mr. Cutter's granddaughter slammed my mom's groceries down in the store with the whole town glaring at me, I couldn't stay another minute. The guilt I carry over Abbie Mae's death is unbearable enough. Add a town full of hate and judgment every time I left home....

I couldn't breathe.

The weight of Bellum's blame sent me spiraling. I hate admitting this to you, even in a pretend letter, but that pressure carried me straight to alcohol. I didn't drink it ... before I took the first sip, the smell reminded me of the nightmare that was rehab. I won't go there again. Deep down, I know I wouldn't survive again.

Reaching for the bottle, though, sent me packing. Now I'm in Columbia, South Carolina, working for a construction company. It's a family business owned by the Millers. You'd love Junior, Ducky, Senior and Mawmaw Mabel. They'd love you, too. Of course, who doesn't?

When I got off the bus here, I had no plan— other than get away and find a job. I had no money, nowhere to stay. Nothing. And then I met Senior. His son, Junior, offered me a construction job, and Senior gave me a place to stay. He opened his home to a total stranger. Who even does that?

Despite their kindness, I am lonely. Junior's son, Ducky, asked me if I had a girlfriend. Missing you in that moment pierced whatever passes as a heart in my chest. I suppose that pain will come less often the further I get from you. Maybe.

Unmailed letters to you might ease the ache and allow me to share my ups and downs. I write to your dad, of course, which is great. He's the guy who came to my ballgames and tossed the ball with me after school. He's the one who helped me kick my addiction and steered me on the right path afterward.

He's also the preacher dad who somehow knew exactly what I was thinking about his daughter and could give me the scariest icy glare in those moments. I can't tell him all my emotions and internal confusions, especially when many of them surround you.

Besides, you have always been my best friend—the only one I told everything.

Back to the Miller's construction company and the work I'm doing: I arrived at the start of foundation work on a group of houses for families down on their luck. The first family we're building for came to the groundbreaking, and the dad spoke. A drunk driver hit the family and left one of the kids—a sweet girl named Tara—in a wheelchair. The dad was beating himself up with guilt.

The more I heard him talk, the more a knot in my gut grew and the angrier I got. He's got no right to blame himself. Guilt's not for a man like him because he did nothing wrong. Guilt's for people like me and that drunk driver.

Rach, I could've put someone in a wheelchair ... or worse ... as many nights as I swerved home while I was drinking. I can't remember most of those drives, but the parts I do remember are blurry images of the wrong side of the road and fast-moving mailboxes in the wrong direction. I'm no different from that driver, and he deserves to be in jail.

Maybe it would've been better if Sheriff Pounds had thrown me in a cell after I killed that little girl. It doesn't matter that I was stone cold sober that day. Too many other times, I wasn't. I could have hurt or killed someone then. That thought rips up my insides.

Every time my mind rewinds to the first accident, I see myself waving that damn beer around while I pushed Steven toward the driver's seat to accept the challenge to drag race. That night wrecked all our lives. Every night in my nightmares, I see Steven and the others who died, then my mind fast-forwards to the second accident, and I see Abbie Mae. Their lifeless faces haunt me.

They should. The word accident doesn't resurrect dead kids.

If I'd never taken that first drink maybe Steven would've listened to his brother instead of me. He wouldn't have raced. He'd have waited for a night on the drag strip when he would've been sober. That would have sent us on an alternate reality where I wouldn't have become a drunk who stole from people like Hyram Cutter's sister.

Or, if I'd given in to Mr. Cutter the day of the second accident and backed up to drive around the long way instead of by his land, I wouldn't have had to pump the gas to get away from his fist. Abbie Mae wouldn't have hidden under my truck. And, that girl with her curls and bright blue eyes would still be alive.

No, guilt doesn't belong on the shoulders of that father who has to watch his daughter live life in a wheelchair and never speak again. I'm the one who deserves guilt.

I feel so restless, Rach, like there's somewhere else I need to go. Somewhere I might be needed. You'd probably have all the answers for me if you were here … or I was there. I miss you more every day; I thought it would be the opposite. I guess it hasn't been that long.

You always reminded me what your mom wrote in that letter you read after she died. We'd finish each other's recitation of that line, "None of us deserves any good thing." Another of your mom's lines keeps replaying in my mind, something about finding one good thing to be thankful for every day.

I've decided to try to do that as often as possible—maybe not every day; that's too much of a commitment.

(I can hear you laugh at that.)

Whenever I write you, though, I will try to do what your mom encouraged: find something to be thankful for. So, here we go …

Today's One Good Thing:
I'm thankful for new starts.
One for me and one for that
family who nearly lost everything.

Tuesday, June 4, 2002

Jack and Daddy think they're slick. Jack mailed a letter to the church, and Daddy brought it home and stuck it in his top drawer—the one I have to open whenever I need tape or the stapler. Really, Daddy?

I'd recognize Jack's goofy handwriting anywhere—half cursive, half print, all his.

All gone.

I haven't ached like this since Mama died. Losing her hurt so bad for so long; it still does.

That pain is deep inside me. In place of my mama, I received a grief transplant, and my body will always fight against the foreign replacement.

The pain of Jack leaving remains closer to the surface, like a knife constantly cutting and leaving my skin open and bleeding. The touch of every thought of him sears that gaping wound.

Jack's letter wasn't to me, of course. He wrote my dad. I had to read it, though.

Now I know where Jack is, I've got half a mind to hop on the same bus he ran away on and show up on his new doorstep. I even walked down the hall to demand Daddy take me to the station when a thought stopped me cold.

What if Jack wasn't only running from this town and his past? What if he intentionally ran from me?

I don't believe he did. I know what we had, and I believe he planned to ask me to marry him that night.

That awful, awful night. I'll never forget seeing him half-dead ... again.

I swear! I should get some credit from him for putting up with the heart attacks he's given me over the past few years. I had to keep him from bleeding out on the road after the drag accident. The next couple of years I watched him nearly drink himself to death. Then, seeing him unconscious after Mr. Cutter threw him into his truck's windshield completed the trifecta of terror.

By the way, what kind of adult does that sort of thing to a kid? I know grief does crazy things to people and I know Mr. Cutter loved Abbie Mae, but he couldn't really believe Jack ran over her on purpose. No one knew she was hiding under his truck. If he wanted to blame someone, he needed to blame himself.

Maybe he did, deep down. Maybe that's why he lashed out at Jack. He couldn't take his guilt and needed to put it on someone else—someone he already hated.

Still ... he was a grown man.

I wonder what Jack would think about how Mr. Cutter died. Daddy's last sermon infuriated him, and he started shouting and making a scene on the church steps. He dropped dead right there—heart attack. Talk about a lesson in the importance of keeping a cool head. Anger and hatred and rage never did anyone any good.

Neither does self-pity.

Mama always told me, whenever I fixated on myself and my problems, I needed to switch my focus. She said, "It's hard to be grumpy and mopey when you're giving thanks or giving help."

Jack did write to Daddy that he's in a good place with a Christian family who are treating him well. He's got a construction job, and they're building a house for a girl in a wheelchair. It's hard to stay mad when he's doing something like that. I mean, I am still mad; maybe not angry, though.

Instead of having a pity party over what Jack's put me through, I'm going to focus on the good Jack has found and pray he quickly learns the lesson God has for him. At the end of the day, Jack can never change, never forgive himself, never stop running, until he gives his life to Christ. Real, lasting change only comes through Christ's comfort, and forgiveness only comes from God's greatest forgiveness of our sins.

If running away and spending time with this family is what Jack needs to hear the gospel in a different way to make it hit home, then it will be worth it. I'm still gonna punch him for saying goodbye in a letter, but his time away will be worthwhile if it brings him to God.

In honor of Mama and her wisdom, I'm going to record ...

Today's One Good Thing:
I'm thankful Jack's with a family who knows God and that he can continue to hear the truth he's been hearing all his life.

Wednesday, June 12, 2002

Daddy thinks he's clever. Tucking the letters in front of the bottom drawer in his file cabinet is only slightly better than in his desk drawer.

Okay, it took me a day to figure out where he'd moved them, but I know now. At least I can keep up with what Jack's doing, since he's still a jerk who won't write me.

He sounds positive. He's going to church with the family he's living with. He's also sleeping without nightmares ... thanks to a dog, apparently. I can't picture Jack snuggling with a fuzzy fluffball.

Pets are something a lot of kids have growing up, but we never did. I'm not sure why. It's not like Jack and I hate animals. We never begged our parents for a puppy like most kids do. I guess we were so content with each other as playmates, we didn't need furry companions.

Maybe sleep—for the first time in three years—will help Jack think deeper and see life more clearly. He may see how stupid running away from all of us was. Perhaps God led him away from the town and people that remind him of his past and who he was and who he thought he'd always have to be so he can heal. This new perspective could help him reevaluate the guilt he's placed on himself.

Thinking Jack's healing makes it easier to accept him being gone. I have to believe he will come back and our relationship will be better because of the time he's been away. Right now, I need to be patient, trust God and think about how I can prepare for my future.

I believe God made Jack and me for each other. God will guide our moving separately to lead us back together, so I should move forward with my life without worrying about losing Jack forever.

Once he adjusts his thinking, Jack can plan for his future. I have to believe I'll still be part of it.

Anna Claire, Shannon and I got together last weekend. They knew I needed a girl's night to talk through Jack leaving. We put their babies down to sleep and then talked through all that's happened.

I'm thankful for fierce friends. I know it's not easy for them to have nights like that—single moms, building their businesses. They're always here for me, though. I will miss them when we move.

Shannon was ready to hunt Jack down, and Anna Claire offered to use Steven's old mechanic tools to teach Jack he made a huge mistake.

After a pint of mint chocolate chip and a few hours of talking, listening to sappy music and watching Monty Python and the Holy Grail, I felt lighter. I have no reason not to expect Jack to come to his senses and grow into the man I've always believed God would make him.

Today's One Good Thing:
I am thankful for the dog that's calmed Jack's nightmares and for the family giving him a place to heal and for a God who will move us forward until we're together forever.

Thursday, July 4, 2002

Dear Rachael,

Have you picked a college yet? I'm sure you have. You're probably buying stuff for your dorm room and packing your clothes. I'm sorry I ruined our plans of doing those things together.

I never said it enough, but I'm proud of you—of all you've done and all you will do. You have the whole world at your fingertips. I hope you grab everything you want. You're the only one who can hold yourself back now. I wish I could know all the great decisions you're making.

Maybe your dad will let things slip in his letters. Yeah, he probably won't. No, I won't ask him. I left my right to know anything about you when I left you behind.

In the last letter, I wrote how restless I feel, like I should be moving toward something. You're not going to approve, but every day I feel stronger that "something" is the Marines. With my dad gone, I grew up looking at Marines in movies as heroes. That recruiter who came to our school made an impression on me, too. You probably didn't know that since I was drinking all the time and had pushed you out of my life.

We never discussed why you didn't want me to join after 9-11. I wish I'd asked your reasons. You always think things through better than I do. You are the planner. I'm more run-headlong-into-the-rain.

Remember the time I drug you out in that summer rain shower and we danced? You pretended to be mad I got your hair wet. You were sexy as hell, though.

Back from a cold shower. Where was I? Oh, yeah ... restless.

Whenever I watch the news, I know I can't sit by with my country going to war. I think you'd understand that if I explained it to you.

Maybe war is where I'll find my purpose, where I can do some good. Even if that good is to take a bullet.

Today's One Good Thing: I'm thankful for the possibility of a purpose for my future.

Saturday, July 13, 2002

Dear Rachael,

If I mailed these letters, I realize you would respond with questions about where I am and what I'm doing and the people I'm staying with. So, I figure I'll tell you more about my daily life.

The Millers are a kind family. You would probably use the word "precious." You definitely would for Mawmaw Mabel's dog, Missy. The first night I was here, I had one of my nightmares and woke up screaming. I felt terrible for waking Senior and Mawmaw Mabel and tried to leave the next day, but they wouldn't hear of it. Anyway, Missy ran in to comfort me, and she's slept by my side ever since. A few mornings after she started, I woke up and realized I'd slept all night without waking in a panic and couldn't remember any nightmares. Dogs are amazing, it turns out.

Senior rarely talks, and it's usually only a few words when he does. The other day, though, he shocked the mess out of me.

We were in his woodshop—oh yeah, he's teaching me carpentry. I'll tell you more about that in a bit. Senior and I were planing out this wood his son had brought in. It had a unique design to it. Senior explained how the imperfection was caused by some trauma in the tree's past—like a disease or hatchet whack or something. Trees grow around whatever happens to them, and their past becomes part of the wood grain.

His lesson contained a semi-hidden moral. I should learn from that tree and not just run from my past but embrace it as part of who I am and allow it to become a piece of my future.

I'm not sure I'm anywhere near as strong as a tree.

Mawmaw Mabel, on the other hand, talks ninety miles an hour all the time, even if Missy's the only one in the room. She's also the best cook I've ever met. I'm worried she's going to make me as fat as her dumplin's.

The Millers' house immediately felt like a home. I suppose that's what I need. I know now I wasn't ready to run off on my own. I need a temporary home, while I figure out my future.

My first two nights alone were terrifying. I spent the first wandering around Columbia in the dark. The second, I slept in one of those manger scene things that was pushed up against a church building.

Senior saw right through me when I showed up at his hardware store looking for a job. He knew I didn't have anywhere to stay or any money.

Since settling in with the Millers, I have been thinking about my next steps. I looked into the civil engineering program at the local college. I'm not sure I can get in, though, with just my GED. If not, I've fallen in love with woodworking. Could I make that a career?

Rach, I wish you could see Senior's woodshop. You would understand why I love it so much. It's the smell of the sawdust and the perfectly aligned rows of tools and the feel of the wood when it's been sanded down just right ... and the feel before.

It's the shimmer of dust in a sunbeam through the window. It's taking something that was once alive, imagining what it can become and then making it that—something new and useful and beautiful and alive again. Something that can become part of a person's home, life, memories.

Transforming something inanimate into a useful, beautiful keepsake or tool or piece of furniture makes me feel productive, in control and creative like I never have before. Watching a piece unfold in my hands and take the shape of an image in my mind is ... well, I don't know the right word for it.

I suppose I've found something to be passionate about ... besides you.

One more bit of news would make you happy, so I've saved it for last. I've been going to church with the Millers every Sunday.

Now I can end this letter imagining your beautiful smile.

Today's One Good Thing: I'm thankful today for the memories I have of you—still so real that I sometimes feel you beside me.

Sunday, July 21, 2002

Daddy and I are moving to Savannah. Both of us wanted a change from Bellum. An almost five-hour drive south sounds like a good start.

He had two phone interviews with the Genesis Mission, and they wanted him to come down for a final in-person one yesterday. I knew they'd offer him the job. He's excited to focus on a mission like that. I can tell because he looks lighter. He always shows the burdens he's carrying—maybe not to everyone, but I notice how the creases around his eyes deepen and how his shoulders droop.

This morning, we went to a service at the Mission. Tomorrow we'll visit Georgia Southern University in Statesboro. We'll look for houses the next few days before we return to Bellum to pack.

After the revival that broke out following Daddy's final sermon in Bellum, the church asked him to reconsider resigning. He told them he didn't need to, and we've been attending church a few counties over where his friend preaches.

Since Daddy's blistering sermon, things have been different in Bellum for me, too. A few people have apologized to me for how they treated Jack. I directed them to Ms. Becky and told them she and Jack were the ones whose forgiveness they should seek.

Ms. Becky is the one person I am heartbroken to leave. We restarted the book club she and Mama used to have—a club of two, with stories to share, a cup or two of tea and always laughter. I will miss that and her.

Of course, I will miss Shannon and Anna Claire, but we're all launching into separate futures. Little Stevie is almost three and Laylah is one. The speed of time fast-forwards when you watch kids grow.

Shannon has started doing more wedding photography in other states. Anna Claire's boutique and clothing design business are booming.

One of the letters Mama wrote me before she died was about the gift of friendship. She wrote that life would be filled with people who aren't true friends, but I'll meet a few who are. They will make life sparkle. Thanks to her example and words, I know the difference.

Shannon and Anna Claire have stood beside me through my hard days and through Jack leaving. I've walked with them through their griefs, addictions, pains, fears and the births of their beautiful babies. We are bonded through tears and committed to a joyful future together. I know, wherever me and my friends go and whatever we do, we'll be each other's sunshine on cloudy days. Always.

Since Jack left, I'd been rethinking my next steps and decided to get more hands-on experience with fitness training at the Wellness Center. After working there, I'm certain I want to pursue a career in fitness. I also want to explore options in nutrition. The two fields go well together, so I think it would be wise to double major. Georgia Southern offers both, which confirms it's the right place for me.

The thought of moving scares me. I've never lived anywhere other than Bellum. Losing Mama—and now Jack—has taught me something. Home isn't a place; home is the people who love you, whose hearts beat in time with your own. Wherever they are is more home than some place where no one cares.

I wonder if that's how Jack felt. Did the bad of the people in Bellum outweigh those of us who love him? Did they trample the feel of home? I can understand that.

He didn't need to leave us without giving us a chance to talk it through—or at least to hug him goodbye. All I can hope is that I will get to hug him again one day, preferably sooner than later.

Daddy and I leave soon for a walking tour. Savannah is a beautiful city, and the food is amazing. I'm ready to see more sights, taste more goodies and enjoy time with my dad.

Today's One Good Thing:
I am thankful for a new place to explore that's slightly closer to where Jack is now. Two and a half hours isn't far.

Monday, August 5, 2002

Dear Rachael,

My skin feels itchy—like when we sat in that fire ant hill in sixth grade—but itchy from the inside. My blood feels like it's getting hotter, and now I know how frogs feel when they're put in water that slowly rises to a boil. I always told you I was going to try that, but you'd tell me, "Don't you dare!" I never dared, and now I'm glad I didn't because, man, this sucks.

It's not just the restlessness, the wondering where the heck I belong or where I need to go next. It's an urge, a need to fight, to defend, to demolish evil. Every night on the news I see his picture—that monster in the desert. How can anyone become a dictator like that? How can anyone live with themselves if they kill innocent people—children, even? He needs to be stopped. I know our country will make that happen, and I want to help.

I'm sorry, Rachael. You didn't want me to join the Marines. I made the decision to leave you so you can have the future you deserve, which I guess is in Savannah now. It's weird to not be able to picture you where you are anymore. That's even more of a reason for me to seize the future I should.

When I got back from work today, I asked Senior some questions about joining—he was in the

Corps—and then asked him to take me to the recruitment depot. He took me right away. Mawmaw Mabel was more than a little flustered to hold our dinner so late, let me tell you.

So you know, I have no regrets. I know I took the right step tonight. When I ran away from Bellum, I had no idea where I was going or what I would find. I was stupid and blind and, honestly, got lucky that the Millers took me in. If they hadn't, well … truth is, I was a helpless, lost kid. I'm not sure what would have happened.

Even though that was only a few weeks ago, I've matured enough to recognize my helplessness, which is something in itself. Now, I need to move forward to something—somewhere—to make a difference, to contribute to the world around me and to do all that with the guidance I know the Marines will give me. They're not going to pull me off the street, slap a gun in my hand and let me loose. They're going to train me and give me a plan to execute. That's the launch into life I need.

I mostly made this decision last night while I was talking with Ducky. I'm pretty sure he disagrees about my choice, but I know it's right. His words of warning keep poking at me, though. He said, "If you run across the world to that darkness, you'll just be adding to the darkness inside you."

You'd probably agree; and you're probably both right. Here's how I look at it, though. I'm already so full of darkness, what difference could more make? Darkness plus darkness is still darkness. At least this time it should be ringed with a halo of light because I'm fighting for a cause. That should stand for something, right?

Maybe that's wishful thinking.

Either way, I'm thankful for …

Today's One Good Thing: … the hope of a halo shimmering around my darkness.

Friday, August 9, 2002

Dear Rachael,

I'm building the most complicated furniture yet—a pair of rocking chairs. You know I never was great with math, so I'm hoping I haven't cut something wrong. I suppose the worst that could happen is they rock crooked or not at all.

Or, they could collapse as soon as someone sits in them.

Don't worry. I'll test them before I gift them.

I'm surprised how sad I am to leave this family, since I haven't been here long. When I go, I want these chairs to be a token of thanks to them for all they've done and given me. You know, they've never let me pay for anything—room, board, even the clothes Mawmaw Mabel insists she pick up for me.

More than thanks to them, though, I'm making these chairs for me. Here I go, being selfish again, I suppose. I figure, when I'm off breaking my back under some heavy pack while running through the mud and the muck, I can think about these two chairs and the couple rocking side by side in them. It'll remind me of home and simpler places and keep me going.

If I'm being completely honest—which is easy to do in letters to your best friend that you'll never send—these chairs remind me of more. They remind me of us.

When I look at Senior and Mawmaw Mabel and their family, I see a real-life picture of how I always envisioned we would be. Theirs is the kind of life I planned to build with you. Even their sunset years are how I saw ours being—still in love decades after the vows.

Today's One Good Thing: I'm thankful for dreams because, even though they never get to be, their visions bring me comfort and remind me of the goodness that lives outside of me—a goodness I got to touch and feel for a brief time—and that I will always cherish.

Thursday, August 15, 2002

I found a new letter to Daddy from Jack. He's joining the Marine Corps, and I can't stop crying.

Until now, I believed he would come to his senses and get in touch with us—with his mama—and then move forward with us in his life. Instead, he's joining the Marines.

Fighting. Gun-toting. Battles and war.

He wrote to Daddy that he hasn't told his mama. How could Jack make such a drastic decision without communicating with Ms. Becky?

And now I've messed up my journal with all these tear splotches. I never thought I'd live without Jack beside me. When he left, I figured he needed time.

I read back through his most recent letters to Daddy. He knows we moved to Savannah. As I tucked the letters back in Daddy's hiding place, I had a thought. Maybe because we moved, he thought I was moving on, too?

Of course, I am moving on, but not intentionally without him. I mean, yes, I am making college plans and, yes, I think Georgia Southern's right for me. If Jack came back in my life today and wanted to pursue Georgia Tech like we'd talked about, I would consider it. I would also share my thoughts on Georgia Southern, and we would work out a plan that would be best for us both. We could do that because that's what we've always done: share, communicate—give and take.

Together ... a word that doesn't seem to describe us anymore. The Marine Corps isn't a future we can share.

I'm afraid Jack's still running, but this time he's running toward a future he might not survive. Why would God let him do this?

Jack's choice seems irresponsible and sudden, especially since he made it without his mom's input. I'm scared and angry. Mostly, I feel helpless.

His decision steamrolled my heart and showed me I'm no longer part of his life. Jack signed us away when he signed up.

Today's One Good Thing:
I am thankful that I can pour out my heart and thoughts and worries in this journal. I'm also thankful Daddy's at work so I can cry while I attempt to process this new reality.

Saturday, August 31, 2002

Dear Rachael,

Tomorrow evening I leave for Parris Island and Boot Camp. I'd be lying if I said I wasn't nervous. Part of me worries I won't be able to cut it. I believe it's what I'm supposed to do, though. No doubts about the decision, just about myself and my abilities.

I'll have to remind myself to keep going, even when I don't think I can. It's all about mind over matter, right?

Something I will miss over the next three months is building—houses with the crew and furniture in the shop with Senior. It's the most thrilling thing I've ever done. (Aside from kissing you, of course.)

What I love about building is the satisfaction of a completed project. Rocking chairs for memory-making. A box to store accounts of a small business, both built by hand. Planters for herbs to make savory meals. Or, an entire house that some family will make a home. While I know I'll find accomplishment in the Corps, I think it will feel different. Maybe I'll find ways to do woodworking there.

I've been wondering how you are doing. Do you like Savannah? Are you going to college there? I'm guessing you changed your mind about Georgia Tech.

That may have been more my goal than yours. I'm sorry for holding you back or pushing my dreams on you.

You deserve space for your dreams and goals, and I know, wherever you are, you'll have so many opportunities. Groups to join—perhaps a sorority? I can't see you as the sorority type. Watch out for those frat guys; they're not good enough for you.

I miss you, Rach.

Today's One Good Thing: I am thankful for the chance to prove myself in one of the toughest training programs—to be more than who I have been and to do more than I thought I could.

Sunday, September 1, 2002

After I found out about Jack joining the Marines, Anna Claire, Shannon and I jumped on IM for much-needed friend therapy. Anna Claire said she would've been terrified if Steven had joined. They reminded me that Jack's trying to find his place in the world, and maybe this is the next step he needs to take.

Jack deserves to follow his dream, but I wish he didn't have such a stupid one.

Am I un-American because I don't want Jack to join the Marines? That's a question that's been nagging at me. Part of me feels selfish and wrong; the other part believes I'm justified. Maybe I can sift through my thoughts if I write them.

Uniforms are great. The saying about liking a man in uniform is true, and I can picture Jack in those fancy dress blues and even the camouflage stuff. He'd be hot as anything ... no doubt. Duty to country and the call to serve are noble. Words like brave and chivalrous come to mind.

The reality, though, is what war does. War changes people and takes lives.

I used to read books set in war times where heroes marched off to battle, while the women waited, patiently and expectantly, and did selfless, helpful tasks back home. I loved the stories of knights in shining armor and the damsels in distress they'd swoop in to save between epic battles. It was romantic literature, for sure.

Real war is ruthless and inhumane, and I don't want that for Jack. Maybe I'm selfish, but I'd rather him do anything else and live than put on a uniform and step into the line of fire.

I've watched him almost die three times already. This decision seems like he's trying to get himself killed.

Even if he survives, he'll only add to his nightmares. I don't want him to have to make choices and decisions that will haunt him every day of his life. I don't want him to watch friends die.

The drag accident was bad enough for all of us. I still remember the stickiness of Jack's blood as I begged God to help me apply enough pressure to keep him from dying in my arms. I remember the sounds and smells of Anna Claire and Jerry vomiting when they saw Steven's brains smeared across his car windows. I still smell the spice of the bonfire, the sting of gasoline and the mixture of clay and blood.

That night haunts us all. And that was a teen hangout on a dirt road. Jack wants to go to war where blood and death are guaranteed.

I don't want to lose him. Even if we're never going to be together, I want to know he's somewhere, alive.

Also, I want him to live to know Christ. I want him to give his life to God and follow Him. These are the things I want for Jack, and they're not things I see happening in a war zone. Sure, you hear about "battlefield conversions," but that's not the shift to a Christian life that I want for Jack. I want him to be able to live the Christian life, not finally, at the last minute, accept it and then be gone without the chance to live here for Christ.

At the end of the day, I want Jack to be whole and alive and happy for the first time in too many years. I want all the best for him in this life and in the next.

And yes, I want him here with me. I love him. I always have, and I know I always will. Having him disappear from my life suddenly with only a goodbye letter split my heart in two. Now, knowing he's doing the one thing I never wanted him to do ... it's like having a shaker of salt poured into that still-fresh wound.

Before, I thought he needed time and space to heal. Now, I worry he believes he is healed and ready to move forward with his life. His decision shows me he has no intention of returning to me. He left me behind and hasn't looked back.

Shannon and Anna Claire reminded me of truths I've spoken to them over the years. They reminded me I'm only responsible for how I react and what I do—not for Jack's choices. As much as I want him to be part of my life again, I know I'm not promised that. What I am promised is that God loves me and that He is in control of Jack's life—whether Jack wants Him to be or not.

Jack's decisions and actions have baffled me, though. Nothing he's done in the past few months makes sense.

These choices also go to show how easily I took things for granted. I accepted our future as certain when it never was. We weren't engaged. We hadn't made vows.

Except we said those words: I love you. We meant them. We had plans for our love. We discussed our future and intended to embrace it together.

I know the truth and depth and promise in every conversation we had. I know the emotions and the commitment of our words. I know Jack—his heart, his soul, his innermost being, his hopes and dreams, his everything. That's what hurts, and that's why I struggle to accept that he has really left.

Except, he has. I guess I never fully knew him. Maybe I didn't know the other things I thought I did either.

Today's one Good Thing:
I am thankful for the love we shared, for the connection we had. I think. I don't know. It's hard to be thankful for something as beautiful as that when it's suddenly gone. Now I'm left fighting the inner battle of was it ever real? Switching from "I know it was." to "I think it was." to "Maybe it never was." might make me crazy. This one good thing went sideways, didn't it?

Sunday, September 8, 2002

Dear Rachael,

As I predicted, Boot Camp is kicking my butt. Apparently I have two left feet. It sounds ridiculous, but I cannot drill without tripping. Not sure what it is about marching in time that I can't get the hang of.

Maybe I shouldn't have made fun of the band geeks. Marching is way harder than it looks.

One thing I am good with, though, is my rifle. They issued them to us early on. Every spare minute I get, I'm cleaning mine. I'm ready to get to the range and shoot. For now, I'll have to content myself with cleaning it and knowing each piece as well as a part of my body.

We had to memorize a poem. Actually, it's a creed—"The Marine Rifleman's Creed." I've already got it down by heart; kind of like you did with your Psalms and other Bible verses. Two of the lines play on repeat in my head all day long, no matter what we're doing or what the DIs are yelling: "My rifle is my best friend. It is my life. I must master it as I must master my life."

I won't pretend to know how to master my life, but this rifle I can master. It's got order and a purpose and makes sense. I know what to expect with it, how to clean and care for it and what's expected of me with it. It's a responsibility I can handle; one I believe I can live up to.

Each part of this weapon has a purpose and a place–kind of like every one of us in my platoon. Separately, we're here for our own reasons and have a place in daily life. But, it's not until we're pieced together properly that we can work for our bigger purpose as Marines.

The together part still worries me. Can I trust other guys with my life?

Can they trust me with theirs?

This letter went deeper than I expected. I only intended to write you about my rifle.

Every time we get letters, I think of you. I know you won't send me one–and yes, that's on me. I still imagine what it would be like to see your pretty handwriting on an envelope with my name on it. Do you still dot your Is and Js with flowers or hearts? I guess we're outgrowing that sort of thing. We are technically adults now. I imagine your writing looks more professional, and I'm over here cleaning a rifle I'll use to kill people. That's about as adult as it gets, I suppose.

I miss becoming an adult with you, Rachael.

Today's One Good Thing: I'm thankful for the purpose and order–and life lessons–I've found in my M16.

Thursday, September 12, 2002

Dear Rachael,

Well, I was a jerk again. No surprise to you, I'm sure.

We've got this kid, Dawson, in India Company. Struggling would be a kind word for how he's making it. He's always the last to finish anything or grasp a new concept. He wants to be here, though. I'll give him that.

He came up to me earlier tonight during square-away time—that's when we get to do what we want or need to do, like writing letters or cleaning our rifles, without the dang DIs screaming at us. Dawson wanted me to teach him how to clean and assemble his rifle as quickly as I do mine.

News flash: he ain't gonna be able to do that. That's not me being arrogant, by the way. I struggle to communicate how slow this guy is.

Anyway, I told him no, but he kept yammering away about what he'd been doing and how it wasn't going well. I finally told him to stop trying. My tone might have been a little rude; I did want to be left alone with my rifle. What I meant to communicate, though, was he was trying too hard. Dude's way too uptight.

Before you roll your eyes and decide I'm still the same ass and always will be, let me finish. I called him and his sad face back.

I told him to slow down, to stop worrying about going fast and to focus on each piece and the process first. Once he learns those, he'll add the speed.

As my recruiter told me, "Slow is smooth; smooth is fast."

Dawson was pumped when he finally got it together right. I mean, he's no me, but ....

Yep, I felt that imaginary punch in the arm. I earned enough of those when we were together that I'll always feel it when I deserve one.

Today's One Good Thing: I'm thankful for a chance to teach someone something and to not be a complete jerk. Who would've thought: me, a teacher?

Monday, September 16, 2002

Dear Rachael,

I can finally drill without tripping all over myself.

The advice I gave Dawson about his rifle cleaning issues came in handy for me on the Parade Deck. We'd been out there all day, and I was pretty much dead on my feet—not how I want to be when I have to march.

Anyway, I told myself, "Lighten up. Breathe. One step at a time." Suddenly, I heard—really heard—the beat of our boots on the pavement, and mine werent off anymore.

You have no idea what a big deal this is for me. If I didn't get it together today, I was going to get mustered out. How embarrassing would it have been for me to get kicked out because I couldn't move my feet in time?

I still don't know what my issue was, but, man, am I glad I've gotten past it. No stopping me now!

When the rhythm clicked into place, I wanted nothing more than to share my victory with you. Sometimes, missing you feels like what I imagine missing a limb would be like. The pain is manageable, though, when I consider all the great stuff I know you can do with your life and how happy I hope you are as you work toward your future.

What challenges are you overcoming right now? It's hard for me to picture you struggling with anything, but I'm sure there will be something that's not easy for you. College must be way harder than high school ever thought of being. You'll be fine, though. You're the most determined person I know. Whatever you put your mind to, you will do.

Today's One Good Thing: It's obvious what I'm thankful for today—getting my groove on the Parade Deck and not getting booted out for two left feet.

Friday, September 20, 2002

Dear Rachael,

Our good buddy Dawson had a breakthrough today. The best part? I helped.

In today's run, Sergeant Marshall put Dawson up front with me and told me to run full out. So you know, my full-out is faster than your average recruit's. And, if you'll recall, Dawson is well below average. You can imagine how my best was going to kick his tail.

When we set off, I watched his face shift from ready to hopeless to stone-like and resigned, like he knew this final run would send him packing. I reminded him how I'd taught him to breathe and focus during earlier runs. I'm always getting sent back to run the last stretch a second time next to him, so I've had plenty of opportunities to teach him those lessons. He has been getting better, slowly.

Dawson wants to be a Marine, probably more than anyone else in our platoon. He proved that today. I watched his mindset shift right there as I kicked up our pace and he matched my strides.

I feel proud when I reflect on the past few weeks. I've been able to share what I know and encourage Dawson. Leading might be something I can do in the Corps one day.

Total honesty: a big part of me has resented Dawson because of how much extra work he costs me. Watching that victory in his eyes made all the extra steps worth it. Of course, I love to run; so that reduces the bitterness as well.

Each lesson I learn and hurdle I overcome enables me to trust myself and the guys around me. I didn't think I could do that, especially with life in the balance. Now that I'm settling into the Marine way of life, I trust the efficiency of the training we're receiving to make us more than who we are alone—to make us a team.

Today's One Good Thing: I'm thankful for Dawson's win and for the lesson I learned. I can be more thankful from now on for the extra running because I've seen how it can benefit others.

Friday, October 4, 2002

I haven't wanted to journal because it makes me think, and every thought begins with Jack. I stopped reading the letters he writes to Daddy.

Knowing his words are nearby maintains a tangible connection to Jack. Not reading them relieves me of the weight of how happy he is in his new life without me.

I don't want to be bitter, but I am. Desire and reality don't always match up when it comes to matters of the heart.

In other life things, I'm getting used to Savannah with all its differences from Bellum. Savannah's history and architecture fascinate me, and I love walking along the water. I can always find something to do, too. Fields and back roads were the only attractions in Bellum. Life here feels more open—like I can breathe deeply. I'm not sure if that's because Savannah is bigger with a more open landscape, or because I'm no longer known by every resident as the Baptist preacher's daughter.

Everyone expects the preacher's daughter to act a certain way, but no one knows what that way is, only that you haven't lived it. Every face you make, word you utter and deed you do become exhibits in your life's public trial. Judgment never ceases, and no final verdict manifests. It's a trial without end or mercy.

Another possibility is, I feel free because all the tragedies and loss of my past reside in Bellum and not here. Regardless of why I feel liberated, Jack wasn't the only imprisoned citizen. I didn't realize how Bellum caged me.

I haven't taken advantage of all Savannah's social opportunities yet. Daddy's worried because I only go to work and hang out at home. He declared over pancakes this morning that he and I have plans all weekend. We'll start after supper with an evening concert; then this weekend is some food festival.

Go figure—the dad's the one forcing us to go out, not the should-be-a-freshman-in-college daughter.

If Jack were here, we'd do something every night. Almost every event I hear about makes me think of us—music festivals, food festivals, film festivals. We could have fun together.

Jack may have left me behind, but I'm not ready to do the same with his memory. It feels too soon to experience new things alone—or with someone else. One day I'll overcome these feelings, so enough of my gloomy thoughts.

I hope Shannon and Anna Claire can visit soon, but I know it's hard for them to break away from work and their kids. I miss babysitting those kiddos and watching them—and their moms—grow.

On the school front, I've been in touch with the admissions office at Georgia Southern. Part of me wishes I had started this fall. Honestly, if I could go back in time, I wouldn't wait on Jack to get his mess together. I would've applied long ago and moved forward before he did. Would that have made Jack's leaving easier?

"What's in the past needs to be passed," as Mama would say.

I choose to focus on new plans now. I have filled out all my admissions and scholarship applications. Fingers crossed, everything goes well, and I not only get accepted for next year but also receive financial aid.

In the meantime, I've been working at a fitness center for women. I appreciate the environment. It makes me feel more comfortable because I'm not worried the dude next to me is getting turned on when I use the butterfly machine. Guys can be such pigs—well, not all men, of course. No need to throw the entire gender under the bus because of a few rotten ones.

That's all I have to write about today, I guess. I've got mama's spaghetti sauce simmering on the stove, and it's smelling ready for a taste-test. Daddy should be home from the Mission soon, so I'll start the pasta. Maybe first I'll dig through the closet for a cute autumn outfit to wear to the concert.

Today's One Good Thing:
I'm thankful for a dad who loves me and isn't afraid to push me when I need it.

Sunday, October 6, 2002

Daddy knew what he was doing Friday night. I hadn't realized how much I needed to immerse myself in our new home.

The concert featured folk and jazz music. Around the park, people danced, and Daddy convinced me to dance with him. I told him I was too old to dance on top of his feet. He said it was about time I started carrying my own weight and then proceeded to twirl me around. I haven't laughed that much in a long time.

Dancing with him reminded me of my childhood—of the dance parties we had when Mama was still with us. I loved dancing on Daddy's feet, but so much more than that, I loved watching Daddy and Mama dance.

We'd push the furniture to the walls, and he'd spin her around our living room. Her cheeks would match our hair, and her smile would shine brighter than the stars. The way they looked at each other made me happy. Their love filled our home.

Soon before Mama died, Daddy heard a new song that reminded him of her. He went straight to the store to buy it so he could dance with her. Even when she got too weak to dance, he'd scoop her up in his arms and sway with her to what had become their favorite George Strait song, "Carried Away."

Dancing with Daddy this weekend also reminded me of Jack. I grew up with the confidence that comes from a family built on a solid foundation. When Jack and I danced together, I felt the way Mama looked at Daddy. I believed we'd dance into our future together.

That's a memory I will hold close but cannot dwell on right now. My mind needs to focus on the present.

Yesterday and today, Daddy and I attended the food festival. We ate so much, I'm not sure I can even work out tomorrow; though, I definitely need to.

Tonight, I thanked Daddy for pushing me to get out and be social. He kissed my forehead and held my hands in his and then he said something I don't want to forget.

"I want my little girl to smile as bright as I know she can and to live her life free from the pain of a broken heart. If dancing and food can help with that, we'll enjoy them together every night of the week. Healing may come more slowly; but I know it will, as long as you cling to the identity you claimed when you were a tiny girl. Remember to Whom you belong. You're a daughter of the King of Kings, and He can heal the most broken of hearts."

His positivity gives me hope. One day, maybe I'll feel whole again.

Maybe.

Today's One Good Thing:
I am thankful for a father who speaks truth in love.

Saturday, October 26, 2002

Dear Rachael,

Grass Week has been outstanding. We spent the entire week in the field with our rifles, learning to shoot from all four firing positions. All my time spent with my weapon since we got them paid off. I'm an expert rifleman.

Even better, we're the top Shooting Platoon. It feels damn good to be top dog at something.

One thing I continue working on is my run time. I'm still above eighteen minutes for a three-mile run. That's not good enough for me. I know I can dip below ... just have to keep shaving the milliseconds off. We've got our final physical coming up, so I've got until then to get my time where I want it.

Even with my time not perfect, I'm feeling pretty daggone proud of myself. Rach, I might be a benefit to the Corps ... with my shooting ability now and, one day, with more leadership. I may finally belong somewhere.

That's a weird feeling; I'm not entirely sure what to do with it. Most people who live one place their whole lives consider it home. I never felt at home in Bellum. Maybe that had to do with the way people treated my mom. Maybe it was because of how people never forgave me for all the pain I caused with my drinking or with the accidents.

Whatever my case, I wonder if you felt the same way. If so, maybe that's another reason our bond was so strong.

Enough of this deep thinking and back to training...

I don't want to dwell on this whole pride thing. There's still plenty of time for me to screw things up with the physical around the corner. Plus, we still have to endure the Crucible. With a name like that, it's gotta be bad.

Can't get lazy now—I have to focus on improving and moving forward. One day at a time, one step at a time—I might make it after all.

Today's One Good Thing: If I have to pick one thing to be thankful for today, I'm going with shooting. My rifle's an extension of my arm at this point. Shooting is the only time I've been 100% confident in myself.

Thursday, November 28, 2002

I called Ms. Becky to wish her Happy Thanksgiving and see when she'll finish the third book in the Love Comes Softly series so we can chat about it. She has me hooked on Janette Oke's books, and I'm ready to move on to the fourth. She and Mama discovered them, and Ms. Becky thought they would be the perfect starting point for our club.

She sounds lonely, which I'm sure she is. Another reason to be angry with Jack—leaving his mama on a holiday. Our families used to celebrate together; now Ms. Becky's alone in Bellum.

We didn't talk about Jack today; I avoided the topic. I did break down and read the letters he's sent Daddy. Thankfully, Jack's finally planning to write Ms. Becky, tell her where he is and invite her to his Boot Camp graduation, which is coming up soon. He invited Daddy, too.

Daddy's already told me a fib about going to a counseling conference. Actually, he may have found one nearby so he doesn't completely lie to me.

I'm thankful Jack's finally reaching out to his mama, and I hope she'll go to see him. Family needs to stick together, especially when it's small.

Total honesty, though: my heart broke all over again when I read his letter to Daddy. He never mentioned inviting me.

After Jack left, I had hope. Even after he joined, I had hope. Reading these letters and seeing not a single mention of me—not even an "Is she okay?"—I have no hope left. It's clear he's moved on and doesn't intend for me to be part of his life again. He's gone, and I'm on my own.

I'm glad he's got Daddy and his mom, but I feel alone because he was my best friend. More than that, he was my only for always.

Heartbreak is part of being a teenager and a young adult—at least that's what all the books and movies show. I thought I had lucked out and avoided all that breakup drama and the dating "game." I thought Jack was it.

Before she died, Mama encouraged me to share my grief and emotions with the people in my life. She couldn't have known about a grief like this. I can't talk to Ms. Becky because it's her son. I can't talk to Daddy because I don't want him to know I've been snooping and reading the letters; plus, I don't know how to share with him the pain of losing the man I love. I'm not sure he'd know how to hear it. My best friends are nearly five hours away.

I've never felt this alone, not even right after Mama died. Then, I had Jack. He held my hand while I cried on his shoulder.

How ironic: the one shoulder I could cry on belongs to the same person who's causing my tears.

Today's One Good Thing:
I am thankful for a holiday that forces us to remember the importance of gratitude. Even when I feel hopeless, I know I have a loving father, a good home and a future—even if it's not what I'd envisioned. Those are all things to give thanks for today and every day, no matter how hurt I feel.

Thursday, December 5, 2002

Dear Rachael,

I'm a United States Marine. Hoorah!

You're a big reason I am, too, and you don't even know. Man, I wish you knew. I would love nothing more than to see you walking out of those stands at graduation. I would sweep you up in my arms and kiss you like I've never kissed you before.

During the Crucible—fifty-four hours with no sleep, little food and constant movement in simulated combat—I was ready to give up. I've never been that exhausted or overwhelmed. Even though they were fake, those bullets and bombs crashing around us almost sent me into an emotional spiral ... until this one moment.

One of my buddies had been "hit" in the simulation, so we had to cross the minefield with him and all our gear. We were dragging tail and ready to tell the DIs to screw it. I looked across that miserable field, into the hazy smoke, and saw you—clear as day.

You were dancing, holding your hand back to me, motioning for me to come to you, to not stop or give up. I saw the sun shine on your gorgeous red hair and heard your laugh. I felt this crazy surge of energy and knew I could make it and so could my buddies.

I reminded them of the Marines we'd been hearing stories about along the way. I told them we could be great, too, but we had to take our final steps toward earning the title. We split up the gear and took turns, two of us carrying McNamara while the other led the way through the minefield, testing as we went. We got through.

Once we reached the final part—the nine-mile hike under forty-five pounds of gear—nothing could've stopped me. I took every step for you.

Every time I thought there was no way I could keep running or crawling or pushing, I'd close my eyes and your face would fill my mind. Your smile gave me the strength and determination to keep going, no matter how I felt.

If I sent this letter, if I apologized and begged for your forgiveness, would you come? Would you let me spend the rest of my life trying to make it up to you? Would you ever forgive me? Could you be proud of me?

I know. I left for a reason, and that reason's still best for you. Besides, my leaving isn't something you should forgive, so I can't ask it of you.

More practically, tomorrow is graduation day, when I will wear my dress blues.

That's a big deal, by the way. I'll be graduating, not as a Private, but as a Private First Class; and I'll be carrying the guidon for my platoon like I have for much of Boot.

I wonder what you'd think if you saw me in uniform. I think you'd change your mind about me being a Marine. After all, chicks dig uniforms; and the dress blues are, hands down, the best.

Of course, earning this uniform is the one thing you asked me not to do. Even if you want to hear from me, you wouldn't want to hear that.

Regardless, I'll be thinking of you—my personal guidon.

Today's One Good Thing: I am thankful to have completed Boot Camp and to have achieved the greatest title—United States Marine.

Thursday, December 5, 2002

Daddy's leaving early tomorrow. He'll be going to Jack's graduation—I mean, a "counseling conference."

I packed my bag. I don't know why; I'm not going.

Jack's letters to Daddy make it clear he doesn't regret leaving me. I need to wise up and focus on my future. First, I need to work on mending my heart. It's in pieces, so my first task is to gather them.

Shannon invited me to meet her in Augusta. She's got a wedding there that she's excited about. I could go; maybe I should. Daddy said he thought it sounded like a great idea, but I don't feel like driving anywhere.

All I feel like doing is having a giant pity party because running after a boy who intentionally left me would be terribly embarrassing and won't help anyone. I know that.

And yet, there's my bag—sitting there, all packed.

Ugh!

Being a girl sucks. We do stupid things when it comes to boys, even when we know they're stupid. I don't want to be stupid.

Today's One Good Thing:

I am thankful for a shimmer of wisdom behind a storm cloud of stupidity.

Friday, December 6, 2002

It's still dark. Daddy's already left. Obviously, I didn't go. Which, of course, was the right decision.

I'm kicking myself though because ... what if? What if he couldn't write my dad how he feels about me? What if he doesn't think I would forgive him for leaving? What if he still loves me as much as I love him?

What if? Two words shouldn't cut so deeply.

It's too late now. I've made my choice, and it wasn't Jack. Now I must live with it. And, I've got to actually live.

This weekend, Daddy will be gone. I've got the place to myself, and I intend to do what everyone else my age does to forget. I intend to get hammered.

Then, on Monday, I'll wake up—probably late—decide what I want to learn the rest of this year at the women's center and if I should look for another job before college.

That's me moving on. Without Jack.

Today's One Good Thing:
I am thankful for the anonymity of a larger city and the ease in finding gas stations that are more than happy to sell to underage drinkers with cash and a mission to forget.

Friday, December 6, 2002

Dear Rachael,

I looked for you today at graduation.

Sad, I know. My disappointment that you weren't there was embarrassing. Part of me thought you'd step out from behind your dad and tell me you were too stubborn to stay away, no matter what I said. But, of course, you didn't ... as you shouldn't.

It killed me to be with your dad and not ask how you are and what you're doing—and if you're dating someone. Way harder than not asking in a letter.

Senior and Mawmaw Mabel, Ducky and Daisy came too. You'll be glad to hear I wrote my mom. I told her where I've been and what I've been doing and asked her to come to graduation.

She did; and I swear I will never shut my mom out of my life again. She gave me a huge hug and smile, but I saw a look in her eyes I've seen once before—soon after Dad left. I will not cause her that kind of pain again.

Honestly, I've never felt this ashamed. The way I tore out of Bellum wasn't immature; it was hateful. I see that now, and I am deeply sorry for my choice. My only hope is my actions didn't cause you the same hurt they inflicted on my mom.

She is worried I'm running from my past. I told her, though, I'm not running away from anything—not anymore. For the first time in my life, I'm running toward a purpose. I know she worries I haven't dealt with everything that happened during high school. If I'm honest, I am too; but I know I'm doing what I'm meant to do.

Maybe whatever I do can't change the past, but it can help the future. Like I helped Dawson, I could help others—people who need someone who can run hard and full out, who can shoot true and who can put down some of the evil in this world.

I enjoyed seeing all the people who—for whatever misguided reasons—love me, but I'm eager to get back in the field to shoot and train. Now that I've earned the title Marine, I've got to live up to it.

Today's One Good Thing: Today I'm thankful for a chance to be a better son and to bring some good to the future and do it in a damn spiffy uniform.

Friday, December 13, 2002

That was a mistake. I should have met Shannon in Augusta instead of staying here alone to get drunk.

I don't know why people run to alcohol to numb their pain. It's been a few days since I stopped drinking and throwing up, and I still feel queasy. How did Jack live like this for so long?

Why did I think a drunken weekend would solve everything? All that pain and anger and confusion and hurt that I tried to drown is still inside me—intensified. Above all that, I feel prickly with shame—a heat rash on my soul.

I've helped addicts restart their lives after rehab. That was the point of Passion Discovery. Anna Claire and I started the program for Shannon when she and Jack were going through the Mission. We helped Shannon launch her business, based on our experiences from starting Anna Claire's boutique.

Plus, I watched Jack nearly kill himself. With all that I witnessed firsthand, I, of all people, should never have tipped up a bottle to relieve pain and find numbness.

Another feeling that's intensified now is separation from God. When I try to pray, all I can think about are my stupid decisions or my anger. Jack's not around for me to direct my rage toward, so I've moved on, it seems. I'm mad at God.

Why would God let all these things happen? Four friends got killed years ago. Jack became an alcoholic. He got sober, but then—right when life began to progress for us—that second accident happened. The crack in the unstable foundation of Bellum opened, and Jack crashed down and tumbled away from me and us. In the process, my future disintegrated.

~

Daddy and I shared a couple of pizzas, and I feel better. Food and time with my dad clear my head and improve my spirits. As I reread the first part of my entry, I know my future hasn't disintegrated—despite my recent poor choices or anything that's happened this year. I still have a future, and it's up to me to make it positive. I do know that, and I won't make the same mistake I did last weekend. Nothing good can come from letting alcohol—or anything else—control me.

Moving forward, though, will not be how I always envisioned. Although I've looked forward to college and a career in fitness, I can't feel anything for my future except resignation and numbness.

I'm not sure why, but it might have to do with my relationship with God. I have no desire to read the Bible or pray or go to church. That's new for me.

When Jack and I were in junior high, I went through a phase where I was indifferent and started doing things I had said before I'd never do—like drink and smoke. Even then, I wasn't angry or numb. I just rebelled.

Then our friends died; Jack almost died. I decided the way I'd been living wasn't worth taking my focus off God. I had grown in my faith and relationship with Him since that time ... until now.

I know God hasn't left me—He never will. I also know I have to find a new church home, regardless of my current emotions. It's weird because I never thought about choosing a church. When your dad's the preacher, you don't have a choice.

He told me I could keep going to the Mission's services, but he and I both know I need a real church home—not a place where a bunch of men are trying to rebuild their lives after addictions.

This Sunday I'll attend Peace Presbyterian Church. It's a white church with a steeple I could stare at all day. It's so tall that when you look to the top, the cross floats in the clouds. The sight reminds me of the peace and joy I once felt and the connection I wonder if I can experience again.

Anyway, I don't fully understand all the differences between the Baptist and Presbyterian churches. Frankly, I don't really care right now—which is not like me. I used to spend hours reading Daddy's commentaries and asking him questions when he was supposed to be studying for his sermons. Now, I only want to sit in a beautiful church and ask God to thaw my frozen heart with a desire to desire Him again.

Today's One Good Thing:
I am thankful for a God who has promised to never let me go and to never leave or forsake me, even when I've turned my eyes from Him.

Friday, December 20, 2002

Dear Rachael,

I scared the crap out of the guys in my squad bay last night. Pretty sure I lost their trust, too. I woke up screaming—not something a Marine should do. Thank goodness we weren't in combat.

It was like that old nightmare I had in the church yard my first night in Columbia. Skeletons and zombie bodies, but mostly Abbie Mae's lifeless face.

Will I ever stop seeing her?

That's the first time since before Missy that I've woken up screaming. I hope it'll be the last. The guys around me either glared at me or looked terrified.

Trayvon Henry's the only one who didn't do either. He's almost as good a rifleman as I am—almost.

After I woke us all up, Tray walked over and sat by me. We talked most of the night; it was an easy conversation, like how it was with you. His grandma lives nearby. Apparently, her cooking could rival Mawmaw Mabel's, so I'm hoping for an invitation. At the least, I'm thankful to have a friend. I haven't had many of those since ... well, since you.

In case you're wondering, sometimes I have amazing dreams. Those are the ones when you visit me. They're bright and shimmery—like a fairy tale. You're always smiling, often laughing. I can't get enough of those sexy red lips of yours. I could spend the rest of my life staring at them, kissing them. I should have told you that.

Hell, if I could go back in time, I wouldn't go down that cursed road where that accident wrecked my life and dreams. I wouldn't have waited until that night after prom to get down on one knee.

I haven't written about that to you before now. I planned to ask you to marry me on prom night. The ring is still in the velvet box in the bottom of my sea bag. Not sure why I've kept it. I know I can never return to you. But, in my dreams—the light, happy ones—I do. I walk right up to you, drop to one knee and open that box. I promise you my life, my heart, my everything and ask you to make me the luckiest man in the universe.

Some dreams let me slip into that alternate life where I pull you into my arms, whisper how much I love you, kiss the top of your head as you laugh and dip your head down … those long, curved lashes of yours falling and rising again to show me the sparkle in your sapphire eyes. That's when I smile back and sink into your kiss.

That's what I would do if dreams came true.

Today's One Good Thing: Today I'm thankful for the blissful dreams that bring you to me.

Wednesday, December 25, 2002

Dear Rachael,

Merry Christmas!

Right about now, your dad's reading the Christmas story. Soon, you'll be opening presents and putting the bows and ribbons on your head. After all, Christmas is the holiday of your colors—emerald and red.

In our past, you and my mom would already have pies and other treats made. You'd be in the kitchen together mixing up a magical meal. I never knew how you two did it. Of course, I couldn't find out since both of you were quick to swat me with a wooden spoon whenever I'd walk in the kitchen to sneak ... I mean to help.

I'm thinking holidays away from Mom and you are going to be harder than I thought.

Thanksgiving would have been tougher, I think, but I was busy getting my butt chewed out by the DIs at Parris Island. That's the holiday I always think most of your mom. I'm guessing you do, too. Did you do a big spread for a bunch of people this year like you used to do in Bellum? You were determined to continue the tradition your mom started.

Thanks to your mom's insistence that we celebrate Thanksgiving together every year, along with anyone else who didn't have much family, I grew up understanding the beauty of a family holiday.

Even before Dad left, Mom and I were usually alone. For my dad, a holiday was an extra day to be left alone to drink. For your mom, it was an opportunity to share joy.

I remember the first Thanksgiving without your mom. You insisted you prepare every dish your mom would have. You smiled and laughed and supervised how your dad cut the turkey and the pies to make sure nothing went sideways. When everyone but me and Mom left, you sat on your deck and looked out to where your mom had planted those sunflowers for you. Then you burst into tears.

So you know, I had no idea what to do or what had happened. I wrapped you in my arms and held you close, because I was afraid the tears would take you away, too.

It took a while, but I'm glad you were able to explain your emotions. You told me all you wanted was to give others joy like your mom did. You didn't realize how much you needed it, too, or how much it would take out of you to try to fill her shoes.

I told you then that you never needed to give me all your joy; we would always find enough of that together.

May your Christmas be full of as much joy as memories of you give me.

Today's One Good Thing: Today I'm thankful for joy and for your mom reminding us to look for that one good thing every day. Finding today's cheered me up.

Tuesday, December 31, 2002

A while back I wrote in here about getting a second part-time job. I've changed my mind. Daddy and I talked through my options and what I want to do. He told me I don't need to worry about earning money right now, and I've already had the equivalent of a couple of internships—complete with references—that have solidified what I want to do with my life.

I've decided to take the freedom of this time in my life to do some good. I applied to be a counselor at a kids' camp this summer. Honestly, I'm not sure why, other than it sounds like a fun way to help.

Kids look for role models. Growing up, we face so many challenges and temptations, and it's easy to give in and let go of what we know is right along the way. I had Daddy and Mama to look up to, but some kids don't have any positive influences in their lives. While I'll only be with the kids for a week at a time, I hope I can be a light they will remember later in their lives when they're struggling with choices.

Of course, I'm certainly not the picture of perfection. I continue to struggle in my relationship with God. I want to be better, do better, live for Him. I want to learn and grow. Maybe, despite my shortcomings, I can spread some good, which leads me to a closer opportunity I've signed up for.

My church is taking an extended mission trip to Peru in a few months, and I'll be going with them and leaving my bubble to see another part of the world.

We'll help some missionaries who planted a church in a rural part of Peru a few years ago. I am learning about the country and the hardships they've faced. A Marxist rebel group caused a couple decades of terror and brutality. Drug trafficking is big there, which leads to many other awful things for the innocent people who are caught in the terrifying net of drug production.

The missionaries need our help to begin some programs. Their goal is to help the Peruvian people have a better quality of life—at least in a few ways. I'll be working with them on a nutrition and exercise program for women to have a healthier lifestyle and encourage their families to do the same. I'll also be helping the pastor's wife start a community garden they can tend and add to each year.

Mama would have loved to help with that. She'd be so much better at it than I will be. I miss her.

Grief never leaves. It might diminish for a time; but every now and then (or sometimes for a stretch of days or weeks on end), it crashes over me like a rogue wave. It knocks me down and flushes all the air from my lungs. Times like right now, in this minute, it pulls me down and holds me, away from the light and air of life. I've learned, when grief seizes me, to not fight it.

Instead, I close my eyes and hold my breath and thank God for the time I had with Mama on this earth. I thank Him for the letters she wrote me before she died and that I will see her again one day. I picture her now, tending a garden without weeds in heaven. I see her face with its beautiful smile; and I ache—a stabbing ache that, some days, I believe will slash me in half.

I think of everything I've missed without her by my side. How would she have guided me through the past few years with all its challenges—losing Jack, moving and postponing college? I'll never not miss her.

Now, as I try to imagine what Peru will be like and how I can most effectively help the people there, I wish she and I were planning together. I would have loved to go on a mission trip with Mama.

Peru and the summer camp will give me chances to pour into others and help them know they're not alone with struggles and frustrations in life. I can also share that God will always be with them—no matter what. Even on my dark days, even in my numbness or anger or grief or loneliness, I know He's here and always will be.

Today's One Good Thing:
I am thankful that God's presence doesn't rely on my emotions. I'm also thankful for the opportunities that are coming.

Friday, January 10, 2003

Dear Rachael,

I blinked and a new year appeared. Training, shooting and learning keep me busy. Whenever we get liberty, Tray and I hang out at Harvey's Range. Harvey served as a Marine, and there's a group of guys who gather to swap war stories and tall tales ... kinda like the men at Senior's hardware store.

Even though they're older, they've welcomed Tray and me into their group—probably because we're fresh ears for their stories.

Tray's become my closest friend. We've got a lot of the same interests—shooting, whittling, sports. We both have 0311 as our specialty—infantry rifleman. This is gonna sound like something we would have said in junior high, but he might be my first best friend—besides you, of course. My buddies on the football team were never true friends. We only shared the common ground of a sport and a school address. That was clear after all the crap happened freshman year and I started drinking.

If it weren't for you—and for watching our moms together—I would never have known true friendship. That's another thing to thank you and our moms for.

Tray is different from most of the guys in my squad bay. He doesn't cuss or drink or sleep around.

He's a Christian, and like you and your dad, he's not a jerk about it.

We have a good time, and I can see myself trusting him if we're ever in combat, which we probably will be. I'm sure you're keeping up with the news.

Tray lost his parents when he was young, and his grandpa died a few years back.

His grandpa, by the way, was one of the Montford Point Marines. Not many people know about them—I didn't. Blacks weren't allowed in the Corps until WWII. They didn't go to Parris Island like everyone else, though. Training was segregated. They had their own base near Camp Lejeune. It really sucked for them, and a lot of white Marines treated them poorly.

Tray sure is proud of his grandpa. He told me the other day, "I get to wear this uniform and stand next to you because my grandpa fought to earn his—here and overseas." Pretty crazy to think how, only a few years ago, Tray and I couldn't train together or hang out like we do.

Anyway, his grandma's all he's got now. Maybe that's why we get along—we've got loneliness in common. I suppose, when you think about it, that's enough of a reason to become friends.

Today's One Good Thing: Today I'm thankful for friendship.

Friday, January 17, 2003

Dear Rachael,

I found out today I might be considered for Scout Sniper School. I'm sure your pretty brow would be wrinkled by a frown right now. You know I like a challenge, though, and this school would be the ultimate one. I think I could do it well, too.

Of course, I don't want to get my hopes up too high. It'll be a while before I rank up enough to officially be considered.

I asked an older Marine if he thinks we're going to war. I'll remember his response the rest of my life. "Prepare like hell to go; pray to heaven we don't."

The prayin' I'll leave up to you. The hell, though, I can handle ... and raise.

Honestly, I'm ready to go. Waiting might get to me. At least I stay busy with training.

In other news, I'm pretty sure Harvey's trying to set me up with his daughter. The guys at the range don't get why I don't want to spend my weekends with girls instead of them. I suppose I should. It's just ... well, that would feel like cheating on you. I know that's crazy, but I still love you. In my heart, you're my girl.

My decisions have been made, and I don't get to call you that. Sometimes, I get lonely and miss the closeness we had. Instead of wallowing, I focus on shooting and running and hanging out with the guys. Maybe that will change one day. I suppose I'll know if I should try to move on to a new relationship.

I can tell you one thing: I don't believe it'll be with Harvey's daughter. I know how well he can shoot; I'm not going to risk ending up on the wrong end of his gun barrel.

Anyway, I'm going back to my reason for writing and will close with ...

Today's One Good Thing: Today I'm thankful for an opportunity to be something more than I thought possible ... even if it's a ways off and not a sure thing.

Friday, February 14, 2003

Dear Rachael,

I'm a nerd.

Bet you never thought I'd say that. I know I always picked on you about how much you liked to read and enjoyed history class, but I get it now. I've been spending a lot of time at the library here at Lejeune.

That's where I'm stationed now, by the way. We wrapped up at Camp Geiger a few days ago. I'm here for a couple weeks of Designated Marksmanship training. Next week's live-fire training on the range. Anytime I get to shoot, I'm happy.

Anyway, learning turns out to be good to go. During the Crucible at the end of Boot, they told us stories about past battles and Marines, their courage and loss, that made me want to know more. I've checked out tons of books about battles—Okinawa, Tarawa, Guadalcanal.

I saw some other books today that I want to check out next time—more about the Marine Corps' overall history and some biographies of specific Marines, like Chesty Puller. I wonder what you'd think about some of the tales they tell about him.

When I started ITB (Infantry Training Battalion) at Geiger, I learned about the Marine Corps Institute, which allows me to take courses.

Turns out, the more extra courses I take, the quicker I could rank up. Of course, I also have to keep up with PT and behave myself. You might find this hard to believe, but I'm following orders and steering clear of any distractions. No time for trouble; I'm a squared-away Marine.

Between the classes during training here and the extra ones I'm taking, plus the books, I'm gonna be so smart, you wouldn't recognize me.

I'm sure you're deep in books, too, wherever you are in college. I got a letter from your dad the other day. He sounds happy at the new mission. I still wonder how close you are to him. Makes sense for him to stick close to his knockout daughter when she's at college. Do one thing for me: if any jerk tries to lay a hand on you, punch him square in the nose. And land another on his jaw for good measure.

You deserve only the best kind of guy and the most happiness life can hold.

Happy Valentine's Day, Rachael.

Today's One Good Thing: Today I'm thankful for books and for all the Marines I can learn from.

Thursday, February 20, 2003

We leave for Peru in a week, and I'm getting nervous. What if I don't know enough to help the women? What if I can't figure out ways for them to get proper nutrition because their resources are more limited than I realize? What if they hate the fitness routines I've prepared?

God will help me; I know that. It's just hard to "let go and let God," as people say. I do better when I can be in control and on top of whatever is going on around me. It's why I plan everything out, down to the tiniest details. I like to consider all the possible things that could go wrong, so I can plan around them. Jack called me a control freak.

Jack.

It's been almost a year since he left. I still love him—as much as ever. He was always the only one for me; I'm beginning to think he always will be.

I may never get married. That thought used to horrify me, but I'm beginning to embrace it. I think about this trip coming up and all the other extra things I could do with my time and energy and talents if I'm not tied down to a husband. That probably sounds like a cynical way to describe marriage, but when a person is married, they're part of a pair. (I know, most obvious statement of the century.)

Each half of a pair must make decisions together for their mutual future. If we both decided to take an extended mission trip, that's great. If I wanted to do something like this, but he had to work or we needed to move or I was pregnant, I wouldn't be flying to Peru.

My point is: marriage requires a couple to make all their decisions together for the mutual good of both or for an entire family instead of a single person who only needs to consider what's possible for them. With that truth in mind, the thought of staying single doesn't seem so bad.

Watching my dad and Ms. Becky gives me two real-life examples of adults who are content to remain single. Daddy throws most of his energy into the counseling he does at the mission and the rest into our time together. Ms. Becky works as hard as she has since Jack's dad left. With Jack gone and the start of our club, though, she reads more than she has in a long time, and she's talked about cutting back to one job and maybe even traveling one day.

When I told her about my trip to Peru, she asked me all sorts of questions about the mission, the church and the people. I think if Ms. Becky could have taken time off work, she would have gone to Peru with us. We spent more of our past two book club phone chats talking about what the country might be like than about the books we've read. We have completed the series we were reading and decided to try some Jane Austen classics when I get back.

I doubt I'll have opportunities for extended trips like this once I start school and when I begin my career. I'll be gone a full month—no job on the planet would be cool with an employee flying to another country for that long. I plan to enjoy this opportunity to the fullest—no more worrying.

Well, maybe a few worries about flying. I've never done that before, and the thought of soaring high in the sky makes me feel more than a little queasy.

Today's One Good Thing:
I am thankful that I found the positive today when my heart could have sent me down a pity party spiral. Maybe I can't forget Jack or stop missing or loving him, but I can choose to realign my thoughts and dwell instead on the good in my life.

Thursday, February 27, 2003

I not only survived takeoff but found it exhilarating! It's crazy that I've never flown before, and my first trip is a nearly twenty-four-hour trek.

We change planes in Atlanta, which I'm nervous about. I've heard how crazy that airport can be, so I'm thankful to be with experienced travelers. From there, we'll fly to Lima to spend the night before a final flight to Iquitos, where the church is.

I've seen pictures of the church and the area around it—it's bordered by the Amazon River and the jungle. Many of the buildings (including the church) float in the water. They look like something out of a fantasy book. To think of the poverty nestled in such beauty blows my mind.

The pastor's wife, Sarah, and I have communicated, so I'm looking forward to meeting her. I'll work with her most of the time. She's the one who asked if a few of us could stay for a full month instead of a little over two weeks. She knows how helpful short-term missionaries can be if we have enough time to solidify new programs or offer care or education to enough people in the area. One month will allow us to accomplish more.

Two other women will stay with me. They have much-needed skills for the more rural parts around Iquitos. One is a nurse; the other's a dentist. Thankfully, one of them speaks Spanish almost fluently. While we'll be with Sarah most of the time, I'm sure there will be times when she can't be with all of us. I'm not sure how much help my high school Spanish will be. I'm hoping to improve my language skills while I'm there, though. As my Spanish teacher always said, immersion makes the best language education.

Today's One Good Thing:
I am thankful for this opportunity to travel, explore and see places and experience things I never thought I would. Most of all, I'm thankful for the opportunity to help others.

Friday, March 14, 2003

Growing up, I thought I had a good enough imagination to picture life in other countries. Now that I've been in Iquitos and surrounding areas for a couple weeks, I realize I wasn't even close.

First, this area truly is spectacular. The jungle is right there; the Amazon River is right there. These places I've seen in books and learned about in school cannot be captured in textbook pictures. Iquitos can only be reached by plane or boat. I try not to think about that fact too much because it makes me anxious.

Next, the people are kind and welcoming, warm and genuine. My Spanish is getting quite the workout, that's for sure. I've improved already.

Of course, I often have to beg, "Más despacio, por favor." I can't always keep up with them, but when they slow down—after laughing at me, of course—I pick out the majority of what they're saying.

I do wish I were fluent, so I could communicate better. Sarah told me it took her a couple of years after moving here to think in Spanish. She said she now mostly thinks in Spanglish.

The children are the best. They love when I run around with them, especially when I pretend to chase them. They squeal and laugh. Children's laughter has no language barriers.

I'm so glad Sarah suggested I pack hair accessories. The girls line up to have me fix their hair—pigtails, braids, buns. They love them all. The older girls are learning from me, and now they're practicing on the younger girls. Hairstyles might seem a silly thing, but I see the joy on their faces and know this activity can lead to bonding among these girls. They will grow in their friendships and—thanks to Sarah and the church—in their relationships with God. Some haven't yet come to know Him; others have and are soaking up Bible verses. In the evenings, all the smaller children sit around me—or in my lap—while I read from the Bible or tell them about Jesus' love in my broken Spanish.

Last, but not least, the women have become dear to me. They all want to care for their children and husbands, and they listen to everything I teach and show them. A couple of the women stood out during our fitness classes. I'm teaching them routines they can continue with their neighbors after I'm gone. I'll send new routines to Sarah, so they can keep growing.

Each afternoon we have food preparation and nutrition education in Sarah's kitchen. She and her husband live in Belén—a neighborhood built on stilts in the water. To get into the houses, we balance across a narrow plank of wood high above the murky water. As clumsy as I am, I can't believe I haven't tumbled in yet.

All the houses and other buildings are close to each other, plus the main walkway between the rows of dwellings is narrow. It's common for neighbors to be on their front porches, usually working or cleaning or preparing food. They'll carry on conversations back and forth with friends across the way. I'm usually lost then because they have no reason to speak slowly.

In the U.S., we go weeks or months without speaking to next-door neighbors, so observing this open, friendly community has taken some getting used to. It's also convicting. I don't even know the names of our neighbors in Savannah.

Having my bubble constantly invaded is something I've had to get used to. At first I struggled. Back home, my skin crawls when someone stands too close in the checkout line. Here, space is limited. Everyone stands so close they often brush against one another. They don't think a thing of it. I'm getting there ... I think.

Nutrition-wise, the Peruvian people don't have to fight the battle of preservatives that we do. They use primarily fresh, natural ingredients, so they are better off in some ways than we are. They may be teaching me more than I'm teaching them.

I have fallen in love with juanes. It's basically a chicken and rice dish served wrapped in a leaf. They use various spices, primarily cumin and turmeric. I've always loved cumin but have never done much with turmeric—I see that changing when I return home. They mix in hardboiled eggs and sometimes olives to round out the dish. Different places or families use other ingredients.

Sarah told me she had it once where the family didn't use chickens; they used guinea pigs. She said thankfully she didn't know until afterward.

On the topic of unusual foods, I built up my courage to taste suri—a popular street food served on a stick. Once again, it's not chicken. It's giant grilled slugs. I didn't care for it, but I can say I tried it.

I have embraced this country and the people. In many ways, it's a more laidback environment. Of course, drugs and drug trafficking make life dangerous in certain areas. The pastor makes sure none of us ever goes off alone. That was his one rule, and he is insistent about us following it.

Most of our team left last night. Now it's just Tiffany, Annah and me. On Monday, we'll start an after-school class with local teen girls about proper self-care and health management. I'm looking forward to spending more time with the women and girls here.

Returning to the United States will probably be weird for me. I'm not sure what to expect when I go home, but I do believe life won't be the same. Doing everything, all day long, with the purpose of sharing God's love and gospel with people both unlike and like me—I've never lived like this before. I would think it would be easier to do this in the U.S., but I'm not sure. I suppose I'll see in a couple weeks.

I don't want to think about that yet because I can already tell I'm going to miss this place when it's our turn to board a plane.

Today's One Good Thing:
I'm thankful for this opportunity to meet and love on these people. I'm thankful for them and their kindness. I'm thankful for Sarah and her husband and their willingness to move far away to make a new home in a place where they aren't always safe and often feel lonely. They have become part of the community and embrace it as their home. I can see how the people here—even if they don't attend the church—love and respect them.

Thursday, March 20, 2003

Dear Rachael,

Last night, we watched President Bush give the speech we've waited for. We're officially at war.

When he addressed the troops already over there, he said something that will stick with me: "... the peace of a troubled world and the hopes of an oppressed people now depend on you."

I'm ready to go, Rach. I want to be there with the guys I went through Boot with. Dawson's already there, and it's killing me that I'm still stateside, chowing down on burgers to celebrate my stupid birthday.

I know ... Tray called me on my sour attitude. You two would be great friends. Of course, I'm pretty sure you would gang up on me and I wouldn't stand a chance in any debates.

He was right about one thing. We'll get our chance. When we do, I'll be ready. I just hope I can do service to the uniform and make you proud.

Since I last wrote, Tray and I filed into the 3/8. That's the 3rd Battalion, 8th Marines. Good news is, we get to stay right here at Lejeune. I know Grandma Ethel—Tray's grandma—is happy. She'd prefer him to be at her kitchen table every Sunday afternoon. I'm pretty sure he's okay with that, too, especially when she bakes her famous sweet potato pie.

It's good to go for me, too, because most of the Corps' history I've been reading was made by the 3/8. I'm eager to add to that history in Iraq.

Today's One Good Thing: Today I'm thankful for the opportunity to let freedom ring out to other countries where innocent people haven't known what that can look like. Here's to carrying peace and hope.

Sunday, March 23, 2003

Dear Rachael,

I've tasted heaven.

This afternoon I finally went to Grandma Ethel's with Tray. Her sweet potato pie is better than he bragged it was, and eating her fried chicken should be considered a religious experience.

Her house reminded me of you and your mom. The front was covered with beds and boxes full of beaming flowers, like your mom's magical garden. I thought about her special rose bush ... you know, the one we sat by when I stole my first kiss. I was so nervous and worried I'd do it wrong or you wouldn't let me kiss you. Once our lips touched, though, I had only one thought: how soft your lips were.

I thought about you again in Grandma Ethel's kitchen. She had pots of herbs hanging everywhere. You would've loved the smell. I know you would make some delicious meals with those handy.

One other part of our visit reminded me of your family—the photos of Tray's parents and grandfather reminded me of all he and his grandma have lost. You'd never know their pain and grief because they live and breathe contentment and peace, like you and your dad. I'm not sure I could have such joy after so much loss.

When Grandma Ethel found out I ran off without letting my mama know where I was—she should work for the government as an interrogator; one piece of that pie and I'd have confessed my deepest, darkest secret—anyway, she gave me the sweetest scolding I've ever had. All I can think about is how I wish I could go back and not do that to my poor mama. I can't remember Grandma Ethel's exact words; honestly, I don't remember her saying much of anything, now that I think about it. I just remember apologizing to her.

She said, "It's not me you owe that apology." When we got back to base, I wrote Mama a letter—quick, fast and in a hurry.

I'm so sorry for how I left you, too, Rach. I will always regret that decision. I do still believe you are better off without me. So, although I hate myself for the way I carried out my decision, I am at peace with letting you live the life you should. I love and miss you, Rach.

Today's One Good Thing: Today, I'm thankful for butter and Grandma Ethel and sweet potatoes … and I'm praying—actually down on my knees—that I don't die tomorrow morning during our run.

Wednesday, March 26, 2003

I cannot believe my time in Iquitos is coming to an end. Not going to lie, I got weepy tonight at prayer meeting. The kids brought me drawings or handmade trinkets. I enjoyed long hugs from the women and teen girls we've worked with daily. They will always hold a special place in my heart.

Spending a month in another country has opened my mind and heart to other places and people and to opportunities for service in unlikely places.

I also feel torn, but I'm not sure I can properly explain why. Part of my heart feels I've been rocked to my core, convicted of what really matters—God and sharing Him with others—and filled with a desire to continue pouring myself out for Him and others like I have here.

The other side of my heart knows that when I return to the U.S., I'll go back to my life as it was, with no giving of myself. I don't want that to happen. At the same time, I already feel myself accepting my old ways because I know it will be easier to be comfortable and do things my way, for me.

My numbness toward the things of God scares me. Part of my decision to take this trip and work at the kids' camp when I return rests in me wanting to do enough for God that I'll desire His word again. I know that's wrong on so many levels. My salvation and relationship with God are not based on anything I can do. On my own, I can never do enough good because, without Christ, I can do nothing good at all. Because Christ paid for my sins and saved me, I know I am His and always will be.

My fickle feelings and the lack of longing for God make me question so much about myself. I must be incredibly selfish and unappreciative to not crave time in God's word. So many people around the world don't have five Bibles that are theirs, written in their own language that they can read any time they want. And yet, I have that but don't seize every opportunity to pick one of them up and soak up every word.

Thinking about this makes me sad and angry at myself, so I'm going to stop writing for now. I think I need to be home to work this all out right in my mind and decide how to tackle it.

Tomorrow, Tiffany, Annah and I become tourists. We will fly to Cusco. From there we'll visit Machu Picchu, zipline in the Sacred Valley and hike in the Andes before we return to Lima on Sunday. And then, it will all be over.

Today's One Good Thing:
I am thankful I have a wonderful home to return to and an amazing father who will be waiting to welcome me, but I will miss this place. I'm leaving part of my heart behind but carrying a piece of Peru home.

Friday, March 28, 2003

Ziplining was incredible! Seriously, why have I never done this before? I'm ready to go again. Tiffany told me about other ziplines around the world—some through jungles or down sides of mountains. I'd like to try them all.

Even more amazing, though, Annah told me about her friend who does BASE jumping off cliffs and mountains. She lives near Savannah, so I'll be looking her up when we get home.

It might sound crazy, but the heights and speed made me feel alive in ways I haven't felt since Jack left. He kept me grounded in the best possible ways, but I've felt restless without him. Some days I've wanted nothing more than to dash out the door and run as long and hard as I can or see how fast my car can go. Today's experience calmed and energized me.

Now that I've had a taste of something wild and crazy, I realize I love the adrenaline rush and can't wait to feel it again.

Today's One Good Thing:
I'm thankful for an experience that woke me up and made me feel alive.

Tuesday, April 1, 2003

Happy Birthday, Rachael!

I hope today is your best birthday yet. How will you celebrate? What's on your wish list?

Life in the Corps is predictable ... run, train, learn, clean. Go to bed, get up at the butt-crack of dawn, do it all again. We have chow a few times between all that.

You'd like this area. We've got some nice views of the Atlantic. You and I would have fun on the beach, as long as they aren't doing amphibious training exercises, of course.

In case you can't tell, I don't miss you any less. I keep thinking one day I'll wake up and you won't be my first thought. Today wasn't that day.

Today's One Good Thing: I'm thankful you were born and I got to know you.

Tuesday, April 1, 2003

Daddy met me at the airport and treated me to a messy American burger for my birthday. I'm glad to be home, but I am exhausted. It's time to sleep in my own bed.

Today's One Good Thing:
I am thankful for my bed and for burgers that require an entire roll of paper towels.

Tuesday, May 5, 2003

This is going to sound weird—it's weird to me anyway. I had some culture shock when I landed in Peru, but I expected that. I wasn't prepared to face bigger shock when I returned.

I find myself frustrated with a lot of the silliness I see around me. Drama and pettiness always annoyed me, but now they make me angry. I feel like I'm getting grumpy before I've hit old age. I suppose my perspectives on life and what's important and what's not have shifted.

That's not a bad thing. I can still have fun and be me, but I can do that without feeling frivolous, if that makes any sense.

Part of me still feels uneasy thinking I should be doing more here—more that matters. I think it's easier to serve God in more noticeable ways when you're in another country. I'm still not sure why that is, but I wonder if working at the kids' camp this summer will help me work through my uncertainties.

Peru unearthed something new in me, though—my inner daredevil. As soon as I returned to Savannah, I met up with Annah's friend who does BASE jumping. She told me I must be trained to skydive first and put me in touch with a team here. They were desperate for an interim office manager since theirs left early for maternity leave. I was eager to fill in—will work for a thrill!

I started skydiving and made my twenty-fifth jump Saturday. I'm well on my way toward the few hundred jumps I need before I can make the leap—pun totally intended—to BASE jumping.

The ascent to jump altitude overloads my senses: the roar of the plane's engine, the blended bouquet of the leather and oil and gear crammed in the small space, the adrenaline coursing through my body and keeping me on edge.

When I leap, the rush of the wind and the ecstatic yells from the crew or shrieks of the first-timers reverberate in my ears. The chutes whoosh out, one by one. They catch on the air and flutter to their full glory, jerking us upright—their floating puppets.

As thrilling as the leap from the plane is, the thing that hooked me my first time up was the total peace and silence after the cord is pulled.

Drifting through the air—the earth, a blur below—I recognized something felt different, but it took me a moment to realize the change was perfect stillness. I struggle to describe the experience because it is a literal absence of all sound.

My senses take a vacation they never can on land. They have no sound, no smell, no sensation to process. All I'm aware of are purest air entering my lungs and extreme silence cocooning me as I hang and drift, ever-so-slowly, back to earth's jarring presence.

Speaking of, I begin as a camp counselor the first week of June. Counselors and staff report right after Memorial Day. We'll have training that week before the kids arrive. Each counselor will have another job in the camp; I'm hoping to work on the ropes course. After my recent adventures, I can handle walking around treetops.

With six weeks of camp, my summer will fly by, and school will start before I know it. I got the scholarship I was hoping for, so finances are covered. Having a year off ended up being a happy accident. I have learned more than I imagined I would and have experienced things I never expected.

Today's One Good Thing:
I am thankful for different perspectives and new skills and thrills.

Sunday, June 1, 2003

I got my choice of camp assignments, so I'm living in the trees this summer.

Ascending into the ropes course reminds me of when Jack and I imagined the woods behind my house were an enchanted forest. Whenever I hook on my harness and climb these giant pine trees, I enter a fairy world. With the shimmery beams of sunlight that sporadically filter through leaves and the nodded greetings of the resident squirrels, it's easy to feel transported to a magical kingdom. So far, I have loved every second in those branches.

Saturday the ropes staff had a competition to see who could go through the entire course and zipline down the fastest. Not to brag, but ... I won!

Once the campers get here tomorrow, much of our treetop peace will be shattered, and I'm sure we'll have our stressful moments. They have tried to prepare us for how to encourage nervous kids while recognizing if they're too scared to continue.

In addition to my day duties on the course, I'm paired with another counselor in a cabin. We'll have twelve to fourteen new girls each week to lead to meals and assemblies and in cabin devotions every evening.

This will be an exhausting summer, but I'm looking forward to it. The other counselors and staff are incredible. I'm excited about all the opportunities we'll have to teach and encourage these kids.

None of the other leaders go to Georgia Southern. I had hoped to make a friend who I'll see again in the fall. Most of them go to Toccoa Falls or Covenant. If not for my scholarship—and the fact that I've already pushed off starting for a year—I would consider going to one of those schools. They're both surrounded by hiking, hang-gliding and other outdoor activities.

Tonight during worship, I thought again about how my relationship with God feels off. I don't know why. I've spent so much time in church or in ministry, especially the past few months with the Peru trip and now camp. I thought doing these things would snap me out of the funk I've been in and return me to how I used to find joy in a hymn or in studying the Greek behind verses in the New Testament. Why do I feel so distant and closed off?

I've got to get this figured out and pull myself together. In the meantime, I can't wait to meet our first campers tomorrow and spend the day in the trees.

Today's One Good Thing:
I'm thankful for a chance to use my passions in service this summer and for a fairyland office.

Friday, June 13, 2003

Dear Rachael,

It's been a while since I last wrote one of these ridiculous unsent letters. I got to thinking maybe stopping would help me forget you. It didn't.

I figure I'll just write every now and then when something happens I think you'd like or that reminds me of you. Never mind, that would be writing more. Let's just see where this goes, okay?

We're about to head out for our morning run. Have I mentioned how much I love running? You and I never ran together after I graduated from the Mission, like we talked about. You always teased that you could beat me running backward. That, I'd like to see.

I get faster every day. When I was getting free from alcohol, running was the thing that helped me feel whole and well again. The breaths I had to take to operate my lungs flowed through me, clearing my head, helping me think deeper than I ever had. Feeling my body grow stronger, day by day—sometimes step by step—boosted my confidence because, after two years of abuse, I was building up my body, not tearing it down.

And now, here I am, a Marine—running all the time. I wonder if I'd have done as well as I did in Boot Camp if I hadn't already started running.

Of course, we can never answer those what ifs because we make the choices we do and live with their consequences.

I still fall into the trap of wondering what if about us. What if I'd stuck around? What if I'd pulled it together and remained surrounded by the whispers and glares and hate of the people in Bellum? What if I'd gotten down on one knee? Would you have said yes? Would you have been happy, though?

Are you happy? I like to believe you are. You should be a sophomore in a couple months at whatever college was lucky enough to have you pick it. I'm sure you've got a ton of new friends.

Is your hair still long? I loved when you wore it down. That's how I see you in my dreams. You're laughing—or at least smiling. Often you're running ahead of me, and you turn back to laugh. That's the image of you that I cling to—pure joy on your face, hair fanning around you as you whip your head forward to keep running … running toward your ever after. I'm betting it will be a beautiful one.

Running—you running forward, me running from … or through … my what ifs.

What if I returned now—today—as I am: Marine PFC Jack Calhoun? Would you accept me as I've become? What if you accepted me, but not the title? What would I do?

More what ifs to contemplate on my morning run.

Man, that was an outstanding run. Runs like these, with my time killing it and my body feeling stronger than ever, make me feel frickin' invincible.

My what ifs ran with me. I'm not sure I came up with many answers, but I did think through them. I've decided that I hope I'm running through, not from, my what ifs. If I'm running through them, then there must be another side—one without what ifs.

I'm also wondering more about what I would choose if that last what if came true. Would I choose you over the Marines? Honestly, I'm not sure. I would want to choose you, but Marine is more than a title. This is who I am now. Given the make-believe opportunity to stand before you today, the choice would be yours. Would you choose Marine me?

With what I know of you and your beautiful heart, I'm going to assume you would. Now I can hit the showers with a smile on my face.

Today's One Good Thing: Today, I'm thankful for running through.

Wednesday, June 18, 2003

We've reached that midway point of summer camp where exhaustion has set in and everyone's idiosyncrasies are grating on each other's nerves. It's bound to happen when you have a group of people who live together for an extended period of time, work together in often stressful situations and are physically, mentally and emotionally drained every day.

Even the sweetest person in camp—our office manager—snapped at one of the guys when he tracked dirt into the office this afternoon. She apologized immediately, but I could see the exhaustion on her face as she teared up. I doubt she's used to apologizing for losing her temper.

Anyway, to add to my exhaustion, I've developed a summer cold. Thank goodness for this flavored water filled with electrolytes and vitamins. Straight water wasn't cutting it, and I almost passed out on the stand Monday. Thankfully I was hooked in to the tree. Working and walking for miles every day in the southern summer heat is tough enough; when you can't breathe? Let's just say I'm looking forward to being well again.

At supper, I was nearly dead on my feet and snapped at a couple of campers who wanted me to solve a disagreement about which boy was cuter. A couple of veteran counselors decided to lecture me on why I should be more patient, even with seemingly unimportant questions and proceeded to give me suggestions of how I should have responded.

Through my brain fog, I said something like, "I don't need your self-righteous high horse advice right now." And then I walked all the way to the camp nurse, food tray in hand. Thankfully, she gave me some medicine and prescribed a night away from our cabin.

I wonder if Jack ever felt like this in Boot Camp. Maybe he still feels this way. Don't Marines train constantly, and don't they pack those guys into close quarters? I doubt he's got a compassionate nurse.

Since I have an evening of quiet, I'll share more about the good of camp. The ropes course has been one of the best experiences I've ever had.

When I'm thirty feet off the ground and the breeze rustles my hair and whispers through the leaves around me, I escape into a mental haven. Regardless of which of the seven stations I work on, I'm surrounded by total serenity. It's just me and the tree and the scattered sunbeams when the kids haven't arrived yet and I'm 15 to 20 feet from the next counselor.

The air flows smoother as it fills my lungs with spicy pine scent. When I look down at the mossy floor below, I feel like I could glide through the forest. I think about skydiving and increasing my jump count until I can finally leap off that mountain in Peru.

For the most part, the kids have been great. They are fun and cute, and they look up to us. Sometimes it's overwhelming to think how much they idolize us. Part of me wants to yell at them not to do that; after all, I'm human and far from perfect. But, I also remember being their age and looking up to the older girls with their makeup and cute clothes and perfect hair.

I also remember watching how they acted in church and at football games—usually opposite behaviors. I remember the feeling of confusion and then betrayal when I recognized their two-sided nature, but it made me appreciate the genuine girls and commit to being like them. I want to be genuine, but I have this ongoing battle inside me.

When we sing worship songs and have devotions, I know all the words, but words are all they are. I cannot seem to feel their truth or have my soul stirred by them like I once did. My emptiness makes me feel no better than those disingenuous girls.

In blissful moments on the ropes course before or after the kids have been with us, my mind clears, and I sense clarity circling my head. I believe it holds an answer or an understanding of this war within me. No sooner than I almost grasp it, the leaves rustle and I lose it again—blown away with the breeze.

Despite my shortcomings, I had one unbelievably joyful opportunity. I had been watching this one quiet girl in our cabin. Her name was Lisa. Last Friday, she walked over to me after the morning assembly. I had to bend close to hear her. She might be the quietest child I've ever met.

Anyway, Lisa told me she knew Jesus died for her sins and she wanted Him to be her Lord as well as her Savior. She asked what it meant for Him to be Lord over her life. I explained to her how she would live her life for God, seeking always to glorify Him in all she does. She'll do that with His help.

I shared with her what my mom told me when I accepted Christ as my Lord and Savior: "You're no longer just Rachael; you're God's princess. Your identity will always rest in Him—in what He did for you and in who you are in Him. Nothing else in your life will be more important than that."

Lisa asked if that meant she was no longer her parents' daughter. I told her that her parents would always be her earthly parents but that now she also has a heavenly father who is the King of Kings, which makes her a special princess. I asked her if she wanted to pray. She said yes and asked if I'd hold her hand while she did.

So, there we sat—between the field and the pool—heads bowed and hearts lifted as Lisa gave her life to God. I am so thankful she chose to share that moment with me. I will never forget the joy in her smile.

Another special moment happened on day one of the second week. I was on the first station of the ropes course that day. The fifth boy climbed up the rope ladder of my tree like a speed demon. Once he stood up, though, every drop of color drained from his face. His eyes widened, and I thought he would faint.

My first thought was to get that poor kid down as fast as possible, but I had a gut feeling he was going to love the ropes if I could guide him through his initial terror. I asked his name and started describing the beauty around us to Bobby. I told him about the funny shadows the sunlight makes on the tree trunks. I told him about the squirrel in my tree and how I often catch him watching the kids and how, one time, I swear I saw him cheer for a girl who went all the way through even though she wasn't sure she could.

Bobby chuckled at that one, so I kept going. I told him to close his eyes and listen to the music the wind made through the trees. After a minute or so, he started to smile, and his knuckles weren't so white around his harness. I explained how the music changes from station to station through the course and how going all the way to the end is like listening to an entire CD of wind music.

He opened his eyes and asked, "Really?"

I smiled and said, "You bet! See that zipline through the trees? That's your goal. I can tell you, there's no feeling like flying through the woods. When you get over there, you'll meet my friends Ethan and Jess. Tell them to use their radios and let me know you made it because I want to watch you soar through the trees. When you do, put out your arms—face to the sun, eyes closed—and become part of the wind music."

His smile outshone the sunbeam on his face. I told him, "Eyes on the goal, then face to the sun."

"Eyes on the goal, then face to the sun," he repeated and then nodded. I heard him saying those two lines over and over as he tightroped from my station to the next, a death-grip around each rope dangling along the way.

A while later, I got a radio call from Jess. She said Bobby wanted me to watch him "face to the sun." I could hear his laughter as he jumped off the tower and soared through the trees. At lunch that day, he ran over and gave me the biggest high five ever, and I told him how proud I was of him.

I'll never forget Bobby or Lisa or how God gave me the right words to guide each of them this summer. Something about helping children makes me feel like, if I accomplish nothing else in life, I will have left something positive behind.

Today's One Good Thing:
I am thankful for a kind nurse and enhanced water. And popsicles. They make me feel better, too. Most of all, I'm thankful to be a small part of something special for a few kids.

Friday, July 4, 2003

Dear Rachael,

Happy Fourth!

Tray and I are heading to Harvey's tonight. His range is only open for our group of regulars. They hang out when fireworks shows sound off. Harvey said something about the explosions sounding too much like war. With our protective ear gear and all the shooting we'll be doing, the only explosions we'll hear are our own.

Speaking of fireworks, the base put on a great show the other night. I noticed all the couples and families around, enjoying the lights. Made me think of you and wish I could share them with you. Are you watching fireworks tonight? Could you be thinking of me?

Enough of that. I ran through those what ifs last time. No retreating, Marine.

I've got to head out. The vets'll be putting back some beers tonight—or maybe whiskey, since it's a special occasion. Anyway, Tray and I have to stock up on some drinks for us. Having a friend who doesn't drink either helps in situations like these, though he's got me addicted to Cheerwine. Rach, you'd love this stuff. It's the best cherry soft drink ever made. Tray and I put down a couple cases in no time flat. I'll be sure to raise a can in your honor tonight.

Today's One Good Thing: Today, I'm thankful we live in a country where we're free to blow shit up to celebrate our freedoms.

Friday, July 4, 2003

Returning staff members have talked all summer about the amazing job the camp staff does with fireworks for the Fourth of July. Honestly, as much as they gushed about it, I expected the show to fall short. Instead ... wow!

These kids saw a show tonight they will never forget. I know I won't. It went on for a good twenty to thirty minutes, and the finale rivaled every professional show I've seen.

I had to walk off midway through to finish watching on my own. I didn't want the kids to see me crying. As the colors exploded across the sky and the patriotic music beat to each flash, thoughts of Jack filled my mind. Jack, in his uniform, on his way to war.

As far as I know, he's still in the States, but he could go any day. He is a Marine, after all. War's kind of their thing.

I couldn't stop picturing him in a uniform. I wonder if he's watching fireworks tonight, too. If he is, I'm sure his arm is around some beautiful girl. And yes, as petty and childish as it sounds, when that thought hit, I hated that imaginary girl.

Why do I still miss Jack? Sometimes the ache I feel for him is so sharp, I fear my heart will stop, even after all this time and distance. He may be gone from my life but never from my heart.

Will I ever live without the pain of missing him? Ugh! I hate writing like this. Being whiny is the last thing I want to be, but here I go again.

The last time I read Jack's letters to Daddy, Jack sounded good. He's made a friend, and they like to whittle and go to a nearby shooting range when they have liberty. I'd think they get enough shooting on the base, but maybe they don't shoot as much as I thought. Honestly, I know very little about the military and how they spend their days. All I know is they wear uniforms, train and go to war.

I hate war. Men die in war—men with their entire lives ahead of them. Men like Jack.

That's enough morbid thinking for today.

Back to the program: we ended the night with our typical closing bonfire. Listening to a couple hundred kids and counselors singing "How Great Is Our God" with no instruments, no walls, nothing but an accompanying chorus of nature was unbelievably beautiful and inspiring.

My heart continues to feel hollow ... dull ... still. When we worship, like tonight, I don't feel the words, the praise, the promises, the truths deep in my soul. Once, these words and the experience of singing as we did would have pressed me to my knees and left me in total awe and full of joy. Instead, my tears flowed, but I felt nothing.

Today's One Good Thing:
I'm thankful for freedom, celebrations, fireworks, bonfires, music and cleansing tears.

Monday, July 28, 2003

This past weekend, I met Shannon in Atlanta. She was shooting a wedding and needed someone to watch Laylah while she worked. In the evenings, we got to catch up.

I told her how I'm not sure I can move on from Jack. She saw us together after he graduated from the Mission; she saw the love we had, so she understands how hard it is for me. She did tell me that just because I don't feel able to move on now doesn't mean I never will be. I know she's right. That's such a distant future, though, I can't even imagine it. She was right about another thing too; when it is time, I'll know.

She still believes she'll never be loved by anyone because of her past. She made poor choices when she was young and got too deep with guys and drugs, but what happened to her later—being sold by the men who took her—that was not her fault. God's forgiven her for the rest, and He's healing her scars.

I told her she needs to see herself the way God does, as His daughter who's been covered by the blood of Christ and given His righteousness. Once she embraces and accepts who she's become in Him, she'll be ready to accept true love from a godly man.

Maybe she believed me. I think she did. I know God has someone amazing for her, and I told her that, too. Sweet Laylah needs a good daddy.

This is the second time this summer I've shared with someone the importance of remembering that, as Christians, our identity doesn't lie in anyone or anything else; it doesn't even rest in ourselves or something we do. A Christian's identity rests solely in Christ and what He's done for us. That knowledge overshadows all the uncertainty and imperfection around and in us.

Shannon asked me about college and if I'm worried about anything. I was surprised that I am nervous about not knowing anyone and uncertain about making new friends. As we talked, though, my worries drifted away. No matter if I make a hundred friends or none, I'll always have Shannon and Anna Claire. They're an IM or call away. Plus, we're close enough to meet up for a weekend every now and then.

As long as Shannon gets put up in fancy hotels to shoot weddings for people with huge budgets, I'm more than happy to drive to wherever she is and hang out with Laylah at the pool.

Today's One Good Thing:
I'm thankful for best friends and weekend getaways.

Monday, August 18, 2003

I'm officially a college freshman. This weekend's been a whirlwind.

Any hopes I had of making lasting friendships at the start of the school year have been dashed. My roommate said two sentences to me the one time I saw her: "I won't be here much. That's my caramel corn, not yours."

Well, okay then.

One of the sororities is holding a party tonight for freshmen. A few of the girls talked to me for a while when they gave me the invitation, but all they wanted to know was if I have a boyfriend and don't I think all the new guys are yummy?

Yes, I'm rolling my eyes.

I have no desire to go to their party. The thought of paying for friends rubs me the wrong way. Besides, I intend to focus as much as possible on my studies. I've got a year to make up for and don't plan to go past spring 2006. That was my original graduation date, and I'm determined it stays that way.

My adviser supports my desire to complete my degree in three years instead of four, even with the double major—Exercise Science and Nutrition and Food Science. She echoed Daddy's advice to take a lighter load this first semester as I adjust to college life, with the plan to add more in the spring if things go well.

Another thing I have no desire to do is date. It's not just because I want to stay focused on my studies. I have given it lots of thought since Shannon and I talked. The thought of dating anyone who's not Jack makes me panicky. He was everything to me. Our history together, our friendship and our bond—I can't imagine having something so special with anyone else.

I don't want to put myself out there with someone who knows nothing about me. With Jack, we knew everything. We'd literally known each other from birth. Our conversations on dates were about memories of things we'd done together and of people we both knew. I'm not sure how to date someone where we have no common past to discuss.

At this point in my life, I'm also not far enough removed from Jack to give dating a shot. It wouldn't be fair to any guy willing to take a chance on me. I'd spend the entire date comparing him to Jack.

My first class starts at ten tomorrow morning, so I should probably put this away and pack my bookbag for class.

Today's One Good Thing:
I'm thankful that most of the distractions I might have encountered at college seem to be non-issues for me right now. Time to get to work.

Wednesday, August 27, 2003

Dear Rachael,

Today's run about killed me. The thermometer lied—no way the high was only 95°. I was sweating worse than I did hammering shingles on roofs in Bellum. Right now, I'm lying on my rack in my skivvies with a fan blowing on high. I sure would love to be splashing around in that cold stream with you like we did that day after work. Man, you drove me crazy! I miss your lips on mine in that arctic stream—fire and ice, just like you.

I know you hated that nickname, but I thought it was perfect for so many reasons. Marc loved to get under your skin, and he knew how much you loathed your pale skin and red hair. When I thought of you as fire and ice, though, I knew it captured your spirit—your passion and your determination and drive—and your perfect skin and long, silky hair. I miss all of that, but most of all, I miss your heart.

Every day, I wonder what you're doing, how you're spending your time. Has school started back? Do you have a roommate? I'm guessing you live in a dorm, unless you're close enough to your dad.

I live in a squad bay with forty other guys. It's not too bad. Sometimes a few of them get loud and obnoxious, but Tray and I mostly stick to ourselves.

When we're not training or working, we sit around base and whittle.

You probably do way more exciting things than we do. Do you have a favorite hangout on campus or off? We can get pretty much any kind of food we want on base. We usually only go off base to shoot at the range or get some of Grandma Ethel's home cooking.

Sometimes, we play basketball with the kids at this center near her home. Tray's like a mentor to them. Some of them will probably enlist because he did. They're good kids who may not have the money or grades for college. Good jobs are limited without a degree, which makes the military a good option for them.

It doesn't pay a ton, but the benefits are decent and housing's included. I manage to send my mom a good bit of money each month. I'm thankful to support her after all she's done for me.

I've realized something about myself. Most of my life, I've viewed myself as a burden. I suppose it began with growing up with a dad who demanded quiet when he was around. He'd ignore me, unless I bothered him. As much as I wanted his attention, I never wanted to upset him. I spent the first few years of my life tiptoeing around our house. When he left us and I finally realized he wouldn't be returning, I figured I was why he left.

When I lived with the Millers, I woke them with my screams early in my stay, which I regret. They fed and clothed me and gave me a home and wouldn't let me pay for anything. All I gave them was another mouth to feed and a few parting gifts. That doesn't seem like enough. I felt so much guilt for all they did, although they invited me and assured me I was no burden.

And finally, thinking about my mom today is what brought all these memories together. I was a burden to her for a long time and put her through so much anguish. Then I left without even saying goodbye.

What I realize now is, sometimes I believed myself to be a burden when I wasn't. My misunderstanding affected my relationships with others and view of myself. My misbeliefs led to poor choices that, ultimately, hurt others more than any perceived burdens I imagined.

Now that I recognize the difference between caring actions from others and attention I coerce from someone, I can embrace kindness and love, release my misconceptions and avoid being an actual burden. Moving forward, I will look for ways to give back to the special people in my life, instead of second-guessing their willingness to share good with me.

I might finally be down under a million degrees. I'm gonna grab a shower and get some sleep.

Maybe tonight I'll dream about you in that stream.

Today's One Good Thing: Today, I am thankful for air conditioning and fans.

Sunday, August 31, 2003

Having a long weekend with Daddy has been great. I needed time together more than I realized. Even though I see him on the weekend or during the week, it's not the same as living at home with him.

Most of the girls in my dorm look forward to the weekends so they can party or hang out with their friends. I'd rather drive home. Maybe it's because I've lost one parent and understand the importance of time together. Or, maybe it's because Daddy and I have fun together.

We spent the past three nights watching the Braves' series against the Pirates. Friday night was a heartbreaker, but the past two nights totally made up for it. We've done a lot of eating—pizza, burgers, Italian. We're going to grab some tacos tomorrow before I head back to Statesboro.

Daddy asked me last night if any boys have "caught my eye." I laughed at his cheesy phrase. Sometimes I wonder if he wants to ask if I still think about Jack. I'm not sure if he wants to tell me about him but doesn't know how or isn't sure if he should.

I wonder if Daddy thinks I should contact Jack. I also wonder if he's ever written to Jack about me. Maybe Jack ignored it; he's still never written my name. I suppose that's proof he's moved on.

Of course, my life is full of enough thrills without Jack or any other guy. In fact, Saturday, Daddy went with me to my skydive school and watched all three of my jumps, including the last—my seventy-fifth. I should hit a hundred over the holidays since I'll be helping more than on the weekends. Soaring out of planes keeps me plenty busy, much to Ms. Becky's chagrin. She still hasn't warmed up to my hobby.

As she told me when I started (and repeats often), "I can't imagine why anyone would want to jump out of a perfectly functional airplane. I'm not going to say Carolina wouldn't approve, but I can't imagine her being thrilled about it."

Speaking of Ms. Becky, I better dive back into Middlemarch, so we can discuss it next week. She chose this book, and I admit I'm struggling. Total honesty: I'll likely fall asleep before I've gone more than a page or two. At least I'll be greeted by dreams of tomorrow's tacos.

Today's One Good Thing:
I am thankful for tacos and time with my dad.

Monday, September 22, 2003

Dear Rachael,

I got outstanding news today. I'm getting promoted to Lance Corporal, and—even better—after the first of the year, I'm heading to Scout Sniper School. Hoorah!

You would probably be crossing your arms at me right now, but this is a huge deal. Plus, Tray's going too.

Being a Marine already gave me a sense of purpose. Being a Marine sniper will lead to a more vital role in our mission. If I succeed in training, surely they'll send us to Iraq sooner. This Devil Dog's ready to fight.

Despite my excitement, I can't keep the what ifs at bay. I know I'm good at shooting, but what if I'm not good enough. In Boot, I was terrified to fail. I haven't had that word in my vocabulary since graduation, but now ....

This training is different. I want this for myself, more than almost anything. I've always managed to let other people down. Now, I'm facing the possibility of letting myself down.

Maybe I should focus on my advice from Boot Camp: "Lighten up. Breathe. One step at a time."

Today's One Good Thing: I think it's obvious ... today, I'm thankful I've got a shot—get it?—at becoming a Marine Scout Sniper.

Sunday, October 19, 2003

Dear Rachael,

You would have loved this weekend. We drove to Raleigh for the North Carolina State Fair. This was the 150th year of the fair.

It's a big deal here, and I can see why. We ate so much food I'm sure I'll regret come tomorrow's run—funnel cakes, turkey legs, messy burgers, plates piled high with these spiral potatoes ...

Rach, I'm gonna be dreaming about those things. They had malt vinegar to put on the potatoes, which I thought was weird ... until I tried it. Best combination ever! I wonder if I could convince the base cafeteria to serve fair foods.

There were rides—Tray turned green a few times—and games, of course. I wasted a ton of money on those things ... all my pay increase, plus some, I'm afraid, but I finally won a giant stuffed bear. The cute little girl I gave it to was thrilled. Her parents might not have been when they tried to get that thing in their car at the end of the night.

You would have made so much fun of me—I milked a cow. It was weird, but I can say I did it. And, if I ever get desperate and need some fresh milk, I know what to do. Just give me a cow and a stool.

I thought about how much fun it would be to enjoy that fair with you. I'd buy you cotton candy, win you something obnoxious (likely after getting in a fight with a carnie), hold your hand between rides and kiss you on top of the Ferris wheel. That would be a good date, wouldn't it?

The fair was such a normal thing to do. It made me realize how much normal I've lost. I've missed dates with you as an adult, weekend getaways and memory making. I signed my life to something immensely bigger than fair rides and fried food.

Have I lost something I can never get back—I mean, something other than you? Have I given up normal to be a Marine?

What am I saying? Being a Marine is way better than any fair. I'd like to see one of those carnies tear down and reassemble an M16 in just north of 10 seconds. They can keep their normal.

Maybe one day I can have normal, too.

Today's One Good Thing: Today, I'm most thankful for spiral potatoes and bottles of malt vinegar. Tomorrow it's back to Marine normal.

Monday, November 10, 2003

Dear Rachael,

Today's the Marine Corps birthday, which is a big deal. They had a birthday ball this past weekend, and we wore our dress blues. Honestly, I had no desire to go. I had to act proper, and I didn't have a date—not that I wanted to go with anyone other than you.

I would have enjoyed escorting you. You'd dress up in a fluffy gown, and we'd dance—like we were going to do the night of the second accident. I'm sorry I ruined your prom, Rach. We should have had such a special night. You, me, this ring and the rest of our lives.

The weather's changing here. The cooler weather makes me run faster, harder ... angrier. That sounds weird, I guess. Sometimes I run out my feelings.

Today I feel unsettled. Restless. I've been training for war so long; I'm ready to fight.

Maybe I'll always be a restless person. Some folks are, right? That's what my mom said about my dad. He didn't have much stick-around in him, as folks in Bellum would say. I don't want to be like him, but I guess some things we don't get to choose.

Whatever the cause, I'm ready to move on. Not from the Corps—never from that. I'm ready to march on with the Corps straight to the desert. It's my turn to take down some bad guys.

Today's One Good Thing: Today, I'm thankful for celebrations … for people who can celebrate them.

Thursday, November 27, 2003

Dear Rachael,

Happy Thanksgiving!

I wish I could be with you today on your mom's favorite holiday. I'd help you cook. Honest! I know I haven't got a clue how, but I'm positive you'd be a great teacher. At the very least, I'd make a helluva taste-tester.

Tray and Grandma Ethel brought me down to Columbia to the Miller's where mom met us. It's been incredible to see her again and be back with Senior and Mawmaw Mabel and their whole family. Grandma Ethel and Mawmaw Mabel hit it off right away, and I'm pretty sure they'll never leave that kitchen ... except to shove more food in my mouth.

As soon as she saw me, Mawmaw Mabel burst into tears and hugged me. She shuffled off, muttering something about "skinny as a rail," and came right back with a platter stacked high with five types of cookies. She can never remember my favorite, so she bakes them all. (Between you and me, they're all my favorite, so I'm perfectly okay with her forgetfulness.)

You should've seen Tray and his grandma and me riding down here—all three of us in his Ford Ranger. Grandma Ethel sat, prim as you please, in the middle, while Tray and I did our best to stick to our doors and give her room, which was extra difficult when Tray had to shift gears.

Anyway, I smell Thanksgiving dinner in there—actually, it's what woke me up this morning. I'm trying not to drool on this paper. I mean, it's not like I haven't eaten. Mawmaw Mabel's not going to NOT cook a huge breakfast when she's got a house full of folks, even when we're about to have the biggest meal of the year. I believe there is something about this house and her cooking—Grandma Ethel's, too—I could eat, sunup to sundown. Their food is so dang delicious.

Of course, PT's gonna suck when we get back to base. But, I did run an extra mile last night in preparation. Tray was pissed, but I made him stick with me. I told him he was soft. That seemed to work, though I'm pretty sure he wasn't having overly Christian thoughts toward me.

I suppose I should wander into the kitchen to see if I can help. And, by help, I mean taste.

Being surrounded by food and family, love and warmth reminds me what could have been with you. When did we lose our shot at this? Your mom's cancer? The first accident? Me drinking? Abbie Mae's death? Or, was our downfall all on me—when I ran, I shattered our futures? I at least fractured mine, but I sure hope yours is whole now. That's all I want.

I love you, Rachael. I wish you were here. Have an amazing Thanksgiving, wherever you are and whoever you're with.

Today's One Good Thing: Today, I'm thankful for food, family and your future.

Thursday, December 25, 2003

This year has flown past ... in more ways than one. I've jumped almost 125 times now. It's easy to get in the time when I work more than weekends.

The semester went well. I was worried about getting back into a school mindset, but it was like I'd never taken a break. Next semester will be more intense, but that's okay. It's my choice to make up for lost time.

Anna Claire and Stevie arrive tomorrow for a few days. I can't wait to see them. Anna Claire said she decided to close the store Christmas Eve through Monday so she could have some extra holiday time with her son. She said she has new clothes and designs to show me. I love looking at and wearing her work. Her talent amazes me.

Since I've been home for the holidays, I've caught up on Jack's letters to Daddy. He's now a Lance Corporal, and he's starting Scout Sniper School after the first of the year. With all I know about Jack—his heart, his mind, his innermost being—I cannot picture him as a sniper. Hiding somewhere, shooting people. I don't know how to process this development. He's a different man now than the boy who ran away from me.

Reading that he spent the holidays with family and friends in Columbia made me happy. I'm thankful he opened his life back to Ms. Becky and that he has other people close to him. He needs them.

He hasn't written anything about a girlfriend. I mean, it doesn't matter, of course. He's gone and we're done. That's that and all. It's just ... I still love him.

Today's One Good Thing:
I'm thankful Jack has people in his life again, even if I'm not one.

Thursday, January 1, 2004

Dear Rachael,

It's 2004!

Did you celebrate last night? Did you watch the ball drop?

We were on base, so it was business as usual. Full confession: I fell asleep around 9. How lame does that sound?

Anyway, I was thinking about you and wondering if you still make resolutions. I'm not a fan; mainly because I suck at keeping them. Big surprise there, huh?

Tray makes the same two resolutions every year, and he keeps them. He reads through his Bible and looks for something good to do for someone at least once a week. Yeah, he's a way better dude than me. He's the kind of guy you better find.

If I were to make a resolution, it would be to work on being more content. Less restless. I need to remember that Lejeune's where I am right now because this is where I'm supposed to be, so I need to do my job to the best of my ability and soak up all the training they'll put me through. We'll get our turn to fight, and I need to be content here until then. Besides, if I'd gone to Iraq before now, I wouldn't be about to become a sniper.

Honestly, I should be able to keep this resolution for the next few weeks, at least. We start Scout Sniper in a few days, so I probably won't write for a while. Tray and I will be busy.

I'm itching to get out in the field and take my shooting skills to a whole other level. This is going to be good, Rach. I mean, it's going to be hard as hell, but I can do this. I really believe I can.

Today's One Good Thing: Today, I'm thankful for the chance to become a sniper.

Sunday, January 4, 2004

I've moved back into my dorm room. Classes start tomorrow, so I'm trying to relax tonight. Apparently I'm not good at that. This semester will be crazy busy and will require a ton of focus and energy to get through with a strong GPA.

Before I forget, I wanted to journal some things that happened over the holidays. Last week, I had a blast with Anna Claire and Stevie. We took Stevie to see the water and watch the boats. I told them they'll have to come back when it's warmer so we can see more boats and have a picnic.

Anna Claire and I talked late every night. I didn't realize how much I miss having good friends nearby. Tears are therapeutic, especially when they're shared. I finally got to cry with someone about Jack joining the Marines. Anna Claire cried about how much she still aches for Steven. I can only imagine the intensity of the pain she feels. If Jack had died, I'm not sure how I could put one foot in front of the other, especially if I had a little one to care for and to remind me of his father with every smile and laugh.

Despite her grief, Anna Claire has followed her passion and launched her dream business to provide for her son. I told her how amazing she is and how proud of her I am. Of course, that brought more tears, but they were the good kind. She hasn't had anyone in her corner, aside from her great-aunt who passed away last spring. I'm thankful I can still be part of her life. Distance doesn't dampen true friendships.

Stevie's four years old and already knows most of his letters. He loves cars, just like his daddy, and will sit for hours playing with those and blocks. He builds roads and tracks and obstacles with his blocks and narrates races.

I think my dad enjoyed having a little one here. He spent most of the time they were here on the floor helping with the races. Daddy will be a wonderful grandpa one day.

If I ever get married, that is. I probably have to get past a date first, which leads me to the other big events during my break.

I went on a couple of dates. A regular at the skydive hangar has been asking me out for a while. I kept saying no, but the past few times I realized how ridiculous it sounded. I'm never going to see Jack again. Holding out hope or heart for him is plain, downright stupid. So, I finally said yes.

We did a few jumps together right after Thanksgiving and then went out for supper. It was fine, I guess. He's a nice enough guy. He's smoking hot; so there's that. But, I felt like our conversation went as deep as it will ever go, and I found myself wanting something more.

Then, at the end of the night, the guy leaned in for a kiss. I totally freaked out. Jack's the only guy I've ever kissed, and as illogical as it is, I felt like I would be cheating on him.

I backed away, whispered "I've gotta go" and bolted. I apologized to him the next day. I explained that I lost my one and only boyfriend and haven't been able to move on. Thankfully, he was nice about it, especially since we jump out of planes together. That could have been awkward.

Another guy who I have some classes with lives in Savannah, so we got together between Christmas and New Year's. I thought maybe I just needed to try again, push myself. It felt the same, though. I do know how foolish this sounds. It would make me so happy to simply move on with my life when it comes to relationships, but my attempts so far feel like slamming my head against a brick wall. They also feel wrong and lacking and impossible.

Ugh!

Why am I like this? Did I allow myself to become dependent on Jack? I've always thought of myself as independent. It's frustrating to want to move on but not be able to. I'm unsure if I need more time or need to force myself forward.

Anna Claire and I talked about my questions while she was here, and then we got on IM with Shannon after the second date. I know Anna Claire understands how I feel. She told me she never intends to date. Steven was her one and only, and the thought of being with anyone else makes her sick. Shannon longs for true love. One day she'll believe it's possible for her, and she will find her one.

After our chat, I decided I'm not going to think about dating anymore this semester. I need to focus on classes anyway. In a few months, I'll reevaluate and consider how I might move forward. Maybe it's not the right time for me, and that's okay. God knows what's right for me and what's not. He's got me. I need to chill.

Today's One Good Thing:
I am thankful for new classes to drown my thoughts in and best friends who understand broken hearts.

Monday, March 1, 2004

I knew this semester was going to be tough, but holy moly!

The classes are great, honestly. I'm keeping up with all the assignments and loving the subject matter, but I don't have any time to slack off or slow down. Let's just say, hitting 200 jumps by the summer isn't going to happen. I haven't been up in the plane in a few weeks now.

Today, I met with my adviser to register for summer classes. We mapped out the next couple of years and have a plan to space things out better. I ended up with all tough classes this semester, which adds to the stress.

This summer will be a good mix, I think. I only have Tuesday/Thursday classes and Savannah's an hour away, so it's going to work out for me to commute. It would be silly to live on campus for two days a week.

That means I'll have more time to work at the airport and jump. I want to get my count as high as I can so I can finally BASE jump. Skydiving is amazing, but I'm ready for something new, something more wild.

Today's One Good Thing:
I'm thankful for the challenge this semester has given me, but I'm also thankful for an adviser who's helped me reduce stress in future semesters.

Friday, March 5, 2004

Dear Rachael,

Today in training, I screwed up—made the kind of decision that would get other Marines killed. Sergeant Thomson ran my butt and made me shoot as punishment. At some point while I was running back and forth, the fog cleared in my brain. That's when I decided something—something you won't like one bit. I am sorry for that, but I have to be honest.

God's not for me. Or, I'm not for him. Not sure which way it goes. I can't believe in a God who lets bad things happen—who let me hurt good people. God's fine for good people like you and Tray. Me, though? I'm beyond that grace y'all sing about being so amazing. If God's as good as everyone says, then he doesn't want me around. No matter how much I think I've grown, I always find some new, more horrifying way to screw up.

Moving on from here, I will be a better Marine—more focused and sure. I will not "lead my team to slaughter," as Thomson said. I cannot have any more innocent lives on my conscience. The enemy? I'll take them down, without blinking. But, my fellow Marines? I won't lose them; I can't. I promised Tray that today. He told me not to make promises

I can't keep, but I'm keeping this one. No more good folks are dying on my watch.

After everything today, I told Tray my whole story. I told him about the alcohol, about Abbie Mae, about you and about me running. He talked about peace and prayer, but I told him my decision and walked away. You and he can't understand how I feel about religion. You've never made the kinds of mistakes I have. Y'all don't see dead kids' faces in your nightmares.

When I was telling him about you, I realized something else. The reason I never ask your dad about you in my letters isn't because I don't want to know or don't care. I do, but I don't want to face that you've done what you should have—moved on and found someone worthy of you.

All I want is for you to be happy, to be whole, to have the life you deserve. But, the selfish part of me wants to scream at the thought of you in another guy's arms. I know every bit of this is my doing, my choice, my leaving. It's just that selfish demon side of me that screams inside my head sometimes—or oftentimes.

Sorry today's letter is so insane. So many thoughts compete for my brain's focus. They needed somewhere to go, and writing them helped.

I'm glad you won't read this, though. I don't want to disappoint you more than I already have.

Today's One Good Thing: Today, I suppose I'm thankful for lessons learned and decisions made.

Saturday, March 20, 2004

Dear Rachael,

I'm no longer a teenager. How'd that happen?

Before you laugh too loud, remember your turn's coming in a week and a half.

I'm also officially a Marine Scout Sniper. I survived training and earned my hog's tooth—a bullet that symbolizes the round out there with my name on it. This symbol around my neck should remind me I could die, but ... I don't know. Right now, I'm feeling pretty daggone invincible.

My hog's tooth reminds me of my promise a couple weeks ago—I won't lose another person. I will deal out death whenever we finally get to Iraq, but it will be to people who deserve it, not the good ones around me. I finally get a say in life and death.

Over the past few months, I had many times I didn't think I would finish. It was, by far, the toughest training I've gone through. Not gonna lie: I'm pretty proud of surviving and of this new title. I feel like I've grasped a higher purpose for my life now.

Tray and I are about to head out to spend the day on the range. Best birthday ever!

Today's One Good Thing: Today, I'm thankful to be one step closer to dealing out justice when and where it's needed.

Thursday, April 1, 2004

Dear Rachael,

Happy twentieth, beautiful woman!

It's weird that we're both twenty. You'll be closing out your sophomore year soon. I could be shipping out to Iraq any time.

I've been thinking. Maybe I need to force myself to try and meet someone. No one could ever replace you, but I need to step forward. I'm sure you have—as you should. Instead of adding to this stack of ridiculous letters I'll never send to the girl I left behind, I should have conversations with a girl I might make a future with.

Your birthday was a bad time to write all this, I suppose. You've been on my mind so much all day, though. I wonder if I should focus less on you and more on this life I ran to. The problem is I don't want to and, honestly, I don't think I'm ready.

If that's the case, though, will I ever be?

At the very least, I can admit I should move on. That feels like progress. Maybe all I need is to make one step forward for now. More steps will come one day.

Today's One Good Thing: Today, I'm thankful for one small step and for whatever amazing things are happening in your life.

Saturday, April 10, 2004

Dear Rachael,

Ducky and Daisy got married today. Those two are so in love. They've had to overcome a whole lot to be together. People sure can be mean when they see them, just because Ducky's got Down syndrome. Daisy doesn't care about that extra chromosome. She looks at Ducky the way you used to look at me.

I tried to move on from you this weekend. There's no good segue for that, is there?

Anyway, I met a bridesmaid who seemed nice. She was pretty. We danced together after the rehearsal dinner. They partied late into the night, and we slipped off together. Things were starting to heat up—yeah, this is weird to write to you, but stick with me. Anyway, we were making out. I started to kiss her neck and shoulder—like I remember you liked. When I did, she threw her head back and laughed, and I stopped.

Her laugh was nothing like yours.

All I wanted in that moment was to hear your laugh, your voice, feel your lips, your skin. I couldn't get away from her fast enough. But, I did apologize. I tried to explain how I thought I was ready to move on but couldn't. I'm pretty sure she was still pissed at me.

I still love you, Rach. I don't think I'll ever not love you.

Your voice and laughter fill the soundtrack of my best dreams. I feel your touch at the strangest times. I can be walking through a crowd or stalking through the woods and swear I feel your hand on my arm. You know that weird moment when you're about to fall asleep, but you're not totally there yet? That's when I feel your head tucked under my chin.

I miss you so much, I physically ache. No one will ever be who you always have been to me. I only wish I could have been who you deserved.

Part of me is glad this happened because I know now, I'm not ready to move on. I feel bad for hurting this girl, though. I wasn't trying to use her. Maybe she'll understand that one day. She was nice at the wedding today. It's probably a good thing I didn't have to escort her down the aisle, though. That could've been awkward.

Tray ragged on me a good deal about it. Talked about how I was hopeless in the romance department. He's one to talk. I've never known him to have a date. Asked him about it once, and he mumbled something about a girl he used to know. Of course, we were at his grandma's. She'd just taken a pie out of the oven, so we both got distracted.

After his jokes, though, he told me it was okay to not be ready. His grandpa told him once that love isn't something to be rushed; it takes time and patience. Tray repeated the advice he'd received.

"Love's got its own mind about things. It doesn't make much sense or give us much of a say in the matter of our heart. Love does what love does, when love chooses to do so."

I certainly don't seem to have any say in the matters of my heart.

Today's One Good Thing: Today, I'm thankful that a laugh taught me a lesson in love.

Sunday, May 2, 2004

I survived my freshman year and kept my GPA up. It's good to be back in my bed at home, though. I've got a lot to pack into ten days before the summer semester starts. Daddy and I have plans to explore the railroad museum and City Market and to take a horse-drawn carriage ride. Plus, I intend to work in some vegging on the sofa.

After church today, I got home before Daddy did, so I caught up on Jack's letters. He's really a sniper now, so there's that. He was a groomsman in a wedding. Still nothing about a girlfriend. He sounds like he loves being a Marine, and every letter had something about looking forward to getting to Iraq or being ready for a piece of the action.

At least he's still in the States and not fighting for his life.

Yet.

Part of me wonders where the Jack I knew went, but I know that's him. He did always talk about the Marines. The thing was I always made him stop talking because I didn't want him to join.

If I couldn't let him talk to me about something he wanted to do, maybe I wasn't right for him.

I'm not sure why it's taken me all this time to figure that out. The important thing is, he's happy. He's doing something he loves, and he has good people in his life. At the end of the day and deep in my heart, that's all I want for him. Okay, yes, I want to be part of his life; but his well-being is the bigger picture desire. I will remember that and find contentment in his peace.

It's weird to think we're adults. Part of me regrets all the big events over the past few years that we've missed sharing. I do know it doesn't matter now, but it still makes me sad. To have reached many of our life milestones separately feels wrong.

This is reality, though, and my life should move forward. I need to uncover who I'm supposed to be. With small steps every day—like meandering through City Market and exploring Savannah's history and convincing Daddy to go into the art museum with me—I will take steps to be the adult God intends me to be ... without Jack. I think part of this journey includes learning who I am apart from Jack.

Today's One Good Thing:
I am thankful for this connection to Jack so I can know where he is and how he is, but I'm also thankful for opportunities to be with my dad and slowly learn who I'm meant to be.

Saturday, July 10, 2004

I've got another semester behind me and almost a whole month before I have to be back on campus for R.A. training. My church is sending a team to Nigeria for two weeks. I didn't think I'd be able to go, so I didn't sign up. one of the team members had to back out because she's pregnant, so they asked me to take her spot.

They want me to work with the women, many with children, who live at a special home and teach them nutrition and fitness, like I taught in Peru. These women come out of situations where they have AIDS because their husbands infected them and then cast them away.

Why do innocent people suffer for the actions of horrible ones?

I'm looking forward to another mission trip, even though more relaxation would be nice. My thought is, I won't always be able to go on trips like this. Now is my time.

Maybe this trip will help me find the pieces of my heart and soul that I seem to have lost these past two years. I think I'm standing in my own way of rediscovery, but I learned in Peru how being in another country can help me see with more clarity. Maybe Nigeria will open my eyes inward.

Today's one Good Thing:
I am thankful for the opportunity to spend time in another country, to learn about the culture and to help more people.

Tuesday, July 27, 2004

Nigeria is full of jaw-dropping landscapes and genuine people. It's also full of instability, fear and uncertainty.

Christians could be under attack at any point from Muslim extremists. Christian and Muslim tribes fight. Innocent people get caught in the crossfire. A few streets from the mission compound only rubble remains of a mostly Christian part of town after recent attacks.

In the bush, people walk for hours in the heat and dust to hear a sermon. I think about all the times back home where I stayed home from church, claiming I was too tired. Here, people will go to any lengths to sit outside under a tree and hear the Bible read, even if it means they'll be killed when they return to their Muslim village.

We've been going nonstop since we've been here, and many things have happened. I'll record two stories.

Sunday, we attended church in a distant village. As we drove up, families rushed out of their huts, most with multiple children. They all waved and smiled. The missionary explained how excited they were that American Christians had come to worship with them. I was surprised by that. We're nothing special—just people who want to help and witness a culture different from our own.

The smiles of the people in the village confirmed the missionary's words. They were genuinely joyful and welcoming. The people's happiness was contagious. When they began to sing—some tunes I recognized around the foreign words—I couldn't help but beam back at them as I listened to their exuberant praise.

Hearing familiar songs in another language was strange, but their singing reminded me of how amazing our world and our God is. No country lines or language barriers exist in heaven. We'll worship Him together—every tongue and tribe—for all eternity.

After the service, the village presented us with a special treat—a few packages of cookies and some bottles of soda to share. The missionary explained again how important hospitality is to the Nigerian people and how they had chipped in to provide a snack they thought Americans would enjoy. Each of those people—including the children—stood around us, smiling and nodding, encouraging us to enjoy their gift.

Let me just tell you: eating cookies and drinking soda in front of kids who may have never had a treat like that was one of the hardest things I've ever done. We wanted to show our appreciation for their selfless kindness, but that lovely cookie turned to dust in my throat as I choked it down.

All I wanted to do was distribute the snack among the children. Their smiles and excitement and joy were so real, so pure, so true. Witnessing such a beautiful picture of selfless giving overwhelmed and reminded me how much I take for granted.

The women I've been working with are equally kind and loving. We have had so much fun with fitness classes and cooking and talking about food. Once we'd been there a few days, several women shared their stories with us. Each of them has been cast away, discarded, by the men who were unfaithful to them and infected them with this awful disease.

They had to find a way to care for themselves and their children. That's where the home helps them. They teach many skills—knitting, sewing, jewelry-making. These women make exquisite handmade items that the missionaries help them sell around the world. This is how they support their families. They also have a true home, surrounded by other women who have faced similar hardships. They are sisters, bonded through adversity. Most of them have come to know Christ, too, and they share their testimonies with others.

After several of the women shared their hearts with us, I noticed one young woman, not much older than me. Tears poured down her face, and pain haunted her eyes. She looked at us and whispered, "It's hard to know no man will ever love me again."

One of the college students with us left his chair to kneel before the crying woman. He said, "I would. This disease could never stop a man of God who meets and gets to know you from loving and caring for you. Don't ever think any of this makes you unworthy of love. God loves you, and any wise man could love you, too."

All of us were crying then, but her tears had turned to ones of joy and hope. I thought of Shannon because she's had similar fears. Watching the woman in Nigeria shift from lonely and hopeless to optimistic is one of the most beautiful transformations I've ever witnessed, second only to salvation.

I think the women's ability to accept positive possibilities centers around an understanding of who they are in Christ. Understanding the great sacrifice the God of the universe made for them enables them to picture their futures without limits. They may have needed a friend or kind stranger to help them make the connection.

Today's One Good Thing:
I am thankful for the beauty and power of love, mercy, peace and hope that transcend the worst situations, the deepest poverty and all geographical boundaries.

Monday, August 9, 2004

R.A. training begins this week. I hope I can handle the responsibility for the residents on my hall in addition to my class load. I know every resident has different struggles and heartaches. Part of me wishes I could help them and be the listening ear they might need; part of me wants to bury my head in the sand again so I don't have to take their burdens on me.

I'm not sure why I'm like that, but when I listen to others' pain, it's like I take it into myself and feel it like they must. Empathy can be an overwhelming burden. Maybe I'll talk to Ms. Becky about it next time we talk. She may have some advice for me or will tell me to knock it off because I'm being crazy.

Since returning from Nigeria, I've felt restless. In some ways I feel like I got close to peace, closure, an epiphany ... I'm not sure what ... while I was there. Whatever it was slipped through my fingers somewhere over the Atlantic, like the sand I sifted on South Beach when Daddy and I visited Tybee Island at the start of the summer.

Instead, I've taken that restiveness and applied it to trying new things. I've been practicing formation jumps with the crew. We've been talking about entering competitions or shows. I would welcome the new challenge.

Today's One Good Thing:
I am thankful for the opportunity to have my own dorm room and new challenges where I can channel my restlessness.

Thursday, November 25, 2004

Dear Rachael,

How is it Thanksgiving again? I hope your holiday has been full of all your favorite foods and people. Do you still cook for anyone without family? I bet you're a master chef by now. You were always great, though. Your mom did an outstanding job teaching you before she died. She also had a brilliant student.

I know it's been a long time since the last letter. I started a few here and there but kept getting interrupted and losing things. It's been insane here. Tray and I started the Urban Sniper Course soon after Ducky's wedding. We're actively training for Iraq at this point. It won't be long.

You wouldn't want to hear that, I'm sure.

Don't worry. I'm in way more danger of dying from a diabetic coma induced by all Grandma Ethel's Thanksgiving food than of a bullet in Iraq. Don't laugh! I'm in mortal danger. Her fridge is full of leftovers, and as soon as Tray comes in from washing his truck, we're going to raid it. I barely made it out alive the first time. At least I'll die with a sweet potato pie smile on my face.

By the way, you should be impressed to know, I'm now a Corporal. At the rate I'm moving up in rank, I'll be able to name my next steps when we win this war. I've decided I want to go to college. I'll get my degree and go through Officer Candidate School. That'd be good to go. I hear the officer clubs have better water than the enlisted ones.

In all seriousness, I plan to make the Corps my career. This is my future now.

Tray walked in with a crazed look on his face. Gotta go before he gobbles up all the pie.

Today's One Good Thing: Today, I'm thankful that Grandma Ethel is incapable of cooking for three people. Here's to gigantic portions ... times two. I'm also thankful for elastic waistbands and extra-large plates.

Saturday, November 27, 2004

This afternoon I talked to Ms. Becky for almost an hour. We don't talk as often as we used to, but when we do it's a snuggle-down-and-chat kind of call. She has to be lonely in Bellum. I asked if she ever thought of moving. She laughed and said that sounds like far too much work, so she'll stay put for now.

I didn't want to let on that I read Jack's letters to Daddy. She and Daddy talk sometimes, so I figured it would be best to keep that under wraps. Part of me wanted to ask her all my burning questions, though. Is he going to war soon? How is he really? Is he dating?

Finally, I simply asked, "Is Jack okay?"

I heard a small smile in her voice when she said, "I think so."

Her answer was enough for now, so I said "Good," and then told her all about formation skydiving. She's still not a fan of my hobby, but she's never told me I shouldn't do it. She asks all the "mama questions" and then mentions safer hobbies—like reading. We always end with a laugh and discuss which book we'd like to try next. We've picked Jan Karon's Mitford series.

I shared with her how I've struggled this semester with offering a listening ear to the girls on my floor or protecting my emotions instead. I told her about the opportunity I had to help a girl get her friend the care she needed to not commit suicide. I'm sure we have many more residents struggling like that girl was, and yet I hesitate to find ways to help.

Ms. Becky told me she understands how I feel, that she struggles with maintaining her ability to live with the empathy she feels toward hurting people. Knowing that someone else—someone I admire—battles the same issue I do helped me immensely.

"Sometimes, people just need to know they're not alone," she told me.

She also told me I can find ways to help without overextending or harming myself. We talked through some ideas I could present to university leadership—counselor availability, suicide prevention campaigns, posters across campus.

Finally, she reminded me of something I should have been doing all along. She told me to pray before, during and after every encounter with a resident. She also encouraged me to pray for my residents every day and told me she would be praying with and for me as well.

Talking to Ms. Becky always makes me miss Mama. Before I go to sleep tonight, I'm going to re-read some of the letters she left me.

Today's One Good Thing:
I am thankful for Ms. Becky. Every girl needs at least a mama figure, and she is mine. I'm also thankful Mama left some of her words for me to hold when I need her most.

Sunday, December 26, 2004

Dear Rachael,

Merry Christmas!

I realize I'm technically a day late—it's past midnight—but this is the first time I've had a moment of peace. Tray and his grandma drove me down to Columbia. I swear this Miller clan gets bigger every time I visit.

Mom's here too. On Christmas Eve, we were keeping an eye on Mawmaw Mabel's fudge ... well, I was eating as much as I could while Mom made sure I didn't eat it all.

Anyway, she asked if I'd reached out to you. I told her no and told her I didn't want to know anything about you, that I'd turned my back on you and that's that. I think she wanted to tell me something about you, but I had the sickest feeling in my stomach because I imagined her telling me you were getting married.

Of course, the sick feeling could have had more to do with an overabundance of rich fudge.

She caught me off guard, you know? I mean, I figured y'all were still in touch. She was like a second mom to you as much as your mom was to me. Her question made me wish again I'd made a different choice two and a half years ago.

I've decided it's best for me to be married to the Corps, though, especially now that we're heading to Iraq. Forgot to mention that ... we got orders a few days back. We'll be heading out after the first of the year. I think a big reason I'm ready to go is I don't have anyone back home to worry about. Of course, I'd hate to leave my mom, but she'll be fine. I've made sure she receives everything of mine once I'm gone. If I were still with you, I'd be terrified of leaving you behind.

Single is good. I can focus 100% on the enemy instead of hesitating in a firefight. If I had a family, I'd be more cautious or reserved and that could end up getting me killed. Headlong and full speed ahead ... take out the bad guy before he registers the hell I'm raining down on him.

It won't be all breaking down doors and killing folks. We'll be spending most of our time gathering intel to report back. I'm sure we'll have many long, boring days and nights, which will make me appreciate the action even more.

We have to return to Jacksonville right after church tomorrow, and it's getting late. It'll be non-stop when we return to base; there's a lot to do before we ship out.

For one thing, I have some other letters to write—the just-in-case kind. I'll write one to my mom, of course, and one to your dad. He's been the closest thing to a dad I've ever had. I'm thinking I'll write you one, too. I'll put it in with your dad's and let him decide. If I do get killed, I'd like you to know how I felt about you when I died.

The good news is, I've had plenty of letter-writing experience over the past few years. My default setting to crack jokes when things turn serious has become more aggressive lately.

I hope—if it comes to it—you'll be willing to read the letter.

Today's One Good Thing: Today, I'm thankful for confidence and closure. And you.

Thursday, January 6, 2005

I'm about to start another semester, and Jack's going to Iraq.

Honestly, I'm not sure how to process the news. When I read the last letter he sent Daddy, part of me thought maybe Jack would show up over the holidays and ask for my forgiveness and to wait for him.

Yes, I had that ridiculous romantic scenario play out in my mind. I even imagined what I would say and how I would let him have it but also wrap my arms around him and kiss him like I've wanted to for almost three years now.

Of course, the holidays are over. I'm back on campus, and Jack hasn't come. And he won't. It was a silly dream.

I've got to put hopeless wishes out of my mind, just like I have to put Jack out of my mind. He's about to be gone, and I have to get a grip on the reality that—one way or another (God, please don't let him die.)—I will never see him again. I cannot repeatedly lose myself in dreams that'll never breathe in reality.

What I can do, though, is pray for him and for his safety—like Ms. Becky advised me to do for my residents. It's not like I will forget him, so I may as well pray my thoughts.

God, please save him—not just from bullets ... or worse ... but also from hell. Bring him to accept you as his Savior; make him your child.

Today's One Good Thing:
I'm thankful for the power of prayer and the possibility of miracles.

Wednesday, January 26, 2005

Dear Rachael,

If there's dirt on this paper, it's Iraqi sand, dust ... whatever the heck this crap is ... that sticks to everything. Tray and I have been in country for a couple weeks now, and I've spent most of my time trying to keep myself and, more importantly, my rifle clean. Not sure that's possible.

I know, I know. I'm grumpy. You'd call me on it, I'm sure, if we were talking. Just know, you'd be grumpy too.

As you can imagine, a lot's happened since we landed here. We had a stopover in Kuwait—that was all a blur, honestly. Tray and I were both relieved to be on the ground and terrified of getting back on one of those death traps. We didn't get the commercial airline tickets like most of the guys heading this way.

How those giant military planes stay in the air, I've got no clue. Sitting beside Humvees while flying toward war was surreal.

That's not the most unbelievable thing we've encountered, though. An overwhelming stench greeted us when we landed. Let's just say, thoughts of Iraq will always remind me of the smell of burning garbage.

Other constants are explosions and gunfire. While we heard those on base, with trainings and all, it's eerily different when you know they're real.

The first guys we met started us out right away on our RIP, which stands for Relief in Place. Basically, the guys who've been here doing what we're about to do and are on their way out show us the ropes. Pretty ominous acronym, though, if you ask me.

Anyway, the image I'll never forget is those guys' eyes. Rach, they're all about my age; some a little older, none super old. Their eyes, though, reminded me of Senior's. It's crazy. I felt like a baby next to them. They've got lines on their faces that I bet weren't there when they landed. Even when they smile or laugh when we're shooting the bull, their emotions don't seem to come from the heart. It's like any joy or happiness they show rests on top of those lines on their faces, like a stack of cards, balancing into a house that could implode at any moment.

I've heard a million times that war changes you. Now I've seen it. I suppose I'm in the process of living it. I wonder how I'll look to the next guys during their RIP.

Tray and I will spend most of our time hunkered down in hides, gathering intel or seeking insurgents. For now, though, we're gearing up to head out near some polling areas. Voting is one of many rights we take for granted. This will be the Iraqis' first democratic election since Hussein stomped his boot on their freedoms. Of course, many people fear for their safety if they vote. That's where we come in—to keep the peace.

Our moms dragged us with them every time there was an election. As much as I complained, I didn't mind. Of course, you know that. You always teased me about "fake complaining." It was fun to get candy and stickers.

Do you remember that one year when we were probably in kindergarten? Mrs. Appleby gave me a flag and told me to wave it proud. You grabbed my hand and shook it and the flag back and forth while you said, "Oh, he will, Mrs. Appleby."

I can't help but wonder what you would think about me defending that flag and the freedoms it stands for. Would you be proud? Would you have gotten over not wanting me to join?

Knowing what I know now—how I've found my purpose and place in the Corps—I wonder what would have happened if I'd stayed in Bellum, asked you to marry me and then decided to join. Would you have supported me, or would you have said no? We never did discuss it, and I never asked why you didn't want me to join. I didn't think I needed to then because I thought I had more options.

Well, I'm here now. I'm glad I am; though, I would rather be with you. That's a choice I do think I'd make differently. But, that's in the past, isn't it?

Something I've realized is, I need these unsent letters, especially in this place. I have a feeling I'm going to face times when I need to write you to calm my nerves and flex my heart. Thinking about you while processing the insanity rolling around us will help me remember that beauty and light remain in the world—beauty and light that the people who live here deserve to know, too.

I love you, Rachael. I wish there was some way I could let you know that without causing problems. Since I can't think of one, I'll look up in the direction of where the stars are and repeatedly think those four words. Maybe somehow they'll sail across the world and land in your heart. \

Today's One Good Thing: Today, I'm thankful for the opportunity to help people in this country have a voice. Here's to freedom!

Sunday, March 20, 2005

Last week was spring break, but I didn't want a break. I've powered through this semester with the goal of never resting, never stopping. In rest and pause comes thinking—something I have no desire to do because my mind always focuses on a desert thousands of miles away or on headlines that pierce like daggers to my heart.

And so I did a lot of free-falling through the atmosphere this week. The crew and I trained and put on a fantastic formation show yesterday.

Today's One Good Thing:
I'm thankful for a diversion from thinking about the possibility of my best friend—and only love—dying in Iraq on his twenty-first birthday.

Sunday, March 20, 2005

Dear Rachael,

Day million-and-two in country and I still hate dirt. It's seriously everywhere and in everything. Places you wouldn't think dirt could get. I'll let you use your imagination for that.

Of all the ways I pictured spending my twenty-first birthday, burrowed in a hide in Iraq was not one of them. That's where I am, though.

Tray gifted me his MRE ("Meal Ready to Eat" to you civilian). He pulled a good one (those are few and far between) and gave it up to me. It was a downright touching moment.

Anyway, we've spent most of our time hidden away, tracking, searching, gathering dirt—literally and figuratively. We're finally getting some decent intel on this Iraqi sniper who's been taking out our guys. I think Tray and I will be moving out to hunt him down soon. It'll be rewarding to finally contribute some rifle action in this war.

Wherever I am on your birthday, I'll be sure to send up a wish for you.

Today's One Good Thing: Today, I'm thankful for chili mac and a thoughtful partner.

Friday, April 1, 2005

Dear Rachael,

Happy twenty-first, beautiful lady!

How are you celebrating this weekend? Have you changed your mind about drinking now that you're a junior in college and legal to boot? Are you going out with friends? Is your dad treating you to a special dinner? Or, is it a lucky guy who's doing that?

I hit a milestone today. Heard a bomb go off nearby and didn't flinch. I'm getting used to life in hell.

It's not all bad, I suppose, as far as war zones go. Tray and I are getting stir-crazy, though. We've been in this one hide for almost two weeks. It sucks, but we know we're in the right spot. We just have to out-wait that Iraqi sniper. I know he's there; I can feel him.

We'll get him. He might be good, but I'm better.

In Bellum, I never got into the whole hunting thing with the other guys. Now, I'm a hunter of men. That's a crazy thing to wrap my mind around, especially when I think about the flip side.

I'm also the hunted.

Lately, I've been thinking a good deal about souls. I realize that sounds odd since I've declared God's not for me. Just because I'm not meant to walk the straight and narrow, though, doesn't mean I don't believe the whole heaven/hell, people-have-eternal-souls thing. As I think about lying in wait for a man, my mind wanders to thoughts of his soul. Honestly, I can't let myself linger there for long because I start to feel jumpy inside.

One thought helps me—though I'm not sure it's a good one. I figure this sniper's already damned himself to hellfire. My bullet will just send him where his name's already written.

He could probably say the same about me … if he contemplates the business of souls, that is.

Today's One Good Thing: Hands down, you are the one good thing in my day. I love and miss you and sure am glad you were born.

Monday, April 4, 2005

Dear Rachael,

I killed a man today. He was breathing. Now he's not.

And now, he can never kill another one of our men.

I know what happened today will not be the last—not by a long shot.

(That's a sniper joke—might be insensitive, but humor's standard issue when you deal out death.)

I also know now every life I take will stick with me. They'll need to be dealt with one day, but today showed me I can live with this. Yes, I took a life; but I took a life that's taken many others. Each enemy I eliminate is one less our guys will face.

Rach, I've seen things here—things you read about in horror books or history books. The things that've been done to innocent people. The things that've been done to other Marines. They're enough to make me want to scream and go Rambo on any enemy I meet.

I've seen other things, too. I've seen kids of all ages, many waving as we drive past. Once, soon after we got here, I noticed two kids standing by the road, holding hands. They probably weren't even five—a boy and a girl.

The girl raised her other hand to wave and dropped her doll. The boy noticed right away and bent to retrieve it. He returned it to her but never let go of her other hand. She clutched that doll tight and gave the boy a smile that said "thank you" more clearly than words in any language. He nodded to her, a hint of a smile in his eyes when they looked at her.

When he turned toward us, Rach, his face was solemn, and his eyes reminded me of those Marines we met our first day in country.

They might have been siblings, but I don't think so. I think they were best friends, like we were. I swear that boy would go to war for his friend if we offered him a weapon.

Every time I hear of another girl taken too soon because of some damn "honor" killing or of a fourteen-year-old girl with a bloody, bruised and swollen face because she displeased her much older husband, I'm ready to take on all these ... well, I don't intend to write what they are to a lady.

In these girls' faces, I see your eyes, your worth. And so, I will do my job. I will take out every enemy I am tasked with eliminating. One by one, I will make the difference I can.

As I do, I will remember your goodness. That's what will get me through. You will remind me of my humanity when I leave this desert and return to a home of freedom and peace and justice. My visions of you will carry me home whole and intact, even if bruised and battered.

Tonight—or this morning—whenever I finally shut my eyes, I'll send up a prayer for you to meet me in my dreams. I need to see you, to feel the warmth of your smile, to hear the chime of your laughter. Those are the things I need tonight.

Because of your memory, I can open my eyes again tomorrow with no regrets. I can go back out in the field. I can clean my rifle for the umpteenth time. And, next time I lock onto a target in my crosshairs, I'll do what I was trained to do. No hesitation. No question.

Every shot fired will be for the freedom of another Iraqi girl or woman who reminds me of you.

Today's One Good Thing: Today, I'm thankful for friendship—those two young friends on the side of the road ... and you. You were my first friend, and you will always be my best friend. Not time, distance or war can change that.

Monday, May 16, 2005

one more semester down; the next starts tomorrow. I decided to stay on campus straight through as a R.A. I've tried more dates over the past few months. Maybe dating's not for me.

Anna Claire, Shannon and I spent the weekend on Tybee Island. Anna Claire understands the whole childhood sweethearts thing; she and Steven had been inseparable nearly as long as me and Jack. She said maybe Jack just needed time and space to mature and maybe we both needed to be our own people apart from each other before we can be together.

Shannon asked what I thought about coming clean with Daddy and asking for his advice. She suggested that he and Jack may talk outside of the letters. Maybe Jack has asked about me after all. Maybe Daddy would have more information or could advise on whether I should send Jack a letter.

They both agreed that it's possible Jack still loves me, too, but it's been so long he figures I've moved on. After all, that's what he told me to do in his goodbye letter. Shannon also gave me the hard truth only a true friend can: Jack may have moved on and discovered who he is and is content in the life he chose ... the life away from me.

I feel like, at this point, it would be weird to be honest with Daddy. I should have done that three years ago. Of course, my friends are right, and I really should do something other than fret.

Would a letter from me now be a terrible distraction for Jack? Whether he'd welcome it or not, I think it could be. I would imagine a man at war needs to be focused more than anyone. Maybe I'll wait until he comes back from Iraq. I can read his letters at that point and decide if it might be a good idea or not. Or, maybe I'll talk to Daddy then. Until then, I'll continue praying for Jack's safety every day.

Several of the other exercise science majors and I are going out for drinks tonight. While I'll never drink like I did that one ill-advised weekend, I may as well enjoy an occasional drink or two now that I'm legal.

Who knows? Maybe it will dull my emotions. Staying busy hasn't accomplished that goal.

Today's One Good Thing:
I'm thankful for friends who speak truth, another semester ahead and post-war possibilities with Jack.

Friday, June 10, 2005

Dear Rachael,

The last several letters I wrote blew away in these damn Shamal winds. I thought the wind was bad before. These things are like frickin' dirt hurricanes.

If the insurgents or a tyrannical government won't get you and the religion doesn't condemn you, nature will blow you off the earth. I'm so thankful you're in the United States. At least we have basic freedoms ... and no killer dirt storms.

Despite the evil I often focus on in my letters, this country has its beauty. Out in the desert, the sky's blue is deeper and more expansive than I've ever seen. As the clouds drift overhead, I find myself overwhelmed with the enormity of the heavens above. In the evenings, the sunset hangs on the edge of the sand and lingers; its brilliance slowly melts across the horizon, and I think it will drape the earth forever. I force myself not to blink until—in one gulp—the desert swallows the splendor, and we're blanketed in night's pitch.

These people are fellow human beings on our vast planet. They have jobs and families, friends and dreams. Every morning, they get up and do their best to live—despite ever-present explosions and threats of death. Though their tomorrows aren't promised, they live in the pursuit of them.

I'm not sure I could do that. I might give in to the hopelessness flashing all around and lose my last thread of faith. Instead, I'm a Marine with confidence in the uniform I wear, the flag I fight for and the training I had.

Beneath that flag, we're marching north toward Syria. We'll be there for a while since the border's still a hot spot for insurgents sneaking across. Our bullets will find some marks there. Hoorah!

Today's One Good Thing: I'm thankful the wind's not blowing … right now, anyway.

Monday, July 4, 2005

Dear Rachael,

Are you watching fireworks tonight? I hope so. I know how much you love them. When I close my eyes tonight, I'll imagine sitting on a blanket with your head on my shoulder to "watch the sky dance," as you used to say.

The explosive sounds around me aren't exactly celebratory. They can be pretty ... if you pretend they don't deal out death.

All the killing is eating Tray up. For the most part, he spots for me, but we switch out now and then. I worry about how it will be for us when we get home. I want to help and comfort him, but I've never even been able to do that for myself. In the moment—in this place—I don't think of our targets as human beings. Tray's too religious for that mind trick to work. I suppose it's a good thing I came to war a heathen.

I know I'll have stuff to sort out when I get home. As much as I lie to myself, I see the blood. I know I'm putting an end to a beating heart—a soul. I won't let myself dwell on that fact. Not sure if that will make home better or worse, but it's what I do to function now.

Speaking of home, I've been thinking about returning stateside. We'll likely be shipped back in the next few months. I'm ready to kiss American soil and pick up a bag of burgers from the closest drive-thru.

More than anything, I want to see you.

Rachael, you are my light and sunshine in every dark and dingy hide. At night when I dream, you are my angel of mercy. You're my redemption from evil—mine and others'.

When I picture returning home, I can't do it without seeing you there, without imagining my arms around you. When I return, I'll talk to your dad first, but I want to see you again.

I know you're about to start your senior year. I'm sure you've found a guy by this point. Any guy who wouldn't at least try to date you is an idiot, and I'm sure most of them looked incredible compared to your loser high school boyfriend. But, I'm hoping—and maybe even praying—that you might give me a chance.

If you do, I'll spend the rest of my days trying to make up for my mistakes and immaturity—for not staying by your side, for not keeping you by my side these past three years. I believe you would have walked beside me all this time.

Either way, I was wrong to not give you that choice. As much as I rage at the lack of choices I've had in my past, I took this one from you.

If all else fails, I've got a fancy uniform with a snazzy white cover. It's effective on most girls. I'm not above pulling out the big guns.

Hell, I'd pull out my rifle, if I thought it'd impress you.

Today's One Good Thing: Today, I'm thankful for the hope of home with you at its heart.

Monday, July 11, 2005

This weekend, I watched a real-life love story unfold.

I went to Augusta to watch Laylah while Shannon shot another wedding. This time, she found the special look she's longed for all these years. I noticed this groomsman watching her while they were taking portraits on the golf course. He was clearly interested.

Once she noticed him, outside of her lens, I knew she was, too. Never have I ever seen Shannon flustered while holding a camera ... until Matthew spoke to her, that is.

The whole scene was like watching one of those love-at-first-sight movies that we roll our eyes at but always pick.

After the wedding, Shannon was like a giggly teenager. She told me she was afraid to hope, but then she was afraid not to hope. She said meeting him was like watching a dream come true, but she still struggled to believe it could be real and happening to her.

She said she knew when he was the right man for her. His first question was if she's a Christian, and that showed her where his heart is.

He asked if he could take her out before she went back to Bellum. After we all went to church together, I took Laylah on a picnic while the two lovebirds got to know each other.

I have a feeling I'll be buying a bridesmaid dress soon, and I could not be more excited for my friend. She has come so far from the girl who defied the odds to survive literal hell on earth.

Watching them together, I am more certain about sending Jack a letter whenever he returns from Iraq.

Maybe, instead of a letter, I'll talk to Daddy, and we can welcome him home in person.

I'm not sure how Jack would react, but I know I'll always wonder what could have been if I don't try.

Today's One Good Thing:
I'm thankful for past, current and potential future love.

Friday, July 15, 2005

Dear Rachael,

We're wrapping up our time at Camp Al Qaim. A couple years ago it was a railroad station. Most of the guys complain about it. I suppose it's a crappy camp. Bathrooms equal piss tubes and catholes. For me and Tray, though, it's at least a four-star establishment. Of course, we spend most of our time in cramped hides we've fashioned out of whatever we can. And, the bathroom thing? Well, let's just say, we're not picky and know how to make do.

Maybe there's not much variety when it comes to food, but we would be happy to eat those chicken enchiladas all day long and twice on Sundays. Of course, you could make much better. We are talking about a glop of pre-made food on a grab-and-go tray.

Heck, I could probably make better. I'll learn to make enchiladas when I get home so I can impress you. I plan to pull out all the stops to coerce you to forgive me.

We'll be heading south soon, probably back toward Fallujah. We won't know what to do with ourselves there. They've got gyms and computers with internet access. I won't miss the incessant drone of generators, that's for sure. That sound will haunt my dreams.

What are you up to? I'm wondering if you've got an internship or something this summer or if you're being a nerd and going to school. Maybe you're enjoying the last summer off you'll ever get. As an adult, I've realized we took summers and holiday breaks for granted. I hope you took that last option. Enjoy it for me, too.

Today's One Good Thing: Today, I'm thankful for the little things ... like tasty slop.

Monday, August 8, 2005

Dear Rachael,

We've been balls to the wall since returning to Camp Baharia, adjusting to sniping in an urban setting instead of the desert. We trained for this, but it takes getting used to, and many details must be learned in the moment. Tray and I make a great team, though. I suppose it helps we've been together through all our training and combat experiences.

It's mid-afternoon, and I should be sleeping. Our sleeping schedule sucks. Actually, it's not really a "schedule." It's more a whenever-we-get-some-time-between-hunting-and-being-hunted situation.

We head out tonight around midnight. We've had some reports of insurgents nearby and have a decent idea where they're hiding. The city's mostly shut down right now with a Shamal dust storm, so this should be the perfect time to slip out with a team and set up across the street from where our sources say they are. Then, we wait and watch. As soon as they show so much as a pinkie, we'll get them.

Switching gears: I've been thinking nonstop since my letter about coming to you when we get home. Honestly, Rach, I cannot wait to see you and have no doubts about hitting my knees and begging your forgiveness.

At the same time, I realize a romantic relationship between us might never be possible. A lot of time has passed—time I caused. So, I understand my consequences, but I do hope with every fiber of my being that I can re-earn our friendship. We were like those two Iraqi kids I wrote you about—inseparable. I would have saved your doll; I would have picked up a rifle to keep you safe.

I still would, whether I get to do that as your boyfriend or your friend or your forever debtor.

You're the only one who's ever shattered my walls and cut to the soul of me. You ripped me open—bare, bleeding, exposed—and I crave that feeling again. With you, that openness set me free. In your eyes, I became someone I always wanted to be but feared I never could.

Without you, I am enclosed—a hollow tomb. Even the remains I carry have become dust in the Shamal winds, choking and blinding until they've passed, never to be seen again. Cursed and then forgotten.

Like I'm sure I am to you.

Even if I'm nothing to you anymore, I have to reach out. I will apologize and acknowledge the pain I caused you.

Tray threw his helmet at me, so I should probably stop scribbling. Maybe I'll get some sleep. If not, that's what mainlining caffeine's for.

Wish me luck.

Today's One Good Thing: Today, I'm thankful for new missions and opportunities to kick some ass.

Monday, August 15, 2005

How do I begin?

I wasn't even supposed to be home last weekend. I had to get special permission to leave on check-in weekend. We had R.A. training last week, and I left right after lunch Friday. Friday and Saturday, we had a skydive demonstration we've been prepping for all summer. Daddy and I enjoyed a steak dinner Saturday night, and then I went to the Mission service with him Sunday morning.

We'd just finished lunch—I had put a pot roast and veggies in the oven before we went to church ... like Mama used to do.

I was in my room, packing, when I heard the phone ring. I don't eavesdrop, but Daddy's first words caught my attention.

"Becky, slow down. Where are they taking him?"

My heart shattered into a million pieces, and I couldn't breathe. I collapsed in my doorway and strained to hear every word on Daddy's side of the conversation.

"How bad is it?"

"Two surgeries ... or three?"

"Yeah, I'm sure they might not know all the details either. The logistics of medical evacuations can be complicated, but I know some chaplains who've told me what a great job they do getting them from place to place."

"When will you go up there?"

"I understand. She's a gem of a woman. I'll get a flight to Jacksonville and accompany her to D.C."

"Becky, I'm going to call Herb. He and Marjorie can get you to Atlanta. I don't want you driving right now."

"Yes, they will. Just let me handle it, okay? Please."

"And, Becky? He'll be okay."

"Okay. See you soon."

I listened, shock numbing every process of my body, as Daddy tapped on his phone, then silence.

"Herb?"

"I'm doing just fine, but I'm calling to ask a favor."

"Could you and Marjorie get Becky to the airport in Atlanta and probably pick her up again?"

"It's Jack. You know he joined the Marines."

"Right. Well, we're not sure. She didn't have specifics. He's had a couple surgeries already—there in Iraq and then in Germany ... that's where he's coming from. It sounds like a shoulder or arm is the big concern. I'm praying that means it's not life-threatening, but we aren't sure. His buddy who was with him didn't make it. I'm meeting the boy's grandma because she wants to go to D.C. to see Jack. They had become like brothers, and Jack spent a lot of time at her house before they deployed."

A bud of hope brightened my heart for a minute, but they weren't sure. If his friend died, then he could be much worse than Daddy made it sound. Shredded heart pieces nearly beat out of my chest. I squeezed my eyes closed and clutched the door frame to keep a panic attack at bay.

"Herb, I appreciate you being there for Becky. I know she's upset, and I don't want her driving alone."

Part of me wanted to rush out and beg Daddy to take me along, and I pulled myself to my knees. I needed to go to Jack, see him. Be with him.

And then, images of what we might find terrified me. He could die on the way home. He could be paralyzed. He could lose a limb. Once-strong men in wheelchairs flashed through my mind, and the shattered bits of my heart blew away with a forceful exhale as I crumpled onto the floor.

I must be a coward because I pulled myself together, zipped my bag and walked into the living room as Daddy got off the phone again. In his eyes, I saw a fear I'd only seen once before.

That time, Mama died.

I couldn't stay. I couldn't go with him. I couldn't face another loss. I had to get out.

He looked like he wanted to ask something as I kissed his cheek and hugged him. The unasked question shifted to an explanation as I turned toward the front door and air ... light ... escape.

"I have to take a trip up to D.C. There's an older woman whose grandson was killed in Iraq." His voice broke across the last three words. "I'm going to fly with her to visit her grandson's best friend. He's ..."

He had to stop talking. I wasn't sure what Daddy was about to tell me, and I was too scared to find out.

I blurted out—too loud to my ears, "That's a good thing for you to do, Daddy. Take care. Call me when you get home?"

He opened his mouth, swallowed more words and nodded before he kissed my forehead. "I love you, baby girl."

I kept my words light; I had to. "Love you, Daddy."

And then, I left.

I don't remember the drive back to the dorm. I don't remember bringing my bags into my room or walking out in the rainstorm.

My first sensory memory is the cold, muddy ground seeping through my jeans as I sank by the creek on my knees. The sensation woke me to the terror, uncertainty and ache I'd been keeping at arm's length. With the pain exploding from my soul, I lifted my face to the merciless rain and screamed at God. Screamed at Jack. Screamed at myself.

The thunder padded my release; the lightning jarred and emptied my tears into the darkness near what the football players call their "magic water." I felt no magic.

For most of my life, Jack was my everything, my reason for living, my all, my one and only. Where he began and I ended blurred. I haven't been whole since he left. Life without him has made no sense. I've been lying to myself—either saying I'm fine or saying it doesn't matter because I hate him for what he did. Honestly, I've been a shell of me since losing him.

I realize now ... this is why I leap out of planes and intend to launch myself off mountains. All I want is to feel something—anything—as exhilarating as his touch, his love, his kiss ... him.

Him and me. Us. It was always us. Now, there may never be a "we" again because Jack could die.

It's one thing to know I might never see him again, but that he is out there somewhere, living, breathing, existing. It's another to know I might never see him again because he's dead. That's not a possibility I want to consider.

Living with Jack dead makes absolutely no sense to me, and, right now, I don't want it to.

Friday, August 19, 2005

Daddy called tonight.

If Jack were dead, he'd tell me. Not on the phone, but he'd tell me.

He sounded tired—beyond tired—but he didn't sound broken. If Jack were dead, he'd sound broken.

If Jack were dead, he wouldn't have called. He'd be here. He'd be holding my hand and telling me.

Because of course I'd go to the funeral.

Black dress. Black shoes. Waterproof mascara. Strong mask up; face the lines of people—the well-wishers, the do-gooders, the in-a-better-placers.

I remember every agonizing second of the day we said goodbye to Mama. It was standing up on the most excruciatingly painful day of my life and having to be the entertainment for an entire town of people who I'm not sure ever cared for me, Daddy or Mama.

But Jack …

Jack was there for me, his shoulder pressed against mine. He held my hand and never let me out of his sight or far from his support.

Jack isn't dead.

What Jack is, I don't know; but dead's not it. If his heart stopped beating, I believe mine would glitch. After all this time, I believe they're as connected as in that cemetery beside Mama's grave when we were twelve years old—when he sensed my need for a hand squeeze, for a fresh tissue and for him to press closer to keep me upright under the relentless waves of grief.

Knowing us—believing in our connection—I just can't …

Every part of me aches for him. The pain he's going through—I wish I could take it all away, not just the physical pain but also the anguish of losing a best friend. I feel him hurting, breaking.

How can I feel his heartache? Am I tethered to him… still, after all these years?

I didn't realize I'd flown to that desert with him. The heat of a barren wasteland is what I've allowed to be my existence.

No more.

I cannot do this anymore. He left me to go off and nearly get himself killed. Just when I decided to ignore his choice and reach out—when I allowed myself to hope—this happened. And so, I have to put him out of my life and keep him that way. I cannot continue dragging him through the already wasted garden of my mind, my heart, my life.

This first week of classes has been my worst ever. I have no idea what any teacher has said. I've barely pulled myself out of bed most days. The last real meal I had, I'm pretty sure, was the one I made for Daddy and me on Sunday.

I can't keep this up. I have a future; I'm almost to my goal—to graduation—and I cannot let Jack wreck that.

I'm done caring, loving, hoping, wishing, hurting, bleeding. I'm done with him.

This semester is too important. Only one more after this, and I get that slip of paper, move on with my life and become whoever I'm supposed to be. I will make my skydive goals. I will save the money to go to Idaho and train to BASE jump. I will buy my own gear. I will return to Peru. I will leap from bridges and mountains and over waterfalls. I will freefall from everything I can, but I will never freely emotionally fall again over Jack.

Never.

He's okay without me, and at least, he's alive.

Today's One Good Thing:
I am thankful Jack's not dead, and I'm thankful I'm finally moving on from the desert to live alongside a stream of reality.

Wednesday, March 15, 2006

Time surprises me. In some moments, I fear they'll never pass. Last semester and the first half of this one, I've felt trapped in a time prison with no hope of release. And yet, as I look at how long it's been since my last entry, that day with its pain feels like seven minutes, not seven months.

This will be my final spring break. I decided to spend it at home with Daddy. The past few years, I've been running, nonstop. He has been patient with me and understanding of my never being here. I realize now how selfish I've been and how lonely he must be.

He lost Mama, and I haven't been around much. I'm not sure he has any super close friends. He spends time with a lot of the guys who've come through the Mission and the ones who work with him there. He meets with other preachers, chaplains and counselors in the area. I don't know how close they are.

Anyway, I'll be moving back here in a few months and finding my own place. I don't want to continue being too busy to spend time with Daddy. We decided to make Sunday nights our scheduled time together. I promised him homecooked meals since he still burns toast.

This morning, I broke down and checked for new letters. Deciding to sever emotional ties to Jack and slashing the knife are separate actions. Wondering where and how he is, how his life has changed, who war and loss have made him—my mind stumbles daily over these thoughts. I find myself facedown in a pile of memories of the man I loved and the terror of who he might have become.

Reading Jack's letters hasn't helped. He's only written two. His handwriting's not the same. It's neater, maybe, but more … deliberate? I don't know; it's hard to describe. He didn't say much in either of them. He referenced his gimpy arm and his wish that he'd learned long ago to be ambidextrous. He said he was adjusting to being a lefty. His second letter was more mellow, pessimistic even. He's no longer a sniper, and he's not okay with that. He's not sure he'll stay in the Corps. He sounds … defeated.

Even with this separation and all the life that's happened—to both of us—I can still read between his lines.

Part of me wonders if he gets out, will he come here? I think he would. At least, to see Daddy. I don't know. I need to see Jack, and that need terrifies me. Honestly, my thoughts are so jumbled; I don't know what's true from my heart and what's not.

I can't think about any of this right now—I'm a few weeks from graduation. This should be a happy time. I'm close to something I've worked hard for, but here I am again—unable to feel—or unwilling to, I suppose. After all, the only thing I seem capable of feeling is unbearable pain.

Today's One Good Thing:
I am thankful Jack can write letters. I'm also thankful for this one last break, and I intend to show my gratitude by sleeping as late as I possibly can tomorrow. That might only be 7 a.m., but I'll take what I can get.

Monday, May 29, 2006

This past month has been amazing, and it's gone by too fast.

May 6 was graduation. Daddy was there, of course. Ms. Becky came and stayed a few days afterward with us.

She looks so tired. Worn may be the better word. I wouldn't say old, though she does look older than she should. Burdened might be the best description. I saw worry in her eyes and the creases around them. I blame Jack for the pain she carries.

I'm not sure Ms. Becky has ever had a vacation. As we toured Savannah, her eyes lit up, and her joy cheered my heart. I imagined how much more fun she would have had if Mama were still with us. Their friendship sparkled. Even as a little girl, I recognized the special relationship they shared. Seeing our moms carefree and giggly made me happy.

We tried new restaurants and foods, saw the sights and shopped in some cute stores. Daddy's not much for shopping, so I hadn't explored that aspect of Savannah.

Ms. Becky bought a new purse and outfit. She looked sheepish as we waited in line. She said she'd never spent so much on something she didn't really need. When she started to turn around and put the items back, I grabbed her hand and asked her what Mama would tell her.

Her smile was filled with misty remembrance as she replied, "She'd say, 'Becky, you're being ridiculous. You never spend a penny on yourself, and a treat now and then is simply fulfilling the definition of the word. Besides, that purse of yours is older than Methusaleh's mother's, and you're looking frumpy. Buy the purse and clothes and stop holding up the line.'"

We talked about books, Savannah, graduation and my future. I asked her about Bellum and if she'd consider moving. She laughed and said that sounded awfully overwhelming, but I wonder if she didn't give it a longer thought. Maybe she'll visit again soon.

While we were out together, I found a couple shops that would be the perfect fit for Anna Claire's clothes. I gave them her information and called my friend right away. We made plans for her to visit soon.

A few times as we walked around, I thought Ms. Becky wanted to tell me something—or maybe ask something. Maybe I should have encouraged her to do that, but I know it wasn't something from Jack. If he'd asked her to tell me something, she immediately would have. I don't want her or Daddy telling me anything Jack doesn't want me to know. If he doesn't want me to know, it means he still doesn't want me in his life.

And that's that.

I spent the rest of that week with Daddy. He asked many questions about BASE jumping. He expressed his concerns but didn't tell me I couldn't train in Idaho.

The following weekend was Shannon and Matthew's wedding. The ceremony was a perfect celebration of a love that was a long time coming. Anna Claire made our dresses and Laylah's dress. Honestly, her talents continue to amaze me.

Laylah resembled a magical fairy as she scattered rose petals down the aisle. When she got to the front of the church, she ran over to Matthew and gave him a big hug before she crossed to her mom's side with us. It might have been the most touching thing I've ever witnessed, and I definitely saw tears in Matthew's eyes. By the time he caught sight of his bride, he wasn't even trying to hide them.

I'm thankful for them and excited to watch their love story continue.

Once I returned to Savannah, I packed for Idaho. My boss from our Savannah skydive crew is from Oregon and put me in contact with his buddies. I did formation jumps with some incredible skydivers while I was there.

Like skydiving, I began with a tandem BASE jump. Compared to skydiving, it was far more intense—which I hadn't thought possible. I began my training the next day. Once I completed that, I jumped as many times as I could and spent the rest of the month traveling around Idaho, Oregon and Washington. It was an all-I-could-do buffet of skydiving, BASE jumping, hiking, rock climbing and so much more.

I'll add rock climbing and hiking in the mountains to my list of hobbies. I'm not sure much in this world can top the view from the peak after a tough climb. Unless, of course, it's the speed of the earth rising to meet me after a jump. I may be an adrenaline junkie.

While I was in Idaho, I visited the valley near Galena Summit where my mom told me God filled her heart with peace and contentment right after the doctor told her she may never have a child. She told me how contentment in God, regardless of what the future held, changed the way she lived.

As I sat there with my face to the sun, like Mama must have done, I tried to pray for contentment and peace, but all I could think about was how much I miss her and Jack.

Can a life after loss experience contentment?

I'm not sure I can answer that question.

The past few months, I've tiptoed toward dating. I'm hopeful that one day I might make it to a second date.

It's still too weird, and I haven't been able—yet—to push myself further. But, I figure practice makes perfect, right?

One date, in particular, surprised me. I met Tyson in Oregon at a skydive show, and we went out to eat afterward. He's one of those people who's super opinionated about everything and loves to share his views but refuses to listen to others' thoughts, especially if they conflict with his.

He launched into a tirade about how we had no business being in Iraq and that war was a control mechanism of the right elitists. He went on to say that all our service members who were over there fighting deserve whatever happens to them because they fell for the lies.

We were eating tacos—which, of course, I love—but I stood up, looked him square in the face and told him he was wrong and that if he had any internal fortitude (I might have used a slightly more vulgar expression that I'm too ashamed to write), he would have enlisted and put himself on the front lines for freedom. And then, I walked away and left my tacos behind.

I had no idea people feel that way about the war and our country's heroes. I also had no idea how strongly I would react to such an opinion. Most of all, I was surprised at how much I disrespected and even loathed him for being such a coward. The interaction showed me how much I admire and how proud I am of Jack's service.

As I think back to my disagreement with Jack over his joining and my anger when he joined, I realize my reactions were those of a scared girl. Though my heart aches at the thought of all that's happened to him, I am proud of him. I respect his sacrifice and commitment and bravery. He and all who put on uniforms—whether they're fighting wars, fires or criminals—are heroes. They deserve our thanks and support. Whether we agree with the politicians moving the players on the board, we have to support our heroes and their sacrifices.

I suppose that's my big epiphany of the month, and if it took a rotten date to materialize, then it was worth it. My only regret is not taking my tacos when I stormed out.

Thursday, I enter the real world and begin training at BodyStrong + Life. As excited as I am about working there, I'm even happier that they're being flexible with my schedule so I can keep up an intense jump schedule and get in another trip to Peru at the end of the summer.

I will jump off that mountain!

Today's One Good Thing:
I'm thankful for so many things ... where do I start? How supportive and loving Daddy is—even though his daughter might be insane. The opportunities I've had this month. I've packed a lifetime of experiences into the past few weeks. A job, ready and waiting, that I know I will love and was made to do. Not everyone is able to make a career out of something they're passionate about, so I don't intend to take that for granted.

Friday, August 25, 2006

Today, I leapt off a mountain in a beautiful country, and I am invincible. I could have jumped fifty more times. The chill of that moment when my feet leave earth and I hang in uncertainty for a split second gets thawed by the fiery thrill of soaring down a mountain face, inches from some of its ledges.

Sleep won't come quickly tonight, but I hope I get some. I'm here with dive and jump acquaintances from my west coast trip. Tomorrow we're getting up early to hike. Our destination is a waterfall, where several of us will be jumping. It's going to be intense—in the best way.

I hate to admit this, but there is one thing that would make this better—Jack. Nothing can drown, bury or blast my need for him out of my core. When I took the leap today, my first thought when I hit land was higher, faster, wilder.

Liquor couldn't drown Jack's memory. Moving on and forgetting aren't possible. Shooting my adrenaline to extremes leaves me restless, gasping for more.

He is my greatest thrill. Always has been. Will he always be?

I'm sick of longing, reaching, seeking, falling. Day after day, I fall again for Jack. He's the last BASE jump—the one that ends it all. The one we all crave and fear, fight against, pretend can't happen but must acknowledge every time our toes hit the air.

Why can't I reach a point where I don't long for him and his presence in my life? Will I ever not love him? Will I ever not feel empty when I remember he's not in my life? Maybe it's just being in a gorgeous land, surrounded by history and culture that fascinate me, that I want to share with someone I love.

Tonight, I pushed those thoughts aside and took a moonlight stroll with Ethan. He told me about some of his favorite jumps. He's been to the Himalayas and jumped a few spots there. He said Angel Falls in Venezuela was a whole other experience.

We talked about what we love about jumping. I realized for me it's the nonsensical mashup of numbness with a combination of all the most intense feelings a human can experience. Yeah, it doesn't make much sense.

I'm not sure how much else Ethan and I have in common beyond similar tastes in thrills and music and a love of travel. He was the first guy I've felt almost comfortable with, and though I know he's not right for me, spending an evening with him was better than any of my previous date attempts.

Progress.

I'll spend a few days next week with Sarah and her husband in Iquitos. I can't wait to see them again and to see how big all the kids have gotten. The ladies who have been teaching fitness classes since I left told Sarah they're looking forward to some new routines. We're going to have a blast.

Today's One Good Thing:
I am thankful for airplanes, mountains, waterfalls, friends, opportunities and progress.

Monday, September 4, 2006

Dear Rachael,

It's been a while. More than a year. A lot's happened. That mission went bad, and for some cruel reason I don't get, I'm the one still alive.

If you could read this, you'd see my writing's different. I've had to learn to use my left hand. I guess that's why I stopped writing. At least, at first.

When I got discharged from the hospital back to Camp Lejeune, I realized the love and hope I felt at the end in Iraq got sprayed all over that street in Fallujah, along with pieces of my team, pools of Tray's blood and the function of my right arm.

I couldn't write you. I knew I could never come to you, like I'd been planning. I'm messed up, Rach. Iraq left me hollow, but not empty. Anger, hate, bitterness, evil and nightmares have returned, more destructive than ever.

My only friend is gone. Mostly, I stick to base and stay busy. That keeps me from chasing my thirst for alcohol. I stopped going to the range. I couldn't shoot, so being around the guys who could would have been unbearable.

Grandma Ethel makes me come for Sunday dinner. How I hate choking down the food Tray loved. Every time I step foot in her home, I feel the man who'll never walk through its door again. Every visit kills me as I revisit him dying in my arms. At least the rest of the week I only hear his final breath at night.

Sometimes the loneliness consumes me. I think that's really why I couldn't write you. It's not hard to find patriotic girls interested in welcoming a Marine home from war. I get so lonely and sad and hope somehow being with someone will help me forget, give me something good to hold on to, even if it's only for a few hours. Every time, I hate myself. I hate the girl, too. I swear it's the last time, but a week or two later, I can't take being alone anymore. When your heart's not in it and you don't care about the person's soul, it's a temporary high with a painful crash.

Writing this out to you makes me hate myself even more, but being honest and open to you—even though I know now I'll never give you these letters or see you again—feels right. These letters help me put some of my mind's confusion in order and focus on my next step.

I'm leaving the Corps, Rachael. My time is done, and I wouldn't re-up. It felt wrong. Without full use of my shooting arm, I'm not worthy of the uniform. I wrote your dad, letting him know I'm going off on my own. I'll keep in touch with Mom, but I'll stay away.

That glimmer of hope I had in the desert was a mirage. Thinking I could return to you—could have a future, a home, a normal life—feels naïve now. Warriors who fight for those rights for others forfeit the same for themselves.

Today's One Good Thing: Despite all my mistakes and everything I've turned to ash, my love for you still burns and shows me I have some humanity remaining. That is all I can be thankful for today.

Sunday, September 10, 2006

Jack sent Daddy another letter. He's leaving the Marine Corps ... and life, apparently? He's going somewhere away from people.

He blames himself for his friend dying in Iraq. He has blamed himself for every tragedy that's ever happened around him, and—yeah—I get that it's been a lot, but how can he be this stupid? He is not to blame; he is not a "poison," as he says. He doesn't have to do this alone.

Why, oh why, does he think he does? He's not thinking straight. He's just not. I'm glad he said he'll keep in touch with his mom, but he's still being a jackass.

When he ran away four-and-a-half years ago, he was a kid who did the only thing he thought he could. And then, he found a future. He became a Marine and grew up. Or, he should have. Now, the fact that he's running again is insane. If I could see him, I'd tell him all of this. I'd probably shake him—maybe that would rattle some sense loose in that thick skull of his.

And then, I'd wrap my arms around him and kiss him with every ounce of the love I've held for him all these years because he finally wrote my name in a letter.

"Don't tell her, of course, but I want you to know I never stopped loving Rachael. She was my guiding star so many times. I hope she's got the happiest life. She deserves it."

Damn you, Jack.

All these years—why? Instead of him doing this alone—going to war, losing his best friend, figuring out who he is—and all the things I did without him, too, we could have faced them together.

And now, he's gone. He skipped out on life and the people who love him, like he's done before. I'm so mad and heartbroken. I wish I were back on campus by Eagle Creek in a thunderstorm, so I could scream out this pain that's twisting my heart.

Part of me wants to call Ms. Becky right now and tell her I need to find her son and straighten him out so we can stop losing time together, so we can move forward into our futures together.

But, I won't do that because the logical, realistic, practical side of me knows that a man who claims love, claims we have a connection, has to be either dense or a liar—or both—because, if he really knew me and truly loved me, he would know that the "happiest life" I deserve is him. He would know that I would have waited for him and that I still love him as much, if not more, as I ever did.

Jack has broken my heart for the final time. He's chosen our future and caused us both to miss what could have been. I am done feeling, aching, praying, wishing, remembering.

Done.

After all this time, I still feel empty. Every Sunday, I sit in the pew and feel ... nothing. I sing the hymns, but joy isn't in my voice. I open my Bible during the week; the words blur on the pages. I bow my head to pour my heart out to God, but the words stick deep where I cannot reach them.

I want to be the girl I used to be. The one who felt joy and peace, even in the days after losing my mother. I don't know what happened to that girl, but I think she ran away with a boy who's gotten them both lost along his path.

Long ago, I wrote in here how I think I chase the wind from planes and mountaintops because I long to feel something as great as being with Jack. I was wrong.

Instead, this whole time I haven't been chasing a feeling; I've been running from all the thoughts, truths, emotions and depths that I claim to want to find. Maybe I don't want them to catch me. Maybe I'm not sure I'll like what they reveal about me.

Today's One Good Thing:
I am thankful for ... closure? Is that what this is? I don't even know and am not sure if I can use the word "thankful" anymore. For Mama, though, I will.

Tuesday, October 31, 2006

Tonight I finally went on a second date. It wasn't terrible, and I made it all the way through without bolting.

Progress.

His name is Tyler. I could tell he was interested, but he works at my gym, so I figured he was a meathead. He was persistent, though, and I finally agreed to a date. I figured it would be only one, like all the others. But, I didn't feel the urge to leap out of the moving car before he dropped me off. So, there was that.

He's not a meathead. He's knowledgeable about fitness and understands the dangers with many of the fads. He's committed to pushing clean eating and lifestyle in conjunction with fitness, like me. Our training styles are similar, and he's a lot of fun to talk to about routines, nutrition and more.

I had every intention of saying no to a second date; in fact, I did—more than once. He persisted and asked questions and showed he wouldn't give up. Finally, I answered him. I told him I had a serious relationship once that I haven't been able to move past. He told me he understood and that he never wanted to push me too hard. He also told me that he intended to wait as long as it took for me to either push him off the elliptical or say yes to the next baby step toward a relationship.

His honesty and listening ear were refreshing. He reminded me that the future I believed was mine has been gone for a long time, but I don't have to blindly accept a future without love. Love could still be for me, too.

Maybe.

Though, even writing that word in relation to someone who's not Jack makes me want to leap from a mountain. While I can't very well leave my bedroom this late at night, I can put down this pen before I scare myself away from Tyler for good.

Today's One Good Thing:
I'm thankful for possibilities. I think.

Sunday, December 24, 2006

I thought I wanted to run at the end of the last entry; I'm far past that after tonight.

Tyler told me he wants to marry me. He wasn't asking, but he wanted me to know he's serious about us, will wait for me to be ready and can't imagine himself with anyone else.

His words sounded like an audible recording of my thoughts about Jack.

The realization in that last sentence only adds weight to my shoulders as I drown in this confusion. Maybe I'm willing to continue taking baby steps with Tyler, but I cannot fathom marriage right now. It's way too fast. We've been dating less than three months, and we haven't known each other much longer than that. I believe he's sincere and only wanted to convey his commitment to me, but ... slow down, dude!

Daddy listened to me freak out for a good hour and a half this evening. Then he went to the kitchen and came back with pints of mint chocolate chip and cookie dough. He's a great dad; mama would be proud.

I opened up to Daddy about my relationship woes. I told him how hard it's been for me to date since Jack. I told him how I feel I'm cheating on Jack, even though that's the most ridiculous thought ever. Then I told him about Tyler and how he seems to genuinely love me, but I'm not sure I'm ready to reciprocate his feelings.

Daddy told me my emotions aren't crazy. He knows how close Jack and I were and how the kind of bond we had isn't something that can be quickly or easily broken. He also told me I don't need to say or do anything I'm not comfortable with simply because I think I have to move forward. He said if Tyler is serious, he'll wait. In the meantime, he said I'd know if Tyler isn't the right person.

"No matter what, trust your gut, baby girl. You've got that same laser-sharp intuition your mama did. You'll know what's right and what's not."

I know one thing for certain: I've got an amazing dad.

Today's One Good Thing:
I'm thankful for Daddy, paper bags, journals and sweet treats that counteract salty tears.

Monday, January 1, 2007

Dear Rachael,

My brain's screwed up worse than I realized. I cannot live around people.

Last night was New Year's Eve. I was in downtown Raleigh. They do a big countdown thing, and people were everywhere—so many people.

Panic replaced the air in my lungs, and I swore I was back in Fallujah. I saw the streets and buildings there. Every noise became enemy fire; every shout of celebration, a screamed curse sure to be followed with a shot. And then, firecrackers snapped nearby.

Somehow, I ended up pinning this teenager down on the sidewalk. Rach, I had my hands on his throat. I almost killed him. What the hell kind of mess is my brain that I almost did that?

I was so scared, I ran. Terror of what had almost happened, of what I'd almost done, chased me.

Once I stopped running, my first reaction was to drink, so I hit the bottle. For the first time in nearly six years, I drank. And then—I hate to admit this to you—I almost killed myself. A train was coming, and I thought how easy it would be to stand on that track and let it end my misery.

Boom! No more pain, no more running.

My mind cleared enough to imagine my mom getting that call, and I stepped back. I've sobered up, and I'm heading west with a new scar on my left cheek from my near-attempt to take the coward's way out. I'll get as far from people as I can. It's the only way I can see to continue existing.

I've been afraid many times in my life, but living in terror of my own brain—what kind of life can I have?

Today's One Good Thing: I'm thankful to write these letters again because being honest—writing out my unfiltered thoughts and actions—makes me better able to function. Even without you physically present in my life, I need you. The good thing is I find you're still inside my heart. You never ran from me.

Monday, January 1, 2007

This New Year's, I am resolved to move forward with Tyler but also allow myself the occasional breath before taking another step.

I spent some time reading back in this journal, and I'm tired of sounding like a whiny junior high kid who thrives on drama.

If I find myself writing in here again, great; if not, that's probably better. Most of my entries center around thoughts of Jack, and I don't believe I can ever give Tyler—or anyone—a fair shot at being part of my life if I keep dwelling on what never can be.

Today's One Good Thing:
I am thankful for resolutions—and for the commitment and dedication to achieve them.

Wednesday, February 14, 2007

Dear Rachael,

I made it to Asheville, and I've fallen in love with these mountains. I've seen them mostly from below at this point, but I plan to hike all over these beauties ... all the way to their peaks.

If you'd have told me during Boot Camp or Scout Sniper when we had to live out in the elements that I'd be choosing to live off the land in the not-so-distant future, I'd have said you were smoking crack.

Living in the wild—taking odd jobs here and there to buy food and supplies—isn't too bad. I've seen parts of this state I never could have seen from a car. Plus, I'm free from the horror of hurting anyone around me since I steer clear of people and crowded places.

Instead I explore mountains and waterfalls and caves.

One thing about living away from civilization is I lose track of time. When I walked into downtown Asheville earlier today, I noticed a bank sign with the date: February 14, Valentine's Day. I thought of you.

I remember how excited you were for that Father/Daughter Valentine's dance when we were thirteen. I remember all the dances we went to together. You always picked the best dresses ... reds or emeralds. You were stunning. Every time, you took my breath away, and I got to be the guy who danced with you. Holding you, hearing your laugh, watching joy coat your face when you looked up at me—those remembered moments fill my heart with warmth.

If I'd never left you, I'd be picking up one of those red hearts full of chocolates. I'd have us a reservation at some candlelit restaurant. Maybe I'd have bought you something shiny. Maybe I'd take you dancing.

I enjoy an occasional trip down the what-might-have-been lane, but now I choose to focus on my immediate future of hiking and climbing.

The nightmares continue. One keeps replaying. I'm standing on top of a mountain, and I can feel all the ghosts of my past creeping behind me, closer and closer until I pitch forward and fall ... and fall. Falling without end; alone in eternal darkness.

Maybe getting on top of a real mountain to witness the beauty will erase that nightmare from my sleep.

Today's One Good Thing: Today I'm thankful for mountains and a sense of home—both here in this new place but also in my heart with memories of you, my forever valentine. Yeah ... that was embarrassingly sappy.

Tuesday, March 20, 2007

Dear Rachael,

Just when I think I can't possibly have a worse nightmare, I do.

In the dream, I floated beside a mountain until I ascended to hover above it, overlooking the peak. I saw those two kids from Iraq—the ones I wrote you about because they reminded me of us. They held hands like they did beside the street in Iraq. They smiled at each other. It was sweet, until ...

The mountain rumbled and vibrated. It split in two, right between the kids. They were knocked apart—one on either side of this chasm that spread farther apart. Suddenly, I collapsed where the boy was. I became him and reached toward where the girl had been. She was gone, though, and that half of the mountain rushed away until I could no longer see it.

Behind me, I heard moans and screams and the gurgles of people choking on their final breaths. I didn't have to look behind me; I knew what was there and didn't want to see them again. Something forced me to face the ghosts of my past—I couldn't fight whatever pushed me, no matter how hard I tried.

There they were ... floating, creeping, crawling toward me. Their lifeless eyes pierced my soul; the sounds they made were deafening, horrific. I wanted to cover my ears.

Worst of all, though, was the smell. I've had a few nightmares where I smelled the dream, but none this intense. All the worst smells of Iraq combined—burning garbage, metallic blood, burnt plastic, seared flesh and rancid grease that's caught on fire … the smells of life and death—in a war zone.

They were so strong, I could taste them. I've smelled them all in waking life, which is why I can never forget them—or the horrors they represent.

I needed to throw up from the sensory overload; but I was trapped in that nightmare, and the ghosts inched closer. The breath of the dead hit my face—an explosion's concussive wind. I was on my backside, frantically crab-crawling, until the ground disappeared and I tumbled into darkness again—like the end of every mountaintop nightmare.

Worse than any emotion or horror in the dream, the feeling of alone overwhelmed me. I believed I would never wake up and would continue plummeting through darkness, completely alone, for the rest of eternity.

I finally thrashed myself awake a good four yards from where I lay down last night. It took me a while to realize I was awake and then to understand where I was. I'd made a mess of my campsite, knocking over my pack and kicking things all over the grove I've called home for a couple weeks.

The next realization was I couldn't breathe.

I guess I was having a panic attack. I got on all fours, trying to catch my breath. It wasn't working, and I became frantic. I must have been rocking back and forth, and my dog tags repeatedly tapped my chin. I jerked them from my neck and fell against a tree.

Slowly, I ran my thumb across the words and numbers stamped on the tags—a lifeline in my hand. I rubbed back and forth, back and forth—until eventually, my breathing evened out and my eyes focused.

My blood type was the first fact I locked on. From there, I read all my details, silently at first, then out loud, over and over. Anybody passing my private part of the mountain would've thought I'd been captured and was reciting name, rank, number, birthdate and nothing else—no matter the torture inflicted.

The repetition eventually calmed my heart and slowed my breathing.

I don't understand why I have such intense dreams. It's an ability I'd give up in a heartbeat, that's for sure.

The next few nights, I'll do some hunting ... tracking, really. That will give me a reason not to sleep. Maybe if I keep myself up for a few days, I'll be able to sleep soundly. I don't think my heart can take another nightmare like that one.

Happy birthday to me, huh?

I picked up a calendar last time I visited a store for supplies. I figured it would be a good idea for me to keep up with the day, especially when I schedule odd jobs for a certain day. While I don't need much money, I sometimes take a job to be near people for a while. I never considered how hard it would be to live in isolation, and it may take me a while longer to get used to complete solitude. I guess we were made to be neighborly.

Speaking of getting used to things: I had a hard time falling asleep when I started living in the woods. As I walked west across the state, I usually stayed close to major highways. The noise of the cars zipping past was enough to drown out the sounds of nature, I suppose. Out here on the mountain, though, nothing masks them. I always thought of woods as quiet and peaceful. Not so much.

Wildlife compose quite the orchestra—howling coyotes, crying bobcats, scampering squirrels and racoons and other rodents that sound as big as elephants in the impenetrable darkness. I'm slowly adjusting, though, and I'm interested in my new neighbors.

It seems I live near a couple of bobcats because I've seen tracks that look like they belong to big cats. I'm pretty sure it's mating season, too, which might be why I've heard so much noise. The coyotes sound close, but apparently they can sound way closer than they are.

Today's One Good Thing: Today I'm thankful for waking up.

Sunday, April 1, 2007

Dear Rachael,

Happy birthday, pretty lady!

If I could give you a gift today, it would be to lead you by the hand on a tour of my mountain home. You would love the beauty, the peace, the animals.

Speaking of ... I finally saw my bobcat neighbor. I wrote in my last letter how I've been seeing tracks and hearing them cry. The tracks aren't much bigger than a regular housecat, and this bobcat isn't much bigger than Old Mrs. Kershaw's tomcat—you remember him? Of course, this cat isn't fat. He's sleek and athletic.

I've spent some of my time—I have a good bit of that, as it turns out—tracking through the woods. I've learned to identify the animal that made each track. Plus, I'm learning to differentiate types of scat—yeah, I know that sounds gross. I've even gotten good at noticing details ... fur stuck on limb ends, broken twigs, disturbed leaves and openings for potential bobcat dens.

Over the past few weeks, I had found some hollow trees and a couple of uprooted ones. Any of them could make good dens, so I checked the areas around them every day. I noticed tracks circling the roots of one of the downed trees and figured that must be his home.

Yesterday afternoon, I hid nearby. Sure enough, right at dusk, he emerged.

He stood and sniffed for a while. Then, he stopped sniffing and stared. I was totally hidden—scout sniper, remember?—but, I swear, Rach, he looked right at me. We locked eyes for a good thirty seconds until he lowered his head, a nod in my direction. He gave a growl and bounded off to do his nightly hunting. My heart was beating so hard. I think he knew I was there and decided we could coexist, as long as we each kept to our sides of the forest.

I stayed in my hide for a few hours, watching and listening. I could hear him in the distance. My guess is he did some hunting and then carried a freshly dead gift to his girlfriend—do cats do that?

This morning I returned to his den and followed tracks in the direction he went last night. I found a few spots where two sets of tracks crisscrossed. He's definitely got himself a lady friend. I might stop by a library next time I go into town and see what I can learn about bobcats. We might have babies soon. I can't say I've ever seen a wild baby anything.

Wonder what the feline equivalent of a cigar would be to congratulate Bob when the big day comes. Yeah, I call him Bob ... creative, right?

I have yet to see any venomous snakes, which makes me nervous. We have at least a couple kinds in these parts, so I'd feel better if I could spot them so I know what to look for.

Plenty of harmless snakes slither around, too. A corn snake lives in my grove. I've named him Chesty. He keeps the mice population at bay, which I much appreciate. One of those little buggers nearly gnawed through my seabag. Maybe Chesty's keeping the bad snakes away from me, too. He's not a bad neighbor.

In case you're thinking I've lost all my marbles since I'm naming wildlife and writing about them like they're my friends, don't worry. I'm as sane as I always was. Writing you reminds me I'm human and makes living in the wild like some sort of caveman feel more acceptable. Almost like I'm on an extended training expedition or camping trip and will return home to you in a few months. No big deal.

Of course, I won't be returning to you. And, I may or may not go home. I would like to see my mom. I'm not sure when or how. It would have to be on my own terms. You know? I don't think I can live with her. I would just visit ... briefly. Being away from people has been good for me. When I go in town now, I feel more in control because I have an escape. The nightmares haven't left, but they haven't been as bad as that one I wrote you about.

Anyway, I suppose that's enough rambling for this letter. It's time for me to exercise, which will require me to strip off this shirt and do some sit-ups. In another lifetime you might have found that hot. I've gained a few muscles since the last time you saw me bare-chested. I often wonder how you've changed over the years. I know you've only become more beautiful.

Today's One Good Thing: Today, I'm thankful for fewer nightmares, a new normal and a chance to write Happy Birthday to you.

Monday, May 28, 2007

Dear Rachael,

I hiked into Burnsville, which may have been a mistake. Turns out today's Memorial Day.

Flags lined both sides of the street. People carried grocery bags full of food to grill. Two women waved at each other across Main Street and called, "Happy Memorial Day!"

If it's a day to remember those we lost, how can it be happy?

I get it; I said the same thing once upon a time. When we were kids, Memorial Day was all about grilling and opening day of the swimming pool and kicking summer off right.

And, honestly, that freedom to enjoy the good things in life is what I fought to protect here and promote elsewhere.

It's just ...

I think about Tray all the time. Every night, I watch him die in my arms again. Over and over, I hear his final words. Grief never leaves me, and guilt won't release me. It's all my fault he's dead.

When the insurgents flipped on those flashlights and raised their rifles, I froze—a deer in headlights. Deer get their own stupid butts killed. Marines who freeze get their brothers killed.

I will never forgive myself for hesitating. I know Grandma Ethel and your dad and my mom and a bunch of guys in the hospital and back at base told me it wasn't my fault. It was probably five seconds ... five frickin' seconds.

In war, five seconds equals eternity ... literally.

And so, this weekend—the flags, the cheerful greetings—reminded me hard of Tray. Of our friendship and of all he meant to me. How he carried me through. How we pushed each other to be the best shooters. More than my friend, he was my brother.

He saved my life.

In my moment of hesitation, Tray acted. He threw himself across me onto that godforsaken street. He took the bullets that should've lodged in my brain and ended my madness there and then.

A few more months—weeks, maybe—we would've returned stateside. He had written to his grandma about this girl he'd loved forever and a day. She wasn't a Christian, and that was a deal-breaker for him; so he'd asked his grandma to talk to her, to share with her and try to get her to go to church. He was hoping she'd have a change of heart, so he could ask her to marry him.

I wrote how I was feeling about you and our future right before that last mission. Tray knew too. I'd told him all about you, of course. He told me I was an idiot

... in a nicer way. Whenever you came up in conversation, he always found a way to remind me what an immature move it had been for me to leave you the way I did.

In the desert, we were both picturing our futures with the girls we loved. Though we never talked about them, we pictured weddings, white picket fences, kids and all that jazz. He would've been my best man; I would've been his.

Now I'll never get to stand up with him, swap war stories or rag on his whittling skills. We had our entire lives ahead of us before I opened that door.

Tray was a great man, Rach. That's the thing that always stops me cold. He was such an upstanding, good guy. You know? He would have been someone great in his community. Preacher, leader, teacher, mentor, someone who made a real difference, who brought home goodness, even after the uniform.

I'm not any of that—not even close. What have I done since returning to the U.S.? Run away ... again. Nearly killed a kid and then myself. Wandered across a state so I could live with wild animals.

Tray should have lived, not me. Honestly, I hate I did.

Today's One Good Thing: Today I'm thankful for a great man.

Monday, September 10, 2007

Dear Rachael,

I've been keeping busy since that depressing day in May. The summers here are way better than on roofs in the Georgia oven. It's cool in the mornings and evenings, which is nice for my daily workouts. Running continues to comfort me. Plus, it's a great way to explore my new home and find things I wouldn't typically discover—like a den of baby bobcats.

Bob's a proud pop. Well, I'm not sure how proud he is, but he has three kittens who are his spitting image. The day after my last letter, I went on an extra-long hike to clear my head. I looped around to the mom's den and spent a while there, watching and listening. Sure enough, I heard their cries. That was either the day they were born or soon after. I got my first look at the little guys on the Fourth of July.

They are like regular kittens, for the most part. Playing, fighting, biting, scampering and getting in trouble. You'd love them. They're weaned now and fending for themselves more and more. I don't know if bobcats stick around or separate to find their own territories. Right now, I'm enjoying the extra company.

The past few weeks, I've been exploring during my runs. Winter's coming, and I need somewhere warm. I've found a few caves that might work. They seem to be unoccupied. The thought of sleeping inside the mountain makes me claustrophobic, though.

While I worry the nightmares will start again, I don't care to freeze to death either. At least I have a few weeks before I have to choose.

Today's One Good Thing: I'm thankful for new life and perfect running weather.

Tuesday, December 25, 2007

Dear Rachael,

I'm watching the snow fall outside my cave. Colder weather makes writing challenging, but not impossible.

Running, hiking and other exercise keep me active and warm during the day. I have a fire site for cooking and warming myself and my cave where I sleep out of the elements. I got one of those sub-zero sleeping bags, too. That thing keeps me toasty.

The issues with writing are, when I'm out, I keep gloves on, and when I go into the cave to sleep, I curl up inside the sleeping bag quickly. I had to wish you Merry Christmas, though, so I'm on top of my bed, gloves off, scribbling away.

I hope your Christmas has been as magical as mine. The snow reminds me that beneath its insulation, the earth sleeps. Animals rest, and seeds and roots wait. In a few months, slumber will cease, and growth will begin—another season of magic.

Perhaps this is my season to hibernate. Maybe one day, I'll bloom.

Hmmm ... I read what I wrote—I'm getting cheesy in my old age.

It's getting harder to hold the pen, since my fingers are going numb. I'll sign off for now and try to write again soon, even if it's just a few lines. Hopefully they'll be less goofy.

Today's One Good Thing: Today, I'm thankful for the wonder and magic of snow and what lies beneath it.

Tuesday, January 1, 2008

Dear Rachael,

It's a new year, and winter in the mountains is a whole other experience. I'm still freezing my mittens off and probably will for a couple more months.

Between the cave and my supply hides that I make wherever I move, I don't have to worry about supplies getting wet. Me getting wet, though? That happens occasionally, but I've learned to avoid it at all costs in these bitter temperatures.

I'm feeling positive about a new year. This has become home. Plus, I figure if I can survive winter here, I can survive most anything.

If I'm going to keep my living streak up, though, I better tuck myself in for the night. I love you still. I'm hoping this year will be your best ever.

Today's One Good Thing: Today I'm thankful for gloves and the know-how to build solid shelters anywhere in the world. Hoorah!

Thursday, March 20, 2008

Dear Rachael,

You'll be pleased to know I've mostly thawed out.

Upon examining my reflection in the stream, I have discovered I'm officially a mountain man. It was the darnedest thing. I was cleaning myself off—braving the frigid temperatures to scrape away some of the winter grime, you know—anyway, I looked down after dousing my head and giving my face a good scrub and didn't recognize the wooly beast staring back at me.

I may be the source of any recent Bigfoot sightings.

My hair had grown below my shoulders, and my beard was tickling my chest. Quite the switch from the clean-shaven Marine look. I think if you had the choice, you'd pick the Marine version in a heartbeat. I'm probably frightening as I look currently. Don't worry, I trimmed everything and won't let my hair get below my shoulders again.

Up here in the hidden parts of the mountain, I get to skinny dip whenever I want. Of course, I don't want to right now ... way too chilly. Last summer, I took a couple dips a day.

The only thing that would make that experience better on a warm afternoon would be to have you splashing beside me. The idea makes me fall into this fantasy world in my mind—a world where we're together on this mountain. We watch the bobcat kittens grow and build ourselves a cabin for when we don't want to sleep under the stars.

And Iraq and car accidents never happened.

Back to reality: I sifted through the letters I've written you since leaving the Corps and realized I've been completely self-absorbed. I need to focus outward, so get ready for some questions, lady.

In the midst of the year after Iraq when I lived in a daze, you would have graduated from college. Congratulations! I have no doubt you did great and are now living out your dreams. Where are you? Do you live near your dad? What's your job like? Do you have a boss you hate, or are you the boss? Have you found someone?

Actually, don't answer that one.

Are you happy? That's all I've ever wished for you.

Do you have big plans for your birthday? I do for mine. I'm chopping up a whole bunch of logs to replenish my firewood stash. Well, technically, I'm taking a break from that to write you—which is way more fun. Then I'll probably take another run.

I might even be brave enough to head around to one of the popular trails and take it to the top. A majestic mountain sunset view would be a nice gift.

How old are we now? Let's see ... twenty-four? We're getting old.

Well, I'm getting old; you're starting to live.

It's hard not to drift back to what ifs again. If all the bad hadn't happened, I bet we'd have graduated from college together. We'd be playing house and figuring out how to be grown-ups. Would we have married during college or waited until graduation? Even if we'd waited, we'd be almost two years married. It's crazy to think how different things would be.

Makes me reflect on how every choice—each decision—leads to so many others. One wrong step can result in a landslide.

When I hike on steep places, I watch every step. When the path starts going mostly vertical, I test every foothold before I trust it. When I was a kid, I just stepped ... never testing how the spot might hold, never looking where I might tumble if it didn't.

Can I learn how to walk right in life? Can I learn how to live carefully and make wise decisions that lead to better outcomes? In Iraq, I thought the Marine Corps had taught me how. But then, that one day, that hesitation, that failure to check the footing and the failure to grab onto an anchor ....

Failures like those keep me doubting. I'm not sure a return to life would be the right step for me. I certainly don't think it would be right now. I'm not ready. Whether I ever will be, I don't know, but I have to believe I'll know if it happens.

That's enough waxing philosophical for now. I suppose that's what happens when you turn twenty-four. You'll find out in twelve days.

I love you, Rachael.

Today's One Good Thing: Today, I'm thankful for footholds and anchors … and the hope of one day having the sense to grab the right ones.

Tuesday, April 1, 2008

Dear Rachael,

Happy birthday!

I've got happy news to share. I'm whittling again.

As you might have noticed, I write better with my left hand than I ever did with my right. Maybe that's the difference between being forced to learn something as a kid and being a determined adult learning something that was almost lost.

Since the damage to my arm stopped me from shooting again, I decided I'd be damned if I let Iraq take woodworking from me too. Once the woods thawed, I dug out my knife and began testing how I could coax animals from wood again.

Not gonna lie—it went awful at first. I've got a gash in my leg from one attempt. The craziest thing happened, though. I was so ready to give up, move on and pretend that part of my soul never existed. I lay on the creek bank to let the sound of the water sing me to the sweet forgetfulness of sleep, when I heard rustling.

A brood of baby birds was getting flying lessons. Before long, three of the four were flying. One, though, well, he had a rougher go of it.

I watched him for a long time. I'll be honest, I doubted he'd figure it out. He was smaller than the others, so it seemed a matter of time before some bigger critter came along and gobbled him up. Circle of life and all.

That little guy didn't give up, though. He kept flapping and hopping until he finally conquered gravity to join his siblings in the freedom of flight.

Watching that victory, I knew I could make a way, too. A love of woodworking was something Tray and I shared, and it's something I can continue in his honor. Also, I miss Senior's woodshop—the smell of sawdust, the feel of the tools in my hands, the movement of the wood as it takes the shape of its purpose. I'll get there. One day.

I've figured out ways to use stumps and logs and other sticks or rocks to brace what I'm working on, while my gimpy arm serves as a paperweight—the one use it serves well.

My first efforts have been small, but I'll improve until I can do the more detailed stuff I used to do. My next step will be to determine how to work on bigger projects. I want to build furniture again—pieces with meaning and details unique to each.

I've got this picture of a four-poster bed in my mind. Actually, I saw it in a dream. You were there. You faced a giant bedframe that looked crafted for a fairy tale. I called your name, and you turned to look at me with those blue eyes that always made me forget to breathe. You smiled, then moved toward the bed. All I wanted was to follow you, be with you, lift you into that comfort and bury myself in your love.

That's about the time a sudden rainstorm whipped up and pulled me back to reality.

But, that bed won't leave my mind. Come hell or high water—as our moms used to say—I'm going to make that bed for you. Even if it's not really for you, I'll be making it with you in mind.

Of course, I've got a lot of work to do before seriously considering making something that big and intricate. I'm getting there, though. Every day I don't chop a finger off is a day of improvement.

I wrote my mom the other day and asked if the hydrangeas are blooming. I remember how much she looked forward to seeing them every year. She told me once that the first blossoms always reminded her that hope never dies. Even when the earth hibernates during the winter, the spring will return to spread color and warmth and wake the land and animals. Hope will bloom again.

What's the weather like where you are? Is it warm enough for a birthday picnic? We always loved picnics. I miss doing everyday things like that with you.

Whatever you're doing and wherever you are, I hope today is full of hope and beauty. I love and miss you more this birthday than last.

Today's One Good Thing: Today I'm thankful for knives. And first aid kits. But mostly I'm thankful for the hope spring brings.

Wednesday, April 23, 2008

Dear Rachael,

I've taken up a new hobby—Bible reading.

Yeah, I'm surprised too. Senior gave me a Bible when I left for Boot Camp. Honestly, I've never given it much of a glance, but once you've lived alone for as long as I have, you start looking for conversation ... even when it's one-sided.

I started in the book of Psalms because I remember how much you loved that book. How many of these have you memorized? Do you still make paintings with verses on them? I remember how pretty that one you made was. It had horses and I don't remember the exact verse, but I know it was from Psalms. Maybe I'll read it one day and remember.

What does daily life look like for you these days? Do you have an 8 to 5 job? Do you work at night instead? Do you still live with your dad? I'm guessing not. You've always been independent; then again, your dad couldn't cook worth a flip. You might still be living with him so he won't starve.

Of course, by now, you must be married. There's no way you're not. I know that, but it's easier to think of you and your dad like you were.

After Iraq, my world stopped spinning. In some ways, I've been in a holding pattern since then; surely time has been standing still as well while I figure out myself and the world. When I think of you, I see you as you were when I dropped out of life.

In the mountains, it's harder to picture life continuing elsewhere, but it's easier to remember that it does. That sounds weird, I suppose. The seasons, though, remind me life continues.

This morning I read Psalm 34. I'm sure you know it. Verse 10 reminded me of that thing your mom wrote that you used to say to me all the time: "none of us deserves any good thing." The verse was "… those who seek the Lord shall not lack any good thing."

I'll be honest, I rolled my eyes. Those words make sense on your lips, but they weren't meant for mine. I've lived a few days, and good on earth is awfully hard to see—even for those seeking Him.

You'd remind me again of your mom's words and then of the second part about accepting those good things when they come. I'm still not convinced God and His Bible are for me. I read that Psalm at least a dozen times this morning because I want what the first few verses talk about: "I sought the Lord, and he heard me, and delivered me from all my fears."

Tray experienced that. You have too. That's why I believe Tray would have been fine after the war. Sure, what we saw—all we did—those things would stick with us; but he would have been okay. Fear remains my constant companion. I believe God would have taken away all Tray's fears and replaced them with peace. He knew God in a way I never can.

Part of me wants to. I suppose that's something new. I'm tired of the nightmares, the constant pain that reminds me of all I've caused, lost and become ... and haven't. Verses like this make me look inside, which I don't want to do. While I feel like that's all I do, this inner look is different somehow. It stretches outward as well and makes me consider what freedom from fear could feel like. I don't want to dwell on that too much, though; it makes my reality so much more depressing.

The good part of reading this book is it reminds me of you and Tray. Not that I ever don't think about you. Somehow reading the words you both read makes me feel closer to you. It gives me comfort in some ways, though it also turns up the dial on my loneliness. It's an unsettling mix of joy and pain.

What have you been reading lately? I know you have been; you inherited the love of reading our moms had. Their laughter was somehow sweeter over shared books. Do you still read your Bible every morning and evening? I'm sure you do. Maybe you're reading Psalm 34, too. I doubt you're watching bear cubs play in the stream while you read, though.

This mama bear and her two cubs appeared a few weeks ago. When I first saw them, I was scared to death. I knew that giant bear was going to rip me to shreds. She sniffed in my direction, stared me down and went on about her day. Now, she ignores me, and I get to watch them up close. My heart doesn't completely leap out of my chest every time I see her, though I don't expect to get as used to her presence as I did to blasting bombs in Iraq.

The cubs are hilarious. They're always sticking their noses where they shouldn't. A few days ago, they got themselves doused by a skunk. This area still stinks.

If I keep improving my whittling, I plan to carve a bear family—see how lifelike I can get them. Each cub has its own personality and features. One cub has more tan around its mouth and nose than the other. That's the one that stands up on its hind legs more often. It's bolder and more impish than the other. As you may have guessed, that's the one that poked its nose in the skunk den.

The bears should be going up the stream soon, and I'll do some fishing while they're gone. Although they have accepted me as part of the landscape, I keep my distance.

Speaking of fishing, I don't like to brag but I'm pretty dang deadly with a gig. I've reached level expert on standing in a stream and waiting for the perfect moment to spear a trout. Sometimes I amaze myself with what I can do with my left hand. When I think back to how helpless I felt when I woke up in that hospital without movement in my right arm, I'm amazed.

Those were dark days, Rach. I wish you'd been with me, but I'm glad you weren't. That's another one of those joy/pain things. So many aspects of life make no sense and seem to contradict, even when they coexist.

Today's One Good Thing: I'm thankful today for comforting, painful reminders and unexpected left-handed skills.

Friday, May 16, 2008

Dear Rachael,

Today would have been Tray's birthday.

I wonder how we would have spent it. I also wonder how Grandma Ethel's doing. She's probably baking sweet potato pies, even though her grandson's not there to eat them.

When we were in Iraq, he and I were hunkered down in hides on our birthdays. He was all about celebrating his birthday, let me tell you. He said when we got back to Lejeune, we were going to have the biggest birthday bashes ever.

You know the one thing he wanted more than anything? A chocolate fountain. He'd never seen one in person and thought that sounded like the fanciest thing you could have at a party. He'd sit there listing out all the foods he wanted to dip under his chocolate fountain.

I remember one night he was going on and on about it. I was frickin' starving, and I knew my stomach was going to start growling any moment. Finally I pulled away from my rifle sight and warned him with my most menacing whisper, "If you don't shut up about chocolate fountain foods, I'm gonna shove my socks in your mouth ... the dirty ones."

He didn't say another word, until we were on the move again. He started up again, like we'd never had a stretch of sleepless nights between.

That was one thing about Tray—he didn't let things go. And that was a good thing, usually. He was relentless in making me talk to him. That's why I shared with him my full past and all the ghosts that haunted me. He was never pushy with his faith, but he didn't pass up a chance to share a verse he was reading or something he'd been praying about. I still remember some of the verses he shared because he tended to share the same ones multiple times. Maybe he did that on purpose.

We never talked a whole lot about what we would do when we got back. I think we both figured we'd make the Corps our career. I know I did. I pictured him always being in that uniform, too. At the same time, I could see him doing many things: being the director of a place like the center, preaching, going on mission trips, building houses for low-income families.

A few times, we talked about sharing a woodworking shop. I'm not sure if we would have built furniture to sell. I think it was more the idea of having a place off base to go and unwind. Maybe we would have taught lessons. Tray would have been way better at the teaching part than me. I was better at the doing, but he had more patience for the teaching.

Contemplating the past with its decisions, both made and rejected, can be a good thing. That line of questioning is a reminder of who's been part of our lives—who's helped make us who we are.

Every now and then, I run through some what ifs. I find it oddly comforting to think of the lives I could have lived. Now that I don't really have one, it's nice to know I had life options once upon a time. It's also a reminder of the things I might still have and part of why I'm filling up a drawing pad with sketches of furniture. I'll need an actual shop to pull off most of these, so it's something to work toward.

The reminders of what Tray and I might have done are also a good nudge to keep moving in that direction. I'm not ready yet, and I'm not sure how long it will take me to be ready, but every day I'm preparing for when I am.

What are you doing today? Do you have a best friend? I know you were close to a couple of the girls from Bellum. Have you replaced them with new friends, or do you have a wider group of friends from your whole life? My guess is the latter. You are a loyal, forever kind of friend.

Do you still think of me? Have you forgiven what I did to you? It's okay if you haven't. I'm not sure it's forgivable to turn your back on your best friend and the love of your life without so much as an in-person explanation. Saying goodbye in a letter was pretty damn cowardly.

For my part, I still love you and think of you as my best friend—not that I deserve to be that, but that I would do anything I could to atone for my mistakes and earn your friendship again.

Today's One Good Thing: Today I'm thankful for all the lives I could have lived and for the friends who made them possible and still encourage me to pursue some type of future.

Friday, July 4, 2008

Dear Rachael,

I feel like I'm back in the desert, barely hanging on to truth and reality. So, once again, here I am, coming to you for salvation. I'll never not need you, Rachael. You ground me, calm me, comfort me ... after all these years and miles.

Every town around here lights up the mountains on the Fourth of July. The booms echo off the mountainsides. I could easily see the explosions of red from every corner of the sky if I let myself look up. Instead, I've tucked myself inside one of my supply hides. It's not ideal, of course. I feel smothered, but the sights and sounds are muffled. Muffled is better than the front row seat I began the night with.

And so, I'm writing to you; I'm focusing on you—your smile, your heart, your love. I miss you every day. It's days like this, though, when my heart feels like it's being squeezed in a vice until it can't stand any more pressure and then, when I can't bear missing you another moment, I see you and your beautiful smile, and my heart explodes inside my chest. My breathing doesn't come easy anymore.

I'd rather my heart disintegrate over your memory than have my head lead me off a cliff. So, I focus on you. I picture how you would have looked that night ... prom night, when I planned to get down on one knee. I was nervous, but I'd never been so certain of anything in my life.

When I look back, I was an idiot. I didn't ask your dad for your hand in marriage. At the time, it seemed old-fashioned. Now, I realize I was a cocky kid who didn't have a clue about what's most important. I was arrogant enough to believe without doubt that you would say yes.

As I reflect on who I know you were (and are), I'm not sure what you would have said. Would you have responded to my proposal like Tray did with the girl he loved? He wouldn't propose to her because she wasn't a Christian. You probably would have said no. I would have been crushed, but you would have been right. That's a big thing to not share.

In some ways, you're more a part of me now than then. I see you most nights. You drive away the terrors. In the worst moments in hell—a more fitting name for Iraq—all I had to do was call you to my mind and there you were, by my side or just ahead, leading me through, always smiling.

I suppose I never completely had you in my life. No, that's not true either. Man! All these flashes and explosions have my brain scrambled.

You and I were bonded in a way that's hard to explain. We'd been each other's someone since we were babies. You loved me, despite my immaturity. I don't know what you would have said if I had asked you. I'm sure you'd have been less than pleased when you found out I hadn't asked your dad. We'll never know, of course.

I'll continue focusing on you and how you would've looked that night and how we would've danced together. How we probably would have made out. Those are the thoughts that drown out everything else. In memories of you, I find myself—who and how I should be.

You calm my fears and settle my nerves. You remind me how to breathe—slowly, deeply; in, out. When I focus on you, I find my center and hear my heart beat slower, steadier, with each breath I drag into my lungs. The rest of the world becomes a shimmer of something outside of me that cannot control or overcome me when I center myself around you.

Again, Rachael, you save me. You hold my identity, who I am … or should be.

Today's One Good Thing: Today I'm thankful for the vision of you. Even in my flight from you, you remained a part of me; and it's that part that grounds and focuses me, saves me from these ever-present demons I can neither control nor flee. Thank you for your guiding light.

Friday, October 17, 2008

Dear Rachael,

These cool mornings and evenings and mild daytime temperatures couldn't be more perfect. I know they won't last much longer.

Winter is coming.

Living in the wild has taught me odd things. Did you know, there's a smell in the air at the change of a season? It sounds crazy, but I swear it's true. I can sense it, too, like my feeling that temperatures will drop consistently now.

It makes sense when you think how the animals know these things too. They don't have calendars or a weather report. They simply know when it's time to prepare for cold weather ... or enjoy the last few days of comfort.

Maybe I'm becoming more animal than human; at the least, I suppose I'm evolving into my role as a mountain man.

I've checked through my winter gear to make sure I'm set. My cave is still available for the coldest nights. Now that I'm ready, I will bask in the mild weather as long as I can. In many ways on the mountain, days stretch on, but months and years fly past.

When we were kids, I didn't think much about the seasons. I mean, I certainly never entertained thoughts of storing up for the winter and considering where I could hibernate. I didn't imagine becoming a bear.

Speaking of bears, the cubs are getting huge. I've enjoyed watching them grow. They eat a ton. I don't know why I thought bears only eat meat. Most of their snacks revolve around plants or berries. They love fish, though, and give me a run for my money in the stream here. They also enjoy splashing as much as I do.

I've noticed them eating even more. They must be fattening up for the winter ahead. They'll snuggle down in their den, I suppose. Early in the summer I visited one of the local libraries and read about black bears. Did you know they're not aggressive and aren't known to attack to defend their cubs? That's the grizzly bear. Black bears are great neighbors—aside from a tendency to snoop in your trash.

We respect each other's space, but I have seen them watching me, like I watch them. We're friends, as much as any human and wild animal can be.

As the season shifts, I find myself gloomy at the thought of being cooped up in the cave, of not seeing the bears and of being alone through another cold winter. I'll be okay, I know. And, of course, the season will shift again; spring will return. Not even winter's darkness lasts forever, right?

Until the cold blankets us, I'll be soaking up every bit of outdoors I can. On that note, the bears emerged from the stream—my turn.

I hope you're enjoying beautiful weather, too, wherever you are.

Today's One Good Thing: Today, I am thankful for the smell of changing seasons and furry friends who share.

Thursday, November 27, 2008

Dear Rachael,

Happy Thanksgiving!

I would love to sit around a table loaded down with good old home cookin'—preferably made with love by you. Turkey, green bean casserole, mashed potatoes—gravy flowing over everything. And, those big ol' dinner rolls to sop up the extra. I'm gonna need a moment.

Honestly, I can't complain. I stocked away some tins of Vienna sausages and picked up a can of cranberry sauce last week. The good part about being alone is I get to eat the whole can myself—don't think I won't—in one sitting.

I'm not actually eating sausages for Thanksgiving. You know I'm a fishing master. I'll be pan frying some fillets and some of those canned whole potatoes. Do you remember how much we loved those things when we were kids? You had frying them down to an art. What was that seasoning you'd always sprinkle on them? I wish I could remember; they were amazing.

Can I be honest with you?

Of course, I can. Even if I weren't writing a letter I'll never send, I have always been able to tell you anything.

I've thought about hunting for something different to give my diet some variety. But, I can't do much with a gun or bow these days. Leaping on a deer or rabbit and slicing its throat doesn't sound appetizing. Even if I could shoot, though, I don't think I would. I've come to know many of the animals here. I know their mannerisms and homes and schedules. I'm seeing nature in a way I never knew was possible.

Since I'm pouring out my guts here …

I haven't told you before, but I could have kept shooting. Well, I could have tried. My physical therapist tried to get me back to holding a rifle. He was confident I could do it—if not with my right arm, definitely with my left.

They also asked me to return to Scout Sniper as an instructor.

I said no to both and never looked back when I ran. Big surprise there, huh? If nothing else, I'm predictable.

When my therapist walked in with a rifle, my surroundings shifted. My heartbeat was the only sound I heard—the only real sound. I heard every shot I ever fired, every shot fired at me, each body-piercing round that sliced into Tray. The soul-shaking boom of the grenade behind us that snuffed out our team startled me back to consciousness in that rehab facility. I shook my head—like that could somehow clear the nightmare reels from my brain—and walked away.

The truth is, the thought of getting behind the sight again terrified me. I've ended so many lives, Rachael. I see them all the time without physically pressing the scope to my eye. Beyond that, I can't close my eyes without seeing Tray covered with the bullet holes that should have covered me.

And—may as well give the full truth—I wasn't entirely sure I wouldn't use my renewed shooting ability to put an end to my guilt for good.

This winter's already been rough on my mind. Cooped up in the cave or huddled close to my fire at one of my campsites, I'm held captive by my mess of a brain. I get restless, but it's much more than the restlessness that's plagued me most of my adult life. I bob along with the restlessness until a wave of loneliness crashes over me. The undertow of guilt and shame and grief holds me until I wonder if I'll ever breathe again.

My admission probably explains why I've been sitting out here in a sub-thirty-degree freezer with my gloves off to write my deepest, darkest secrets to you.

Winter's only beginning.

I'll be okay. I promise. Some days overwhelm me more than others.

On a happier note, how are you celebrating today? Are you pan frying fish and canned potatoes? I'm sure you've got the proper spread going on, and I'm sure you're surrounded by family and friends.

I'm going to picture you smiling and laughing beside a giant turkey. That'll make this day warmer.

Today's One Good Thing: Today, I'm thankful for cranberry sauce and canned taters.

Thursday, January 1, 2009

Dear Rachael,

It seems like just yesterday I wished you Happy New Year, and here we are again.

Today is warmer ... not quite as warm as Christmas, though. Any day above freezing, I go for a run. I might take a longer route today.

Have you made any resolutions? I've decided to make one this year—there's a first time for everything, I suppose.

I resolve to get around people this year. I need to see if I still have wild reactions to noises and crowds. As much as I love this mountain that has become home, I need to return to a real life—or at least try.

At the end of my life, I don't want to wonder if I could have truly lived but was too scared of my own damn mind to try.

Why the sudden desire to make a resolution? You.

I know too much time has passed, and I don't expect to have you in my life again the way you once were. But, what if?

What if you aren't already married? What if I could earn your forgiveness? Or, what if, I had a chance to tell you—in person—how sorry I am for everything?

That's my resolution. Nothing crazy or impossible ... in theory anyway. I simply want to put myself near people again. The towns around here have festivals and gatherings throughout the year, so I'll choose some events to attend once the weather warms up.

I mean, I'm not planning to introduce myself to the mayors. I doubt they'd like to know there's an unhinged war vet running wild in the mountains with his buddies, the bears and bobcats. They'd probably lock me up and steal my vast stores of sausages.

May your resolutions be less insane than mine and may you achieve them all. I love you.

Today's One Good Thing: Today I'm thankful for goals and plans. Going without either for all these years may not have been the wisest choice. Who knows? Perhaps starting with this small resolution might lead me, one day, to something I stupidly left behind.

Wednesday, April 1, 2009

Dear Rachael,

If I forgot about my birthday, does that mean I didn't age? Too bad for you, I didn't forget yours.

Happy birthday, pretty lady!

I would love to take you out for dinner. What's your favorite these days—catfish, barbecue, something fancy? I vote for Memaw's. Her hush puppies and cheese sauce always made me hush my mouth!

On second thought, I would prefer the barbecue. I've grown tired of fish. The thought of a juicy pulled pork sandwich on a big ol' bun with extra barbecue sauce ....

Now I'm drooling. I need to add a second resolution for when I return to civilization: learn to make a killer pulled pork.

I haven't forgotten my first resolution. The farmers' markets are up and running, and I saw some fliers for festivals and concerts. You'll be pleased to know my social calendar is booked solid.

Of course, I'll keep a safe distance. I don't trust myself to do more than hang around the edges of the action. Being there, though, is more than I have done. I've only ever gone into town long enough for supplies—and never at busy times. These ventures will be small steps, but ones in the right direction.

Can I call this my birthday gift to you? Maybe one day I'll get to give you a real gift. Heck, if I ever get that privilege, I'll have a whole lot of buying—or pulled pork making—to pay for lost time.

Today's One Good Thing: Today, I'm thankful for you and the motivation you give me, even when you don't know.

Wednesday, July 15, 2009

Dear Rachael,

I've got a new neighbor; actually, he's more like a roommate. He's big, shaggy and smelly. Oh, and he agreed I should call him Scout.

Scout's an Irish wolfhound who's adopted me for some reason.

The other night, I went to a music festival in Asheville, complete with bluegrass bands, cloggers and more. Shindig on the Green was the biggest gathering I've braved yet for my resolution.

I kept my distance from the crowds, but the overwhelm and loneliness hit me hard, especially when I saw a woman who looked like you from the back. She was with this guy, and they were dancing like we used to do. He spun her around, and for a moment, her bright smile matched the red hair that first made me think she was you. I almost ran to scoop her up in my arms. Thankfully, reality snapped me out of my impulse.

As I scanned the crowds, I noticed how carefree everyone was—untouched by war. I wondered if I'll ever find a place in this free world again. That's when the reminder of my aloneness near that mass of people washed over me.

That's also when I felt this cold, wet ... thing ... on my hand. I looked down—technically, over (he's a massive dog)—and saw Scout. His fur was matted, and he was thinner than I thought he should be. I assumed he must belong to someone and would eventually drift back to them. Instead, he followed me from downtown to the woods, all the way to my campsite.

He's been with me ever since.

That night, I had a nightmare (as I usually do). Scout padded over and laid on my chest. His giant tongue licked my neck and cheek until my heartrate slowed and I drifted off to sleep. He tucked his snout under my chin, and that's how we spent our first night together.

He's significantly heavier than Missy was, and I welcome his presence.

Scout has kept me terror-free, and I can't remember feeling this rested. He's incredible. I have a sneaking suspicion you two would love each other. He's a giant, but a gentle one, who loves nothing more than a good belly scratch.

Today's One Good Thing: Today, I'm thankful for a guardian, my Scout.

Monday, August 3, 2009

Dear Rachael,

Scout's a great companion. He's also a goofball who loves the stream as much as I do. It's probably a good thing the baby bears graduated to life on their own earlier this summer. My guess is the three of them would get in more trouble than they could handle.

I'll be honest, I was sad—lonely even—when the cubs left. Scout found me at a perfect time.

Soon after we met, we walked to Weaverville. I alternate which stores and towns I go to or who I approach about odd jobs, by the way. Anyway, I figured if I was going to have a dog, I better get him a collar and leash. The leash laws can be strict.

I wasn't sure how he would react, but Scout was so proud of his new leather collar, he jumped up and licked me—right there on the sidewalk. You would have laughed. When he stands on his hind feet, he puts his paws on my shoulders and towers over me. We probably drew more attention than I would have liked that day, but I enjoyed our first outing together.

We picked out a brush for him as well. He loves to be brushed, and we've almost got all the matted bits out of his hair. One of the first things I discovered about him was a giant scar. It runs all the way up from his front leg, over his shoulder and disappears somewhere in his long beard—an exact match to my scar from the first accident.

Scout whimpered when I found it. Since it's healed, I imagine he was remembering how he got it. Not sure what kind of monster could slice open a dog.

I promised I would never hurt him, but I warned him I'm cursed and to beware of getting mixed up with me.

Sorry about the smudges ... Scout decided my letter-writing is over for today. He keeps nudging me to go for a swim. It's hot, and a dip sounds like a great idea. He might be smarter than me. No jokes—I realize that bar's not high.

Anyway, I hope you're having an amazing summer and you have a friend in your life as great as this slobbery hound.

Today's One Good Thing: Today I'm thankful for the perfect timing of Scout entering my life.

Thursday, September 10, 2009

Dear Rachael,

Scout has befriended most of the creatures around here. He and Chesty, our corn snake neighbor, have formed an agreement—they keep their distance and tolerate one another's existences.

The most unlikely bond formed between Scout and the rabbits that call this area their home. There are so many; that whole "breeding like rabbits" saying holds true to life.

Anyway, I fully expected him to chase them down and have himself a rabbit dinner. One of the bigger ones—I think it's a male—and Scout got everything started. The rabbit popped out into the glade where Scout and I were lounging. The big-eared fellow stopped and stared. I imagine he was trying to figure out what on earth Scout was—bear ... wolf ... giant hairy rabbit on all fours. Scout stopped panting and did his whole intent stare thing. I figured Mr. Rabbit was about to meet his demise.

Instead, Scout considered the smaller creature as he tilted his head back and forth, back and forth. The rabbit stared right back, occasionally twitching his nose, his snow-white belly moving up and down ... he was breathing heavily—I wonder why.

He had the most interesting black marking between his ears. Most of the rabbits I've seen have a dot or splash, but his is star shaped. After a while, the rabbit hopped off slowly, stopping every now and then to look back—perhaps to make sure he wasn't about to be gobbled up.

This continued every day for a few weeks. The rabbit would pop out at some point. The animals kept their distance while eyeing one another. Each day, they inched closer. Finally, last week, they got up close and personal—nose to nose. Since then, they've been best buds. They play together. Right now, they're napping. Scout's curled around the little guy and has his snout tucked close, like he's protecting his smaller friend.

The other rabbits have started hanging out near us, too—none of the others as close as the first one, but close nonetheless, and without fear. It's fascinating how wildlife accepts neighbors who don't bother them or disturb their homes.

Besides befriending rabbits, Scout joins me on my hikes. We've explored the woods and scaled some steeper points I hadn't examined before. He's a great companion and makes my jaunts more fun. Wandering alone loses its shine.

I realize it's been a while since I've asked you any questions, which feels rude. Questions also make these silly letters feel more conversational.

Where are you right now? Do you work in a gym? Maybe you work with people one on one and drive around, visiting all your clients. Maybe you're famous and work with celebrities. Maybe you got to meet Jonathan Taylor Thomas. Your room was covered in his posters from the ridiculous teen magazines you girls always giggled over in study hall.

Whatever you're doing today, one thing's certain: you could have done anything you wanted to do. You've always been one of the most confident and driven people I know.

You would never believe something is too hard for you; you'd tackle it head-on. I always admired that.

My whittling continues to improve, and I'm sketching ideas for bigger furniture pieces.

I should clarify that I whittle when I can wrestle my sticks out of Scout's mouth. He doesn't chew them; he simply takes whatever I'm working on or am about to work on, just to be a jerk. He has a strong personality, that's for sure.

Fall is coming; I smell it in the breeze. That means winter's around the next corner. I'm not looking forward to that. As much as I love it here, I can't embrace cold's confinement. At least this year, I won't be stuck alone with my nightmares in a cave. Scout continues to keep me calm at night. I haven't slept this well since Iraq.

I had to wrestle my pen from Scout. He knocked it to the ground with his giant paw and kept it firmly pinned down. He's ready for a run, so I better keep him happy. He might not let me have my half of fish tonight.

Have a great afternoon wherever you are and whatever you're doing.

Today's One Good Thing: Today, I'm thankful for Scout's crazy personality and comforting presence.

Tuesday, November 10, 2009

Dear Rachael,

Happy Birthday to the Marine Corps.

My life as a Marine feels far away—like I've been given someone else's hazy memories. I miss who I was in that uniform and the purpose I found in my rifle.

The dropping temperatures draw out the philosophical in me, for some reason. Writing my thoughts to you warms my fingers. When my mind is occupied on translating my feelings and confusion into concrete words, I can't think about how frickin' cold my toes are, so here I go.

Myself, my place, my purpose—I'm not sure how to find them again. I feel like I've been chasing my reason for being my entire life. My purpose forms as fog. No matter how fast I run toward or into it, I can never grasp anything solid. Sometimes I've thought my purpose has enveloped me, but I never fully attain it.

This core aspect of who a person is determines how they live; yet I'm devoid of control over mine.

I often dwell on that concept of purpose. Can I have one again? I believe I can work with my hands again. My whittling continues to improve. I don't feel awkward anymore with how I have to set everything up to work around my gimpy arm. The work feels almost natural, and I'm itching to get to a shop like Senior's to attempt bigger projects. I've nearly filled this sketchbook with all the ideas in my head of bed frames and chests and chairs and tables. These are things I believe I can make, and that work would hold purpose for me. I can even imagine being content.

What I'm unsure of is if I can reenter society. Having Scout by my side gives me some confidence, but I keep flashing back to that night in Raleigh.

Yes, I understand some of my triggers now. No, I don't have to immerse myself in crowds.

I'm still fearful of losing control of reality, of believing myself in Iraq and resorting to my training. God help whoever's near me when that happens.

And, that's the problem. God doesn't seem to be much help.

I know you'd disagree, Rach. I do. Words from your dad's sermons or talks with him at the mission and words from you and your mom and my mom constantly replay in my mind. I've read many of them again in this Bible. You've all told me what you believe to be true. Part of me wants to believe, too, but most of me can't accept your truth.

At least not for myself. I keep returning to the fact that I'm too far gone. All the death, all the killing, all the mistakes. I've gone too far. I can accept my reality as I've experienced it, not the one you present as possible.

That's enough gloomy talk. How about a Scout story?

I've written to you before about the hides where I store supplies. I was fall-cleaning one of them, pulling out cans of sausages to transfer to the cave for the colder months. I had just pulled out the final flat to dump in my seabag for transport up the mountain.

All of a sudden, I hear a scuffling behind me and turn around to see Scout's giant scruffy behind sticking up in the air. He thought he'd crawl in to help—or to get himself a snack, more likely—and got himself good and stuck.

He tugged and pulled until his backside flopped down and he just laid there. His grumbling growl switched to more of a resigned whimper, and all I could do was laugh. I haven't laughed like that in years.

Don't worry; I'm not a total jerk. I pulled him out—after I laughed for a while, of course. And then, I laughed for a while longer. Scout plopped onto his rump and glared at me. I felt bad, so I opened a can and tossed most of the sausages his way. He forgave me pretty quickly after that. Scout can definitely be bought with food.

My fingertips may or may not still be here. I wouldn't know since I can't feel them. I'll write sometime … probably around the holidays. I'm sure Scout will keep me warmer this year. He's a helpful companion.

I do miss you. The fire red, orange and yellow leaves glistening in the sunshine around me remind me of you, with your red hair sparkling in the Georgia sunlight. That vision warmed me right up, so I'll have to recall it often the next few months.

Today's One Good Thing: Today I'm thankful for the ability to laugh, for a warm companion and for warmer memories.

Thursday, December 31, 2009

Dear Rachael,

This holiday season has been colder than an insurgent's heart.

Scout does his best to keep me warm. I sure am thankful for him—and not just for his heating capabilities.

He's helping me cling to a final strand of sanity. When it's as cold as recent temperatures have been, we spend most of the time in our cave. I swear those walls squeeze in on me after the first few days of being stuck inside. I watch them close in on me and push out the air little by little, until panic sets in and convinces my mind that this is how I'll die—suffocated by a python cave.

When the fear takes over, Scout knows. He lays on me—on my legs, my chest, wherever—and puts as much of his weight on me as he can. Feeling him grounds me, reminds me of reality and snaps me out of the foggy terror clouding my mind.

I'm thankful as hell for Scout. Without him, Rachael, I don't think I'd still be alive. Why this winter has been harder, I don't know. Maybe a human can only live in isolation for so long before he snaps, and I've maxed out my time. Maybe it's colder this year. Maybe the cave really is possessed. Whatever the reason, I need to reevaluate my life come spring.

With Scout's help, my next letter to you—probably not until we thaw out—won't be such a downer. I have to believe he and memories of you will see me through the next few months. I wish you the happiest of holidays and hope your Christmas was the best yet and your New Year's will be even better. I love you still.

Today's One Good Thing: Today I'm thankful for Scout's faithfulness, loyalty and presence.

Saturday, March 20, 2010

Dear Rachael,

We survived for another spring. Warmer temperatures positively alter my mindset and emotions.

The gloomy depths of winter nearly pulled me under for keeps. Thanks to Scout's company and reassuring presence, I stayed afloat. I don't think I will last another winter, though. I have some decisions to make.

Those choices can wait for a few weeks while Scout and I soak up every ray of sunshine while we explore something besides cave walls.

Scout has renewed his friendships with our woodland neighbors. He and his rabbit friend are currently chasing one another in circles and deranged zigzags.

I swear, Scout just hopped like his friend. He's the goofiest dog I've ever met.

A couple days ago, I trekked into one of the nearby towns to restock supplies. I splurged and picked up chocolate chip cupcakes for my birthday. They won't be anywhere near as good as the ones you and Mom make, of course. Still, I'm pretty daggone excited about something sweet that doesn't have a lifetime shelf life. Canned food loses its appeal after a while.

Right now, I'm going to celebrate my birthday by taking a nap in this sweet-smelling grass while the sun thaws my heart and soul.

I hope you feel the sun on your face today and know somehow that I'm thinking of you and wishing only warmth and beauty in your life. I love you.

Today's One Good Thing: Today, I'm thankful for sunshine and chocolate chips.

Wednesday, May 19, 2010

It's been a while since I've journaled. Where to begin?

I did what I resolved in my last entry: I moved forward, one step at a time, with Tyler. He never pushed me and has been exceedingly patient. We're now engaged, and our wedding is one month from today.

Should I be giddy? Aren't most brides? Or, is there no such thing as one normal feeling?

None of Mama's letters told me exactly how I should feel at this stage. Well, I guess she kind of did, but that was about being in love. I'm sure I love Tyler; I mean, why wouldn't I? Plus, she wrote with more emphasis about love being an action than she did about it as a feeling. Action I can do.

That's another thing that worries me.

Backing up—I've been all over the place to skydive and BASE jump. I go to the mountains to hike and rock climb a few times a year, at least. I've returned to Peru and Nigeria a total of a half dozen more times between them. At this point, I've watched girls who looked up to me in those countries become moms who follow my fitness routines. I've even got namesakes in both countries. How crazy is that?

Whenever life overwhelms me, I run off to jump or travel or climb. I leave with a purpose and a plan, but leave I must. I can't do that once I'm married, can I?

Every time I think of being married to Tyler, I freak out. Is this normal? Mama didn't have a letter for "When the thought of marriage makes you hyperventilate." I wish she were here. I'm not sure I will be good at this marriage thing.

Back to what's happened over the past three-and-a-half years: I feel like I've been living two lives. I've been the independent daredevil adrenaline junkie who's constantly on the lookout for the next thrill and rush—who now rides a cherry red Yamaha R6, by the way. I've also been the girlfriend/fiancée who picks out china and bridesmaid dresses and shows off her ring—all with a smile that somehow feels like someone else's.

My trips to Peru or Nigeria have become a respite for me. Tyler asks to go with me, and every time I tell him no. Why do I do that? Why do I hold him at a distance?

We've been together nearly four years. He's only ever been loving and understanding. Why can I not turn my heart over to him? He's such a good, kind man. He loves me, unconditionally. He is faithful and caring. Honestly, he is the dream. He's so many things I do not deserve and have not reciprocated.

But why?

Is Jack still screwing me up? After all the long years of silence from him—yes, I still check Daddy's letter drawer every now and then.

Why is my heart guarded? I don't know. Maybe because I'm stuck and cannot reopen my heart. Maybe we only get one true love. Maybe I'm being stubborn.

That's it.

I'm stubborn—like Jack. Well, no more—I refuse to be like him, and I will figure out how to completely open my heart to Tyler. He's a good man who deserves far more than I've given him to this point.

In one month, I will be his wife, and I want to be the kind of wife he deserves.

Today's One Good Thing:

I am thankful for more love than I deserve.

Sunday, June 6, 2010

Dear Rachael,

I thought about you today.

Of course, I think about you every day.

Scout and I have spent the past few months exploring farther around the mountains. On one of our adventures, we discovered a retreat. We've seen all sorts of people milling around—kids, families, older folks. They never see us. Scout and I blend into our wilderness home.

This is the first Sunday we've hiked there. Scout and I sat near the stream that separates us from the retreat area. I recognized the notes of an old hymn we always sang during church in Bellum. When I closed my eyes, there was your face—glowing beneath a sunbeam filtered through the stained glass. You turned to look at me and smiled as you sang the words—familiar to me, part of you. I couldn't tell you the name of the hymn, but I feel certain it was one of your favorites ... a solid guess considering how much you love hymns.

I sat beside that stream, grinning like an idiot, as I pictured you singing every one of the songs we heard. Nature always brings me peace and solitude, but music added something extra today.

Maybe remembrance, comfort? The tunes wrapped around me like a comfortable old blanket.

I suppose the music makes me melancholy, too. Ever since we returned to our campsite, I've thought about you and me and our lives to this point. When I think of you,

I hope with all I have that you're happy, but I wish I'd never walked away.

Where would we be today? What if I hadn't joined the Marines, never met Tray or went to Iraq? He might still be alive. I'd still have two fully functioning arms.

Would I still have you?

You were the best of me. By a lot. You were ... incredible. Fire and ice; love and peace. My comfort and rock who always believed in me. What did you see in me? I doubt whatever you saw—or thought you did—still exists. But you ... you were a dream walking.

Perhaps time and distance create great fiction.

Except ... I know with more certainty than I know anything that you are every bit as spectacular as I remember. I also know you are the one I should have been with. I threw that possibility away and will regret it every day of my life. I wish I could have been the man you deserved, who earned the right to ask for your hand.

I didn't have that peace or forgiveness that you, your dad and my mom have. I know that would've kept us apart, too, because I know you and your conviction. You would've been right. Your dad made that clear; he didn't want his daughter to marry someone who didn't share her faith. The problem is I don't think I ever will. I continue to read this Bible but still—its promises don't sound meant for me.

That's my comfort on this side of things, I suppose. Even if my life hadn't gone to hell, I never would have been right for you. And now, I'm only fit for the outdoors and the outskirts of society.

Yes, I think I can do civilization ... from a distance. Seeing campers and hikers from a ways away reminds me what it's like to be a human. That probably sounds weird, but the ability to be near life and not be afraid of wrecking it is comforting and emboldening. Scout and I will probably return on Sundays to hear the music and watch the lives interact before us.

The goofy dog enjoys spying, too. He lays with his head up and alert, his ears wiggling toward different sounds and his nose twitching when the wind carries a scent of something tasty our way. His eyes constantly scan the scene before us—never missing a motion. Once, a younger boy was running and tripped. Scout hopped up immediately, ready to spring to the rescue, and only laid back down once the little fellow had been properly scooped up, comforted and restored to his previous full-speed-ahead activities.

Scout is quite the empathetic creature, which makes me wonder about his past. There was clearly some trauma there. I doubt his gnarly scar that matches mine was from a drag racing wreck.

How are you doing? That's a question I haven't asked in a while, though I wonder about the answer daily. I hope you had an amazing birthday.

All of April was warm and beautiful. We slept for only a few hours each night, but we slept deeply because our days were full. I would venture a guess that Scout and I have made our way around most of these mountains by now. We've seen some views that have stopped me in my tracks. I wish I could bring you here and show you the beauty I've lived in all these years.

Today's One Good Thing: Today I'm thankful for the power of music and the chance to slowly reintroduce myself to civilization.

Saturday, June 19, 2010

I couldn't do it.

My "put one foot in front of the other," "just keep moving forward," "he's such a great guy" routine has done nothing but make the past few years an emotional rollercoaster for me and result in Tyler having his heart broken in a way I will regret forever.

At our wedding, I fainted ... actually fainted!

When the pipe organ announced my entrance, the doors opened. Daddy and I took our first step; my next one never happened. Instead, down I went—out cold.

No one knew what happened. Some people thought I was sick; others, pregnant—ha! Tyler thought I was either sick or absolutely worn from the stress and excitement of the past few months with registries, showers, events, pre-marital counseling and so much more.

What really happened was the thought of saying "I do" to someone who hasn't been a ghost for nearly four years was more than I could bear. And so, I said no. I backed out and broke a beautiful heart.

I should have called it off long ago. I should never have started it.

Yes, I thought Jack was someone I had to push past to have a real future. Yes, I thought I was being stubborn. At what point should I have realized the ridiculousness of those statements?

When every line about love and commitment that Mama wrote to me in her letters immediately made me think of Jack—never my almost husband?

When the letter she wrote me for my wedding day screamed one name—and not the one to whom I had promised to pledge my love?

When I couldn't force myself to give Tyler the letter Mama wrote for the man who would marry me?

I cannot believe I dragged a kind and loving man through my lunacy. I am ashamed of myself and heartbroken for him.

At the same time, I haven't felt this free in nearly four years. I can breathe deeply. Looking back, I realize I existed with a weight on my chest that's magically lifted.

I have no idea what all this means for me or my future. Right now, I'm leaning toward my previous plan to be single. If I'd stuck to that and not agreed to date, I wouldn't have hurt a good man.

But, how could I know?

I am confused about my future and who I am but certain in my decision.

Today's One Good Thing: I
am thankful for this chance to walk away, though it feels selfish to admit.

Monday, August 30, 2010

Dear Rachael,

Yesterday, Scout and I revisited the retreat. We heard "Amazing Grace," and something inside me snapped.

Mama sang that song so many times, I still hear her soothing voice, lulling me to sleep. My reaction this time was opposite.

It's hard to explain, but the words made me angry, as angry as I felt the last night I was drunk in high school ... before your dad took me into the mission. This afternoon's experience was an overload of the messages of grace and forgiveness and healing that I've been reading in that Bible Senior gave me, carried on a song that reminds me of you and all the people I've betrayed over the years.

You would remind me how great God is, but I live a life where hell and horror is daily reality. Dead toddlers. Teens' bodies mangled in senseless accidents. War. Great men slain; useless ones not.

I still can't fuse the two in my mind. It's like two sides of me are warring within, and neither's winning.

In my fury, I rushed up the mountain. Scout and I are part mountain goat by now, so it wasn't overly difficult. We raced until we hit a trail. It's not one I've used because it's busy; the top is a tourist attraction. I'm not sure why I followed it this time.

Scout and I had most of the way to ourselves. I wasn't prepared for what we found when we reached the top.

You remember that nightmare I wrote you about—the one where the ghosts chase me off the cliff that split in two between those Iraqi kids? That exact mountain peak exists at the top of the trail.

How is it possible to dream about a real place you've never seen?

I sat on the edge with my feet dangling toward the valley bottom I couldn't see because of the clouds beneath me. Utter uselessness overwhelmed me.

Rach, I've been away from life for so long, not doing anything for anyone, existing without reason. The realization raised an unanswerable question.

Is a man without a purpose still a person?

I couldn't answer, or maybe I didn't want to. My next thought was how easy it would be to let my nightmare become reality and slide over the edge toward eternal nothingness.

Scout whimpered as he pawed at me. I told you—the dog is crazy smart. I swear he reads my mind. Anyway, I sat there for a while longer, petting the giant furry head that he'd plopped intentionally in my lap.

As I gazed out at one of the most beautiful places I have ever seen, I committed to figuring out why those two sides of my brain keep battling. I need to find a way to call a truce, end the war, open the door for peace.

I also decided to claim a new purpose in this life. If Scout's determined to keep me from flying off a cliff, I need to have a reason to live. I need to be useful. Somehow.

With this resolve in mind, Scout and I have begun the process of clearing out my hides and polishing off cans of sausages. Pretty soon, we'll be traveling, and I prefer to hike light.

To answer the questions warring in my brain, I need your dad. I'm not totally sure how to work my way back to life around others, but the first step is to put myself in more populated areas. It may be a while still before I get all the way to Savannah, but I'm moving that way. One step at a time, one test at a time.

Once I finally reach your dad and work out those answers, I think the search for purpose will become less hazy. I hope so anyway. At the very least, I'm positive he'll have some guidance for me. And, perhaps, that's all I need. Someone to guide me. To listen. To answer. To lead.

The Marines gave me that. I didn't have to figure out my life. They told me where to go, how to act and respond and what to wear while doing so. If Iraq had ended differently, I would have been leading by now. Life and purpose were becoming clearer before that ambush shot everything to hell.

And so, here I am, starting over ... again. Now, though, I believe I can start again. That's a huge step for me. I know your dad doesn't have every answer, but he's the best counselor I've ever known. He'll do all he can to help me.

One more thing happened last night. For the first time in I don't know how long, I had a dream full of light and beauty. I was on my peak again, but it was bright—radiant, even. I felt something moving toward me, but when I turned, I didn't face decaying corpses and the terrors of my past.

I saw you. My Rachael—older, but more beautiful than ever, if that's possible.

You smiled as you approached. I longed to hold you close and kiss your rose-colored lips, but before you reached my open arms, the light shimmering from you wrapped around me, filling me with peace, confidence and joy.

When I woke up with a smile on my face and the lingering warmth of your light in my heart, I realized that I always thought you were the answer to all my problems. And, as much as you have been the most secure hide in the emotional wilderness of my life, I finally understand my faith and hope and reason for life might need to rest somewhere else.

Today's One Good Thing: Today I'm thankful for the lowest moments on the highest peaks, especially when they lead to forward motion.

Thursday, November 25, 2010

I just got back from Peru. Ever since that disastrous day in June, I've been more restless than I have been over the past eight years—and that's saying something.

While I was there, I hiked and climbed and explored and jumped and did all the things I love. I pushed my physical limits; I pushed safety limits—not proud to admit that one. Above all those things, though, I pushed myself mentally, emotionally and spiritually. I spent hours sitting atop mountains, forcing myself to think deeply through all the questions about myself and my actions over the past several years. One by one, I chipped away at the answers.

As I chopped my way through underbrush on our hike to the mountaintop for our first jump, I also hacked through a nagging question about Tyler.

Why did I continue the relationship
with him when I never loved him?

Looking back, I do know I didn't love him, but I honestly wanted to. He was a gift, and I wanted him to be the man for me. I longed to move forward, instead of being stuck in the quagmire of Jack's disappearance. I believed what I was doing was right, that I had to push myself forward to care for someone else. What I know now is that was never the right approach.

True love—the kind that shores up a marriage—never needs to be forced. True love manifests itself mysteriously but grows into maturity through mutual hard work.

I wanted to love Tyler, but wanting to love isn't loving.

As I ziplined through the trees, I shut my eyes and felt the sun on my face and the wind in my hair and let the breeze cool another burning question.

Why can't I move beyond my love
and longing for a man who left me
eight-and-a-half years ago?

For more than half my life, Jack was the other side of my heart coin. The love we shared ran deep. Its roots entwined with griefs we carried each other through and shared memories of joyful moments. Something so intrinsic doesn't easily wash away.

Despite his decision to run, Jack didn't shed his love for me either. He said that in his final letter to Daddy. So, I know now that I was not alone. Our love was true. Holding onto it wasn't crazy, and I wasn't imagining something that wasn't there.

It was at Machu Picchu where I experienced my breaking point with the answer to my final question.

Why am I perpetually restless and
feel separated from God?

As I looked across that ancient site, once home to a culture and people we can only speculate about, I thought about legacy—what we leave behind. The sun shimmered in the ragged tops of the mountains across from me, and their splendor overwhelmed me. Breathing was difficult as I drank in the majesty and realized how small I am in the grand scheme of life and the world around me. And then, that final answer jarred me harder than a rough jump landing.

I've been constantly restless because I haven't rested in God—the only Constant, the only Absolute. Instead of trusting Him, I've trusted myself and my good deeds. I've been habitually escaping into extreme sports and my job.

When that realization sunk in, I collapsed and bawled like a baby as the truth of my past hit me square in the heart.

Thinking deeper, I realized that I defined myself by a man—Jack, Tyler—or by the accomplishments I've achieved or the thrills I've manufactured instead of by God.

I was emotionally broken and collapsed onto God's amazing grace. I remembered, first and foremost, I am a daughter of the King of Kings. That is who I am, period.

It doesn't matter if I marry or not. If I do, my identity will remain in God. If I don't, it will rest in the same place. No hobby or adrenaline rush or job or mission trip or anything or anyone else will ever hold my identity. No amount of good deeds in foreign countries or achievements in extreme sports can ever save or define me.

Since that moment when the truth broke into my jagged heart, I've known beyond a shadow of a doubt, my identity must always and only rest in God. No one and nothing else can ever be my resting place.

The crazy thing about all this? The truth of identity is the same one I recognized in the woman in Nigeria and shared with that little girl at camp years ago and with Shannon at the first wedding I went to with her. I told them how important it was to remember, as believers, their identities rest in Christ alone.

Why didn't I listen to myself? It's unbelievable how we can thoroughly know such an amazing truth and yet walk through life like it isn't true.

Another thing I've always known but haven't applied to my life has to do with faith and feelings. Feelings are fickle. Faith is not a feeling, and it sure as heck isn't fickle.

Faith in God is sure, steady; it's the foundation for my life and all the things I do in it and the people I do them alongside. Faith comes as Christ's gift to me and, like Him, is unchanging, regardless of how my feelings may waver.

Today's One Good Thing:
I am thankful for amazing grace, an unchanging identity and a God who never lets go but always forgives and strengthens my feeble faith.

Saturday, January 1, 2011

It's a bright new year, and I am filled with hope and confidence in whatever God has in store for me. For the first time in years, I am content in resting in him and trusting his plans for me. What a feeling of security that brings!

The past couple months in church and in reading my Bible have been incredible. It's like I'd been walking across a desert all these years, parched and near-death, and now, finally, I'm lapping up the water that's been there all along. Every day, I'm noticing things in the Bible that I've never seen before—it's like experiencing a black-and-white movie in full color. I'm learning more about God, his relationship to me and my responsibility to Him.

During the Christmas Eve candlelight service, I decided I have much in common with those white candles. I'm not always the strongest or brightest, but I can make a difference in the darkness around me, especially when I'm surrounded by all the other lights in my church.

I will attend a women's Bible study this week. Surrounding myself with lights—other Christians—will help me shine brighter and will encourage me on the days I'm tempted to dim my light.

Daddy was surprised at my request for new paintbrushes, paints and canvases for Christmas. Long ago, I loved to draw and paint. Animals and landscapes were always my favorite subjects to paint, and I usually paired them with Bible verses. Somewhere along the way—maybe our move to Savannah or the busyness of college—I stopped.

While I was in Peru, I wished I had paints to attempt to capture the beauty there. I am still quite rusty, but each attempt shows improvement. I plan to make something for Ms. Becky as soon as I feel more confident in my abilities. Maybe I can improve enough by Mother's Day. If not, I have almost an entire year until her next birthday.

I just checked to see if my last painting is dry and examined it with a more critical eye. December 10 might be a better goal for Ms. Becky's gift.

My cheesecake for tomorrow smells amazing and should be ready in another fifteen minutes. Every Sunday evening, I cook for Daddy, either at my place or his. We've started earlier in the afternoon, so we can talk while I prep food.

He was so worried about me after the wedding. When he dropped me off at the airport for my trip to Peru, his face looked creased like a crumpled paper. Fast-forward to our reunion after my getaway, he saw my change of spirit as soon as I emerged from the airport. I watched his worries roll back to reveal the smooth, radiant face I've grown up with and relied on my entire life. I believe his "Welcome back!" held more than one meaning.

In the car, I told him about my Machu Picchu epiphany. His eyes overflowed as he told me he had been praying harder the past few months than he ever had. He had seen the pain and felt the despair in me.

This past month, we've talked more about Tyler and Jack, but mostly about my future and how I approach each day differently. I told him it was odd how free I felt.

He said, "That's what life with and for Christ gives us—the sweet air of freedom, contentment and peace."

No matter what lies ahead for me this year, I know God has a plan and purpose through it all. In whatever that may be, my identity will remain unchanged because it rests in a God who never has and never will change.

Today's One Good Thing:
I am thankful for a new year to rest in God and grow in my understanding of Him and relationship with Him.

Friday, March 18, 2011

Dear Rachael,

I buried my father today.

So many things have happened since the last letter; it's hard to know where to begin. I suppose I should start with where I am and how I got here. For the past few months, I've been living in a homeless community in Durham.

Last fall, I eased my way back into civilization—or maybe I catapulted myself into it; it's hard to say for certain. That's a time I don't care to recall or write about. It was eerily similar to alcohol withdrawals. All the toxic thoughts and terrors from my entire life oozed out of me at once with no filters. I honestly wasn't sure what would be left when—or if—all that horror escaped. Scout is why I survived.

Once I detoxed from a life of solitude, I slowly put myself into more populated areas around Durham. It's easy to blend into a bigger city. People don't have eyes for anything they don't want to see. Believe me, a sketchy dude in ragged clothes with a giant scraggly dog isn't something they care to notice.

Thankfully, each interaction and situation got easier as I went. By Christmas, I decided I was ready for the next step.

I had noticed other homeless people and realized they had communities of sorts. With the fireworks of New Year's Eve approaching and the concern of how that could unleash the monster within, despite my hard work to cast it out, I headed east to live in the woods one last time.

Mid-January, I entered a community. Even in an unconventional society, leaders emerge. This one gentleman—Jay, he called himself—looked out for the others, especially the older folks and those who couldn't care for or protect themselves. He'd established a system for getting day-old foods from local restaurants and grocery stores and distributing it fairly throughout the community. He appreciated my muscles and dedication to the cause. For my part, it was nice to be useful again.

He was a nice guy, but he lived for his bottles. The look in his eyes toward the end of our food runs reminded me of the mirror during my drinking days. He had to have it.

Whenever he settled in with the bottle, he'd chat with me. He told me about the family he left behind and how he wished he could return to the woman he still loved. He talked about how he'd justified his leaving as being "best for them" and how he was no good for them.

Damn, if that's not almost exactly the same things I've said all these years since I ran away from my life and you.

His words hit home in my mind and my heart that I've been so wrong—about many things. I had to get back to my mom, no doubt. But, I decided I wanted to help Jay first. It was obvious he was seriously ill—I saw him cough up blood. Another reason I had to help him was I had to believe it wasn't too late for him ... or for me.

Before I had figured out a plan to approach him about his past, where he was from and how I could get him there to make amends, he overheard me telling the kids a story from home. When I mentioned Bellum, a crash brought my tale to a shattering halt.

I rushed to help Jay clean up the dropped bottle—and to make sure he didn't cut himself. He mumbled some lame excuse and then looked at me for an eternal second. Staring eye to eye raised that mirror image again, and the strangest feeling fell over me. His eyes held a lifetime of regret and sadness and something I couldn't name.

Next, he spoke to me in the most sober tone I'd heard from him. He told me to go home, to not make the same mistakes he'd made. He said my mom's name and told me it was an honor to meet me. Before he walked away, he laid down an old wallet.

You remember that family picture I kept on my nightstand for so many years? You noticed when I put it away—out of sight, like my dad. That was the first day you held my hand for a reason other than to lead me somewhere. You knew I'd realized my dad was never coming back, and your touch helped me believe I might be okay despite that fact.

Anyway, Jay's wallet contained one picture ... that one.

I suppose my dad had a thing about using initials as names. He insisted I have a middle initial that stood for nothing, and he ditched the Jack Senior for the simpler "J." I'll never get to ask him why.

It took me a while to recover from the shock of meeting my dad. When I started looking around, no one had seen him that afternoon. My friend Jed and I and some of the other guys headed out to look for him, but we were too late.

His time ran out.

The cancer took him before I could ask the lifetime of questions swirling in my mind, before I had the chance to actually have a dad in my life. I wish our reunion had been different. If I had figured it out sooner or asked him where he was from or something. I mean, I lived with the man for three months.

Now, mom will never see him again.

The shock of who he was and the grief of what had slipped through my fingers got quickly replaced with rage.

He'd lived in Durham for years, caring for his makeshift family and looking after them. Why couldn't he stick around for his real family? Why did he have to run off on the wife and son who needed him? Why couldn't he return to us? Why couldn't he be who we needed him to be? Were we not enough for him?

The one bright spot is I was able to give him a proper burial. He won't be nameless for eternity.

One day, I'll bring mom here. But first, I have to continue journeying toward her. Mom needs me, and I'm determined not to let her down anymore. I will not leave her alone forever like he did. It's not too late for me, and I will not tempt the fates of time anymore.

First, I need your dad's wisdom as I seek answers to move toward some semblance of lasting purpose.

I'm coming home, Rachael. Finally. I know that doesn't mean you. I gave that right up too long ago. But, in my heart, you—Rachael Jane Burns—will always be my home.

Though I may not have the right to hope for a home, I know now I can return to life and that I need to do it before it's too late. No more excuses. No more procrastinating. I'm going to make sure things are arranged for the food pickups to continue here, and then I'll be heading out on my birthday toward a new life.

That's more than I deserve, but I'm finally taking your advice. I'm going to accept this good thing.

Something will shift with my return, not sure which way. Of course, I can't stop my heart from longing for the impossible—you. But you're not why I'm heading south.

Today's One Good Thing: Today, I am thankful I got to know my dad as an adult, even if I didn't know it was him. I'm thankful, too, that I can return to my mom and bring her closure she never would have had otherwise. I suppose there's always something to be thankful for, even in the face of death and unexpected renewal of a loss I thought was distant history.

Sunday, March 20, 2011

Today, Jack is 27. He's been on my mind a lot the past month, but not like he used to be. I don't ache anymore when I think of him. I don't long for him either—not in the way I did. He's not the missing part of me because who I am isn't wrapped up in him.

I do still love him. I believe I always will.

Even in that statement, I feel peace, contentment. I'm no longer broken and restless; I am who God created me to be, and I will serve Him and live for Him alone. And whether or not I ever see the man I still love again, those truths will never change.

Today's One Good Thing:
I am thankful for contentment and a new outlook on life.

Monday, March 21, 2011

Dear Rachael,

Your dad said the seven most beautiful words I never dared to dream I'd hear: "She's never given her heart to another."

You waited? No, not waited; just didn't give your heart away. I can't let myself hope. Won't.

But maybe ...

I have to put you out of my mind right now, though. The reason I came to your dad was to work on answering these questions about life and purpose and faith. I'm here to seek a treaty or a surrender in the war that's been waging inside me all these years.

Until I accomplish that, nothing's changed for me, which means I'm still unfit for you.

But maybe ...

Today's One Good Thing: Today I'm thankful for the impossible and for a place to find answers.

Saturday, March 26, 2011

Dear Rachael,

Tomorrow I'll attend church with your dad. We've had some good talks this week. He's opened his home to me without a single thought. He's never scolded me for setting out again. He even wished me happy birthday when I showed up, smelly vagabond drifter that I was.

My insides feel jumpy, like when I put coffee grounds in my mouth before an all-night mission. I sense I'm on the verge of ... something.

Perhaps an understanding? A breakthrough?

I'm not sure what it will be, but I hope whatever it is eases my troubled soul and brings me comfort or at least guidance on how to live. All your dad's answers have, of course, pointed to God. I knew they would. I haven't pieced together my thoughts about that, though.

Staying in your room has been strange. Scout and I sleep on the floor. For one thing, I don't want to mess up your bed. The deeper reason is, after living in the woods for so long, the idea of sleeping in a soft, cushy bed feels foreign.

I can feel your presence, which is both unsettling and comforting. I hope you don't barge in one day. I'm not sure surprising you in your dad's house is the right reunion.

Also, I'm not ready to see you; my heart is still too wild. Answers whip around me, out of grasp. If I could catch one or two and gain more control over my life, perhaps I'd feel more prepared to present my deepest apology.

Today's One Good Thing: Today I'm thankful for your dad and his gracious wisdom.

Sunday, March 27, 2011

Dear Rachael,

You told me long ago that you prayed for my salvation. Today, your prayer was answered.

I have true peace for the first time in my life. It's a peace I can continue to have because it comes from Someone unchangeable. That's tough to wrap my mind around.

No matter what your relationship status means for our future, my contentment and future and purpose exist in this new relationship. In God. This new peace came apart from you. That's going to take some getting used to, but I know the truth now, and I'm seeking to understand it.

As I look back, I see how God guided and guarded and led me along my journey. He was the one who sent the comfort and strength when I needed it. The visions and memories may have been of you, but He sent them.

Something I'm wrestling with understanding is that, now, my identity rests in God, not you. I suppose, honestly, no one should make another human the source of who they are. We all let each other down and can't always be there, right?

You were the one I looked to all these years, and my vision of you got me through. Now, though, I'm learning that who I am—and who I'm going to be—must center around God ... not you or anyone.

I have much to learn on this new journey, but the Marine Corps taught me how to study. I asked your dad for advice on reading my Bible. He gave me some verses to start with, and part of one spoke directly to my thoughts and soothed my restless spirit. "This hope we have as an anchor of the soul, both sure and steadfast ...."

Once, my purpose rested in the Eagle, Globe and Anchor. Now, Jesus has given me an eternal anchor to cling to and relief from restlessness to rest in Him.

Today's One Good Thing: Today, I'm thankful for salvation and forgiveness. I'm forgiven. Unbelievable!

Sunday, March 27, 2011

Tonight, I went to Daddy's for our weekly dinner. I know it's not possible, but I believe Jack has been there. It's hard to explain, but it's something like a smell.

That's not right. It's more like a sense of his presence. I said it was hard to explain. I know it's weird, too.

It's more than that, though. Daddy has a mischievous gleam in his eye and acts like he wants to tell me something. Actually, he looks like he does every year right before Christmas or my birthday—when he knows what my present is and can barely contain the secret.

Of course, my birthday is only a few days away. I'm sure that's all there is to it. I won't dwell on my craziness because there's no reason to, and it all seems silly now that I've written it out.

God is in control, and that's all that matters. Even if Jack were to show up here, he doesn't change who I am or what's most important to me. I pray he's okay wherever he is and that he comes to know Christ and peace in this life. That's one prayer that hasn't changed all this time.

Today's One Good Thing:
I am thankful for the ability to pray for people, even when I haven't seen them in nearly a decade, and I'm thankful God hears those prayers and sees that person, wherever they are.

Sunday, April 3, 2011

Dear Rachael,

I joined the Millers and my mom at church today. It was different from any other church experience with them. This time I worshipped with them instead of standing there.

Earlier this week, sitting with my mom and talking about the past several years healed wounds I didn't realize I had. I talked to her about what I've learned about identity in God alone. She said it wasn't an easy lesson for her to learn but perhaps came earlier for her than others. Her words exuded wisdom and truth.

She said, "When you lose what you've planted your identity in, grasping the concept of placing who you are and who defines your future in an unchanging, eternal, ever-present God makes perfect sense."

Telling her about my dad was harder on me than her, I think. I broke down as I tried to tell her all I knew about him and explain where he'd been. She still loved him, even though he ran out on us, and I believe she forgave him long ago. She has a beautiful heart.

Talking through all the heartbreak—as well as the few good memories my dad left behind—revealed something unexpected. I needed to see him again. I not only needed closure but also clarity. Most of my life, I thought I had no choice in certain things—drinking, running. I decided somewhere along the way that I was stuck becoming my dad.

Maybe I felt that way because others whispered it around me from the time I was old enough to start picking out words like "drunk," "good-for-nothing" and "drifter."

Honestly, though, in the end, I used that misbelief as a crutch—an excuse. I didn't want to admit I'm responsible for my own actions and can't blame my mistakes and missteps on anyone but me.

Funny, isn't it? I have no problem blaming myself for killing a little girl—the worst tragedy that could have happened and that I had no control over—and yet, when it comes to something I can control and am truly responsible for, I pass the buck without so much as a blink.

I apologized to my mom again for all the ways I've hurt her over the years. I'm not ashamed to admit, her smile and words made me cry. "You've been forgiven for longer than you even realized you needed to be, my sweet boy."

Talk about a picture of grace on earth.

Mom and I talked about you, too. She agrees with Ducky that I should go to you. Since I plan on being baptized next weekend, that might be an invitation I could extend. I'll talk to your dad about it tonight.

Speaking of, I better head into the kitchen to work on supper. I decided to thank him for his hospitality by cooking him dinner. Of course, I'm not sure what kind of cook I will be, so this may or may not be a good thanks.

Today's One Good Thing: Today I'm thankful for time spent with my mom.

Sunday, April 3, 2011

Jack came home!

I walked into Daddy's house tonight, and Jack was there. Long hair, bearded face, more scars. Same gold-flecked eyes and crooked smile. Still gorgeous.

When I saw him, time slipped like sand through my fingers, and it felt like just yesterday he kissed me on graduation day.

He said hello, and I catapulted myself into his arms. I held him tightly, afraid to let go as I praised God for this miracle.

I'm hopeful and overflowing with love and thankfulness because, not only is Jack here and well and healing, but he knows Christ as his Lord and Savior. That's the greatest news I could ever receive.

He apologized for running, and I told him I forgave him long ago. We have so much time to make up for and much to learn about each other. Because neither of us moved on from or stopped loving the other, we're picking up, in some ways, where we left off.

Unlike before, we're older, wiser and both Christians. Now, our relationship can rest on our individual relationships with God, and neither of us will be defined by the other.

Honestly, tonight's events and these thoughts about the future are surreal. Of course, why would I doubt? Isn't this what I've prayed for all these years: Jack's salvation, his return, our restoration, a future together?

God is amazing, and He works all things out in His time.

Today's One Good Thing:
I am thankful that God saved Jack and brought him back to me.

Monday, April 4, 2011

Dear Rachael,

Seeing you last night was like living my dreams—the good ones. Your voice drew me down that hall, and that first look at you: your slightly messy red hair, that motorcycle helmet dangling in your hand, stopped me in my tracks and wiped out any intelligent words.

I was a mess. You were not.

Part of me was pissed at your dad for springing you on me, but I would still be trying to figure out if I should contact you and what I would say if I did. So, I suppose I owe him.

Did I really greet you with "Hey there?" Man, I've lost my game.

Everything you said, though, was everything I needed to hear. The way you talked about relationships—being willing to jump together, even though we've got no clue if we'll soar or splat. You said it better.

With God as our wind, I'm ready to soar with you, Rachael. Finally.

I couldn't sleep last night. I kept thanking God for all He's done in my life and yours to bring us together at the perfect moment.

Today's One Good Thing: Today I'm thankful I no longer need to write you letters. I'll see you later today, pretty lady.

Saturday, August 6, 2011

The past four months have been a living dream. Jack and I have rediscovered each other and relayed stories from our time apart. He told me more about Scout and the mountain. He spoke about Iraq, especially, about Trayvon and what a close friend he had become. Jack explained about his grief, losing Trayvon and his dad and all the other things he lost after Iraq. I wish I could have known them both.

As we've reacquainted ourselves with each other, we've also grown in our faith. I couldn't believe it when Jack pulled out his Bible on an early date. We usually read a passage or two together while we're out or over the phone before we go to sleep.

Attending church has given us another fresh shared experience. Unlike when we were kids, both of us sing the hymns and mean them, listen to the sermons with faith in the words behind them and seek to understand whatever we don't.

Jack and I have joked about how weird our story must sound to people: "We're childhood sweethearts who took a nearly decade hiatus to soar from airplanes and mountains and disappear into the mountain wilderness. What? It worked for us."

Double dates with Ducky and Daisy have been the activity that's made us feel most like a normal couple. We genuinely enjoy spending time together, and they've given us some great tips for married life one day. Most involve being honest about pet peeves and instructing the other person on ways to avoid said pet peeves.

Ducky's advice was my favorite. He said, "If you get upset about something silly, remember you get to live with the love of your life. That'll turn your frown upside down!"

Speaking of future married life ...

Tonight, Jack asked me to spend a long weekend with him in Asheville over Labor Day. I believe he plans to propose!

Writing that stirs flutters in my heart. While I am content to wait as long as necessary, I am eager and ready to become Mrs. Jack Calhoun. The name change is a long time coming.

Today's One Good Thing:
I'm thankful to experience an old, comfortable relationship in a new way and for the potential upcoming change in our status.

Monday, September 5, 2011

After all this time and all our journeys, Jack and I are engaged!

Friday, we drove to Asheville. The weather cleared after an afternoon downpour, and we hiked to the peak of Jack's mountain where his nightmares were set and where he ultimately made the realizations that led him home to God ... and to me.

The rain ended up being a blessing because the summit wasn't overly crowded and a rainbow painted the sky—the perfect backdrop for Jack to get down on one knee.

Our night was perfect; our weekend was perfect. We are ready for this next stage of our life together.

Today's One Good Thing:
I'm thankful for the commitment and promise to and from the man of my dreams.

Monday, December 31, 2012

The past year has flown by, and we recently set a wedding date: April 6. Some people question why we would wait so long. For us, though, waiting another year or two is no time at all. This time has given Jack space to focus on returning to the real world and to work toward the opening of Becky & Jack's.

Can I just say how much I adore that he and his mom opened a store together? I've never seen Ms. Becky so animated and … alive. Mama would be so proud of her friend and would be her top customer, if not her business partner. I could see Mama selling books alongside her friend and finding a corner of the shop for a plant section.

Jack put so much hard work into the pieces of furniture and home décor he sells on his side. Honestly, though, I think he most enjoys the custom orders. They keep him on his toes, and he loves a challenge.

He and I uncovered the most gorgeous gazebo in the courtyard behind the shop, and I convinced him we should get married there. Actually, that didn't require much persuasion. As soon as I asked, I could tell he was completely on board.

Wedding planning has been a blast. One of the girls at work turned up her nose when I mentioned how we're planning everything together. She said, "The wedding is for the bride. I would never let the groom call any of the shots." She's entitled to her opinion, but doesn't that sound sad?

Jack and I giggle like we're in junior high as we flip through wedding magazines, and we had way too much fun with that gun thing you use to register for gifts. He added a few things to our registry that I would never have chosen, but he loves them. The worst that can happen is that I may have to stare at a hideous lamp until I get used to it ... or it mysteriously goes missing.

Shannon came in from Savannah to take our engagement photos. She does an amazing job of setting up perfect posed shots that don't feel or look posed while also capturing totally candid moments that encapsulate who we are as a couple. The only trouble is choosing which ones go in the frames.

Life isn't all laughs and ease, of course. We continue to grow as individuals and in our relationship. After my epiphanies in Peru two years ago, I mostly hung up my jump gear. I've maintained my skydive certification and have done a few shows with the team here, but I haven't done any BASE jumping. It turns out, my thrill-seeking really was an attempt to fill God's place in my soul. That spot is properly filled.

I'm also eager to focus my spare time on activities I can share with Jack. As much as I love my motorcycle, I'm not upset about making a more practical vehicle purchase. Jack and I plan on doing a lot of hiking and mountain climbing, so I'm leaning toward a rugged vehicle.

While Jack has adjusted well to life off his mountain, his past will always be part of him. Watching his PTSD and flashbacks kick in during the store's grand opening showed me the severity of the war's effects on him. As much as his panic and my inability to help him terrified me, watching Scout calm my hero assured me he isn't alone. Scout is incredible, and we will work through these challenges as a team.

Jack seems focused on controlling his issues. My concern is that no one can fully control anything, certainly not something this huge. He also puts things off that I think would help, like meeting with his friend Randy who's a veteran. Jack tells me, "After this event, I'll go." The problem is there's always another event. I'm not sure how to help or what to do, but I will listen and be here.

Being observant of Jack is important because, although he has told me some things about his time in Iraq, he hasn't told me everything and he doesn't always share how he feels about certain things. When I joked with him about us having babies, his face paled, and his eyes widened. I thought for sure I was going to hear his knees knocking. He tried to hide his emotions, but I know what I saw. I'm not sure what it means, but we should probably discuss it. That can wait until after we're married, though.

Speaking of, when I wake up in the morning, I'll be able to say, "I'm marrying Jack this year!"

Today's One Good Thing:
I'm thankful for the incredible partner God has given me, and I'm thankful that we give and take, listen and speak truth. We can build one another up and take turns being the strength the other needs.

Friday, April 5, 2013

Tomorrow I marry my best friend and one true love. Jack is my only for always, and God carried us to this day.

My mind is filled with peace and certainty. I'm also confident that this step aligns with God's will.

Giving Jack the letter Mama wrote for my future husband was further confirmation this marriage is right. That letter was always meant for him. I wonder if Mama knew that when she wrote it.

The only thing that would have made tonight's rehearsal dinner more perfect would have been having Mama there. She would have loved every second of our night. Reminders of her love smoothed away the sadness that arose during the speeches and conversations.

Today's One Good Thing:
I'm thankful for peace and no doubts.

Friday, April 5, 2013

Dear Rachael,

I've waited all my nearly thirty years on this earth for the moments we say, "I do." Tomorrow, we will.

Regardless of the mistakes I'm sure I'll make along our journey, I promise you this: I will strive every day, with every breath I take and each beat of my heart, to follow Ducky's advice and "be worthy."

As we begin this new chapter of our lives together, I keep thinking about the parents we're missing.

I've read the letter from your mom every evening since you gave it to me. I wonder if she guessed I'd be the future son-in-law reading it. I miss her so much, though I know my grief is nothing compared to yours. I wish she could be here for our special day, to help you with your dress and hair. I understand in part how you must feel. I wish I could look out and see my dad standing with his arm around my mom. I know Mom would love that, too.

Our parents gave us examples to learn from and emulate. Despite my dad's mistakes, which taught me so much, our parents exemplified "'til death do us part." Their loves remained true to the end; no leaving or cancer could change their commitments.

I keep thinking backward at all we've survived, the storms we've ridden out. Even in the bad and the ugly of our future, I believe we can do this. I believe it because I believe in you and, finally, I trust your confidence in me.

Most important, I believe in God and know He'll guide us through every challenge. Our vows today are before Him first and foremost. We have committed our lives and our marriage to Him, and He will not fail us. He never has.

I want to be your rock—like you've been for me our whole life. I'm scared to death that I will never be that for you, that I'll always lean on you. I don't want to be your burden. I want, instead, to heed your mom's words and carry your burdens, sacrifice my all for you. That's what I desire to do and will endeavor to do from today into our forever.

Another thing your mom's letter reminded me of is our marriage isn't going to be picture perfect. Life won't be the hazy, all-smile daydreams I've entertained. We won't always smile. I'm going to screw up; that's inevitable. And, as much as I think you are, you aren't entirely perfect. We'll face tough times, too. I know that, and your mom reminded me of that.

But God. He will hold us and guide us.

As I sit here tonight, eager and anxious and sleepless, I'm sifting through a lifetime of memories, real and imagined: us as kids, playing tag around your mom's garden; our teen years when keeping our hands off each other was torture (and still is ... don't think my mind doesn't keep drifting to tomorrow night and the bed I made you); and then there are the illusions that kept me going and alive during training, war and the loneliness of the mountain; my first look at you again after too many years—you standing there with that motorcycle helmet, looking like the sexiest daredevil; our mountain peak where you said yes; and, finally, how I imagine you'll look in your wedding dress.

I can't wait to commit myself to you for the rest of our life. To leap off the cliff and soar with your hand in mine.

Rach, I've loved you always and always will. You're a gift—an amazing "good thing," and I give myself to you from my knees with open arms and heart.

I am excited and nervous that you will read this letter and all the others. Parts of the letters won't be easy for you to absorb; they're hard for me to turn over to you. They are all part of my past, though ... my history, which I'm binding to yours tomorrow. I will place them all into the chest I made you as a surprise wedding gift.

Good, bad and horrifying, my past, present and future belong to you.

Today's One Good Thing: Today, I'm thankful for the gift of your love. I'm also thankful to spend the rest of my life seeking to love, cherish and honor you in all I do.

Friday, September 6, 2013

Sorrow and joy coexist in life, like bitter combines with sweet to produce a richer flavor profile. We may not willingly accept tragedies and pain in life, but they mold us, grow us, make us deeper versions of ourselves. Sometimes we simply need to pause, recognize the emotions—and our need for them—and let the feelings flood over us.

Our wedding five months ago today was more beautiful than I could have ever imagined. Without a doubt, it was the happiest day of my life. Of course, it wasn't without tears. We made time for the pain because we needed to acknowledge our grief and allow it to breathe.

Jack and I share the common bond of a lost parent. Our solidarity allowed us the opportunity to grieve their absence together. We knew we needed to acknowledge that grief on our joyful day, so we shed tears together for all the moments our absent parents have missed in our lives and all they will miss.

We will continue to grieve their absence. No monumental life event can arise without that heartache when I long for Mama to be beside me. We just passed another anniversary of her death. Seventeen long years without her. Seventeen years of firsts and lasts, hopes and dreams, hard work, laughter and tears.

In many ways those seventeen years feel like seventeen minutes. I still feel the strength of her hand on my shoulder when I face a fear. I hear her laugh and feel the sunshine of her smile. When I smell fresh-turned dirt or see a row of proudly lifted sunflowers, her warmth washes over me. Mama may be gone from this earth, but she's always with me.

I know Jack feels similar. Though his relationship with his dad was different, their reconnection in his father's last days showed Jack how things might have been. He's mentioned a sense of regret that he never thought to look for his dad and that he didn't recognize him before it was too late. I think Jack wonders if he could have learned more from his dad about how to not repeat past mistakes—his and his dad's.

As brave as my handsome warrior is, fear haunts the edges of his eyes. I think it has to do with worry that he'll mess up again or that he won't be able to be everything I need him to be.

How do you convince someone they are more than enough and always will be? That, even in his future mistakes, he will be exactly who I need him to be, and that whatever challenges our later years hold, we will tackle them together with God? We hold a threefold bond that can never be severed.

I fear not being able to calm his nightmares. I may not have all the answers or know how to calm his troubled soul, but I can pray for him and cover him with all the love I have nurtured for him our entire lives.

We've talked about the importance of not dwelling on the should haves. Knowing truth doesn't always keep us from revisiting the lies. Perhaps we'll both struggle with the ghosts of our pasts and the nagging questions of how things may have been. Thankfully, we have each other to lean on, talk to—and talk at, when necessary.

I'm also thankful for Jack's amazing gifts. He blew me away with the canopy bed he built us—it far surpasses any fairytale princess bed ever imagined. He told me he was building our bed, but I never imagined something so extravagant. I love waking up in it, my head resting on Jack's chest and hearing his steady heartbeat, as I examine the detailed scrollwork on each of the posts and all along the inside of the top supports. I can't imagine how many hours such artistic work took him.

The fact that he dreamed about that bed and me while we were apart makes it even more special. God kept his arms around not only us, but also over our relationship.

And then, Jack surprised me with the cedar chest he built and totally floored me with eleven years' worth of letters from him to me. It wasn't until that moment of feeling the weight of his love in my hands that I accepted he never forgot me or stopped loving me.

I've been reading them, slowly ... savoring them. Each one raises a mixture of emotions. They've brought on tears more than once. Jack has been through ten lifetimes of hardships.

Sometimes while reading, I've barely resisted the urge to strangle or punch him. He put himself through so much he never had to endure alone. At times, I wish we could go back, do all our life again—together this time. Of course, I know that wasn't God's plan.

God used our mistakes to transform us into the adults he wanted us to be for Him ... and for each other. We had to learn tough lessons, and God knew we needed to learn them separately and often the hard way. He also brought us together as soon as we were both ready and not a moment before.

As we lived out each scene of our lives apart, God was editing our hearts and souls to polish our love story.

Reading Jack's letters shows me who he was and is. His words help me feel his emotions, his nightmares, his hope. As I read the letters during his seasons of hopelessness when he lacked purpose, I praised God that

He still had a purpose for Jack. God wasn't done with him, and He wasn't done with us.

I understand now how broken Jack was when he left Bellum. He carried more ragged scars than the one on his neck. I recognize that he has even more invisible scars now, deep inside the core of who he is.

God has and will heal them, but scar tissue never goes away. It will likely remind Jack of his past's pain from time to time. Reading about that pain in his own words will help me help him. I can watch for triggers, hold him with more understanding when his fears take over and he can't explain why and love him through the ups and downs.

Jack's letters also fill in the gaps of our time apart and give me a better picture of all the guardians God sent to guide and protect Jack along his journey—the Millers and the Bible they gave him, Tray and his grandma, Scout and Missy Mee. I am grateful for each one and for the God who orchestrated them all.

The records of his terrifying nightmares of eternal aloneness with his demons tore at my heart. I am thankful he never has to be alone again. I can walk beside him, hold him and remind him I will be his only for always, like he is mine.

Between Jack's letters and my journals, we have a record of God's great work in us, through us and between us. I can't wait to see how God will polish the rest of our life's story.

Of course, reading his letters also makes me wonder about other important things ... like when Jack will make me chicken enchiladas or kiss me on top of the Ferris wheel at a state fair.

Today's One Good Thing: I'm thankful for Jack's gifts and God's greatest gift.

Monday, April 7, 2014

Sometimes we don't know what we don't know until it blindsides us.

I should have known Jack wasn't ready to hear the news I hit him with yesterday. We never discussed his fears about having children, and our baby almost became fatherless last night.

Thank God and mama's letter about becoming a dad, Jack came to his senses and put the gun away. He ran to my dad, and they stayed up all night talking through Jack's fears and inner beasts. Randy joined them, and the three of them formed a plan for regular meetings for veterans. Randy and Jack have the personal experiences and understanding to bring to the picture, and Daddy knows some chaplains and counselors who specialize in PTSD.

Today feels like the brightest sunrise after the darkest night of our lives.

Jack and I talked and cried and prayed all afternoon. He revealed the root of his fears over having children and explained the lesson about "leading his team to slaughter" that he learned during scout sniper training. He's terrified of bringing harm to our children or of not being able to protect them from life's tragedies, like those he lived through.

We discussed how we cannot fall for the lie that we can control anything. I apologized to him for not acting sooner. I saw his fears and said nothing, did nothing. Like Jack, I played the never-ending "once we're not so busy, after this event is over" game.

Turns out, that game can be deadly.

We promised one another that any time something feels off—whether we can explain what it is or not—we will act immediately. We will listen. We will ask. We will not wait to get less busy because we'll never be less busy. That's not how life works.

And, we accepted the fact that we aren't going to be able to control a single thing about this baby growing inside me. Like Mama wrote in her letter to Jack, all we have to do is show up for this little one. God's got us, and He's in control when we never can be.

Today's One Good Thing:
I'm thankful God stayed Jack's hand and brought him home to us, and I'm thankful for the gift of a child to love and lead to Him.

Monday, July 7, 2014

To our Precious Son,

This morning we found out you're a boy! We can't wait to meet you. We look forward to watching you grow toward whatever God's got in store for your life. I know it will be something amazing.

That's your mom, bud, always positive and glass overflowing. This is your old man; I'm more hole-in-the-bottom-of-the-glass. We are crazy excited, though, to see you for the first time. I'm gonna go ahead and get this out there for you: your dad's a lot of a mess, but your mama and Grandpa and Nana make sure I stay on the right path. I've spent my whole life learning lessons and likely always will be. The good thing about that is, I can help you learn some of them without you making the same stupid mistakes I did.

Jack B. Calhoun, we're going to have to work on your language before this baby is born. "Stupid" is not a nice word, son. I'll have a word with your father about that.

I call it like I see it, ma'am.

Also, your father is not as much of a train wreck as he makes it sound. You should've seen him before I got my hands on him.

It wasn't pretty. The thing is, son, we want you to know that neither one of us is perfect—though your mama dang near is. And, we want you to know you won't be either, but that's okay. We're here for you. We're here to teach you and guide you and listen to you.

The good thing about having a messed up old man is, chances are, I've been through whatever valleys you might wander one day. No matter the struggles you face in your future, I'll be here to listen, to pray, to encourage. I can also share how God's carried me through my own challenges, and we can rejoice when God carries you through yours, too.

One more thought for your future: you can never do something that will make us stop loving you. We're not going anywhere.

We'll be right here, waiting on you.

We love you, Benjamin Trayvon Calhoun

A GIFT FOR YOU

RESOURCES

Within the pages of this fictional account, you'll find much truth in the pain and struggles of our main character. For that reason, we have included a list with some resources in the United States for your own battles and beasts. For more local guidance and assistance, contact a church near you. Help awaits, friend. Accept it!

SUICIDE PREVENTION: 1-800-273-8255
suicidepreventionlifeline.org

SUBSTANCE ABUSE: 1-888-633-3239
http://drughelpline.org

HOMELESSNESS: 211
www.211.org/services/housing-and-utilities

PTSD & OTHER VETERAN-SPECIFIC CHALLENGES: 211
www.woundedwarriorproject.org

VETERANS CRISIS LINE: Dial 988, then 1
https://www.veteranscrisisline.net/

CREDITS & PERMISSIONS

The hymn "AMAZING GRACE" is public domain.

"THE MARINE RIFLEMAN'S CREED" was written by Major General William Rupertus following the 1941 attack on Pearl Harbor. Since that time, countless Marines have memorized it. It's only fitting to include parts of it here in a fictional account of a young man whose first purpose came with the title United States Marine. Thank you to KAREN JENSEN, editor for WWII Magazine, and MICHAEL HASKEW, editor for WWII History Magazine, for their advice on providing proper credit for this iconic poem.

Use of the trademarked name CHEERWINE comes with gracious permission by the soft drink makers and Carolina Beverage Corp. No story set in the southeastern United States is complete without inclusion of "the South's unique cherry soft drink."

Disclaimer: "Neither the United States Marine Corps nor any other component of the Department of Defense has approved, endorsed, or authorized this book."

ACKNOWLEDGMENTS

The journey to the release of *One Good Thing* has been unexpected in many ways. A standalone novel turned into a four-book collection. (I blame the characters.) I have learned and grown into the title *author* through this adventure. As I sit here, knowing all four books will soon be in my hands, I am immensely grateful.

To everyone who has supported and encouraged me over the seven years of drafting, revising, editing and releasing, thank you. To everyone who has requested or purchased, read, reviewed and recommended my books, thank you. To all who have attended events, asked about the next book and sent emails of kindness, thank you.

To *you*, reading this now, thank you.

Each person who has supported this collection in any way is more a part of it than they may realize. While I can't name every one of you—I know I'd leave someone off—I am eternally grateful because you saw invisible me and took a chance on these stories. I hope you find us worthwhile.

I wouldn't get to write this note if it weren't for God's gifts of creativity, imagination, drive and ability and all His strength, guidance and mercies along the way.

We give thee but thine own, whate'er the gift may be;
all that we have is thine alone, a trust, O Lord, from thee.
"We Give Thee But Thine Own" by William W. How

My husband, *Tony*, has had many opportunities over the past year to look at me and say, "I knew you would." Thank you for believing I will before I do, and thank you for reading everything I write and helping me write the soul with heart. You're my lobster.

My *children* remind me to take breaks and enjoy life. They also cheer me on and still want to spend time with me. I love you both!

Six more special readers have eagerly given their time and care and love to all four of these books. I am humbled by and thankful for your advice, attention to detail, helpful feedback and genuine care. To my critique partners, *Mea Smith* and *Kelsey Atkins*, and to my beta readers, *Terri Sweetland, Justin Stodghill, Gabrielle Hill* and E*ric Demmer*, "I thank my God upon every remembrance of you ...." (Philippians 1:3)

Rachael Ritchey, my cover designer and formatter and dear friend, has also been with me from the beginning. Thank you for your generous spirit and kind heart. I will never forget how you reached out to me when I was drowning in the formatting of *Any Good Thing* and rescued me. I am thrilled to see all four of your gorgeous covers in the world together!

To the members of our new church home, *Redeemer Lutheran (LCMS)*, thank you for welcoming us with open arms, for faithfully proclaiming law and gospel, for supporting the creatives in your midst, for listening to our journey and for asking, "And how long have you been Lutheran?" Our top priority for last year was to find our theological home, and you (along with brothers and sisters at *Salem Lutheran* and *Lamb of God*) helped us do that.

Soli Deo Gloria.

COLOPHON

The typeface used with gracious permission in the cover design and throughout various pages of the book is Bentham, created by designer and developer, Ben Weiner. Some interior formatting is primarily 12 point sizing. Headings and subheads fluctuate between 16 and 34 point sizing. For more on this typeface, read the creator's description:

"I like the lettering on nineteenth-century maps, on gravestones and on the maker's plates of cast-iron machinery. It is characterised by expressive flowing and bulging curves, mannered awkwardness and the bobbles on the terminals of its characters. The letterform conventionally called 'modern face' is the typographical equivalent, and it can be found in books printed throughout the nineteenth century. Its descendants survived into educational textbooks produced into the late twentieth century, and it is preserved in computer science as the style which Donald Knuth adopted for his TeX typesetting system.

"Bentham is a half-way design; it's true neither to the type produced during the nineteenth century, nor to the letterforms of cartographers, stonecutters, or engravers. It's really a sort of examination of the characteristics these letters share, coloured by my approach to type drawing."

Alberobello Script, used for Rachael's journal dates, is an elegant and modern font duo with casual chic flair and is designed bySarwo Edhi Prayitno, reprsented through his company Hasken.

Other fonts used in the creation of this print book are open source selections as follows:

- The Girl Next Door (Rachael's letters) designed by Kimberly Geswein
- Ink Free (Jack's later letters) designed by Steve Matteson
- Give You Glory (Jack's transitionary letters) by Kimberly Geswein
- Reenie Beanie (Jack's earlier letters) by James Grieshaber
- Allura (some headings) by Robert Leuschke
- Baskervville (for some italicized words) by ANRT

MEET THE AUTHOR

Photo: Casie Jones Photography

Legacy and identity, founded on hope-filled faith, infuse the tales of the soul written from the heart of JOY E. RANCATORE. Her Carolina's Legacy Collection embraces everyday moments that constitute a lifetime and its heritage. Told around multiple related characters, this collection explores faith, life, death and the demons within through four mediums—novel, novella, short stories and epistolary.

An avid reader, student of human behaviors and unwitting empath, Joy absorbs emotions and spills them onto the pages of her work. Joy's technical background includes more than two decades of professional writing and editing. Ongoing training in writing, publishing, business and counseling enables her to package soul-filled stories for her readers. An award-winning, multi-genre Indie Author, Joy believes extraordinary things await her characters and their tales.

Despite a fondness for her roles as author, editor, podcaster and speaker, Joy is a hobbit at heart with Bilbo's zeal for mountains. She enjoys a life of quiet stillness with her husband, two children, dog and cat and more books than she's willing to count. When daily homeschool lessons are complete, she eagerly prepares for teatime before writing your next favorite story.

Visit Joy for Book News, Free Stories, Book Club Kits and More:
www.joyerancatore.com/links

Have a Book Club?

READ:

Any Good Thing

(or any book in Carolina's Legacy Collection) together.

REQUEST:

- a Book Club Kit
- a virtual or in-person chat with the author

VISIT:

www.joyerancatore.com/book-clubs

Did You Enjoy This Book?

Reviews from readers make the most precious gift for authors and help fellow readers discover fantastic new reads. Please take a moment to leave a simple star review or a few thoughts on Goodreads and any bookseller sites.

Another way to share your appreciation is to tell all your reader friends and request that your local bookstore and library shelve it.

Share your reviews and book selfies with Joy and Logos & Mythos Press on your favorite social media outlets. #OneGoodThing

Want More?

For more information on upcoming releases from LOGOS & MYTHOS PRESS, visit logosandmythospress.com/links and subscribe to their email list.

Have a book club? Read *One Good Thing* (or any book in Carolina's Legacy Collection) together and request a Book Club Kit and/or a Skype or in-person chat with the author. Email editorial@logosandmythospress.com for more information.

Did you enjoy this book? Reviews from readers make the most precious gift for authors and help fellow readers discover fantastic new reads. Please take a moment to leave a simple star review or a few thoughts on Goodreads and any bookseller sites.

Another way to share your appreciation is to tell all your reader friends and request that your local bookstore and library shelve it.

Share your reviews and book selfies with Joy and Logos & Mythos Press on your favorite social media outlets. #OneGoodThing

Thank you for reading!

LOGOS & MYTHOS PRESS
SLIDELL, LA, USA

www.ingramcontent.com/pod-product-compliance
Lightning Source LLC
Chambersburg PA
CBHW021245190726
48289CB00005B/1492

* 9 7 8 1 7 3 3 1 3 8 7 9 6 *